# A RECIPE FOR DISASTER

Charissa went on handing out assignments and sending kids to the far corners of the camp. Finally, only she and Gladys were left.

"I saved yours for last on purpose," she said with a grin, "because it's so awesome. Anticipation is just the best feeling ever, don't you think?"

Gladys, who wanted to shake Charissa by her purple-clad shoulders, didn't think that at all, but she managed just to give her friend a tiny nod.

"Okay, your CIT assignment is . . . kitchen assistant! See, I knew you'd love it!"

Gladys hadn't even had time to react, but for once she could admit that Charissa was right—that did sound like the perfect assignment for her. "Wow, thanks," Gladys said, taking her card.

"Now, I have to warn you: Our camp cook can be a little . . . prickly," Charissa said. "Like, she insists that we call her 'Mrs. Spinelli,' even though all the other counselors go by their first names. And, well"—Charissa glanced toward the kitchen, then lowered her voice—"her last couple of CITs haven't exactly worked out."

"Oh," Gladys said.

## OTHER BOOKS YOU MAY ENJOY

# THE STARS OF
# SUMMER

# THE STARS OF
# SUMMER

Tara Dairman

PUFFIN BOOKS

PUFFIN BOOKS
An imprint of Penguin Random House LLC
375 Hudson Street
New York, New York 10014

First published in the United States of America by G. P. Putnam's Sons,
an imprint of Penguin Group (USA) LLC, 2015
Published by Puffin Books, an imprint of Penguin Random House LLC, 2016

THE LIBRARY OF CONGRESS HAS CATALOGED THE G. P. PUTNAM'S SONS EDITION AS FOLLOWS:
Dairman, Tara.
The stars of summer / Tara Dairman.
pages cm
Sequel to: All Four Stars.
Summary: Dragged to summer camp by her friend Charissa,
twelve-year-old Gladys Gatsby, an undercover restaurant reviewer for
a big New York City newspaper, meets a young bestselling author and
finds a way to practice her cooking and restaurant reviewing skills.
ISBN 978-0-399-17069-0 (hardcover)
[1. Camps—Fiction. 2. Cooking—Fiction.
3. Journalism—Fiction. 4. Friendship—Fiction.]
I. Title
PZ7.D1521127St 2015 [Fic]—dc23 2014031819

Puffin Books ISBN 978-0-14-751318-2

Printed in the United States of America

3 5 7 9 10 8 6 4

Design by Marikka Tamura

*For Andy*

# Chapter 1

## BITTER BIRTHDAY

GLADYS GATSBY'S TWELFTH BIRTHDAY should have been her happiest one yet.

She was at a fabulous new restaurant in Manhattan on an outing she'd been planning for weeks. Back at home, a three-tiered, strawberry-lime birthday cake (which, of course, Gladys had baked herself) was waiting to be eaten. And best of all, Gladys's parents had allowed her to invite her friends along for the festivities. A year ago, Gladys hadn't had any friends to invite to a birthday party—but now she had three, and they were all here at Fusión Tapas with her.

Too bad they weren't speaking to one another.

Gladys glanced around the table. Parm Singh's thick black eyebrows knit into an angry scrunch as she scowled alternately at Charissa Bentley and Sandy Anderson. Next to her, Charissa was flicking her high brown ponytail over her shoulder about ten times a minute, shooting sneers in Sandy's or Parm's direction each time. And Sandy—whose round cheeks were flushed almost as red as the bottle of spicy sauce in the middle of the table—had scooted his chair so far away from both girls that he was now practically sitting in Gladys's dad's lap.

All this bitterness, and they hadn't even gotten their food yet!

The evening had started off much more smoothly, with the Gatsbys piling into their station wagon to drive into the city. "Hey, I don't remember agreeing to throw a party like this," Gladys's dad had joked as he turned the key in the ignition. "Gladdy, I knew that hanging around with that Bentley girl was going to give you big ideas."

Gladys smiled. It was true that she'd gotten the idea to spend her birthday at a restaurant in the city from Charissa, who'd brought Gladys into Manhattan on a birthday outing just three months earlier. But Gladys's ulterior motive had nothing to do with wanting to be popular like Charissa.

It had everything to do with her top secret job as a restaurant critic for New York City's biggest newspaper.

It wasn't a job she had even meant to apply for, but a few months back, Gladys's entry for the *New York Standard* sixth-grade essay contest had somehow ended up on the desk of Fiona Inglethorpe, chief editor of the *Standard*'s Dining section. Fiona must have liked what she read—and must have assumed that Gladys was a professional adult writer—because she had e-mailed Gladys with a reviewing assignment for the paper.

Almost overnight, Gladys had morphed from a regular sixth-grader into a sort of foodie secret agent. She couldn't let her editor know her age, or she'd get in trouble for being too young. She couldn't let the restaurants find out she was a critic, or they'd give her special treatment, trying to influence her reviews. And, most important, she couldn't let her parents know about her new job. These days, they only let her indulge her love of cooking at home because they thought she spent the rest of her time being a "normal kid." If they found out that she *actually* spent most of her free time writing about food for the country's biggest newspaper . . . well, she could kiss those kitchen privileges good-bye forever.

So Gladys's parents didn't know that she'd chosen this restaurant for her birthday dinner because she needed to review it for next week's Dining section. But Sandy did, and since he lived next door, he was the first of her friends to join them. Jogging up to their car, he looked different than usual: He wore pressed khaki pants instead of shorts, and his usually mussed-up blond hair had been sculpted with gel into a severe wave. But underneath all that was the same old Sandy.

"Happy birthday, Gatsby!" He fist-bumped her as he climbed into the car, then shoved a wrapped package into her lap. "Hey, Mr. and Mrs. Gatsby, thanks for having me. This is gonna be excellent—I can't wait to try the tapas!"

He was overplaying things a little, Gladys thought, but her mom seemed to buy it. Swiveling around in her seat, she beamed at him. Gladys's mom thought that having an active social life was very important, so she grinned at just about everything that came out of Gladys's friends' mouths—even if it was enthusiasm for tiny plates of Spanish-inspired cuisine.

"You're very welcome, Sandy," she said. "We're just thrilled to have you along."

"You've got your notebook?" Sandy whispered as the car turned onto Landfill View Road. Gladys gave him a tiny nod and patted her dress pocket. Inside were the materials she needed to carry off her secret mission: a tiny reviewing journal and two sharp golf pencils.

"And you've got the charts?" Gladys whispered back. She and Sandy had spent the last week—every day since summer vacation had begun—at his house, scouring the Fusión Tapas menu online and plotting who should order what. The menu featured eighteen different dishes, so if Gladys wanted to taste them all, every person in their party would have to order three different things. Luckily, "tapas" were small plates, so Gladys knew that the portions wouldn't be huge.

Sandy nodded and slid two folded-up printouts out of his pocket. Gladys quickly stuffed them into her journal. She and Sandy already had their orders memorized, as did Parm, who also knew about Gladys's secret work for the *Standard*. As for the other diners, Gladys had been dropping hints about what they should order all week and hoped she'd planted seeds in their minds: seeds that would grow into roasted asparagus for her mom, fried eggplant for her dad, and stuffed peppers for Charissa.

Soon the Gatsbys' car pulled into the Singhs' driveway. Parm stepped outside wearing a beautiful salwar kameez of green chiffon, but she kept her head tucked down as though she were embarrassed. When Sandy pushed open the back door, she grabbed a fistful of her fluttery scarf and nearly vaulted into the far backseat.

"Happy birthday, Gladys," she said, handing over a small gift bag tied shut with a curl of ribbon. "And sorry about . . . this." She glanced down at her outfit, which consisted of flowing pants and a matching top. "My mom looked at the restaurant's website, and when she saw how fancy it is, she made me dress up."

"That's okay," Gladys said, pointing to her own striped sundress. "Mine did, too, see? Anyway, you look really nice."

"Yeah," Sandy chimed in. "You look like a princess!"

Parm's eyes narrowed. *Uh-oh*, Gladys thought. That was definitely the wrong thing to say to a girl who spent most of recess either kicking around a soccer ball or punching Owen Green.

Sandy, though, seemed oblivious to Parm's glare. "I'm Sandy, by the way," he said. "Sandy Anderson. Maybe your parents know my mom? She teaches at East Dumpsford Yoga, and she studied in India."

"Well, if she studied there, then she *must* have met my parents," Parm said witheringly. "It's not like there's over *a billion people* in India or anything."

Sandy twisted to look at Gladys, a bewildered expression on his face. "I thought she was supposed to be the nice one," he muttered.

Gladys couldn't think of how to respond. Sandy went to a private school, so he had never met Gladys's other friends. But if Sandy and Parm already weren't getting along, then adding Charissa to the mix definitely wasn't going to help.

And just as she suspected, Gladys heard both of her friends groan audibly as Charissa flounced down her front walk five minutes later. She wore an elaborate red dress trimmed in black lace with matching high heels, and carried an enormous present wrapped in shiny gold paper.

"Is she wearing *gloves*?" Parm asked incredulously. "It's eighty degrees outside!"

Gladys looked closer and saw that Charissa *was* wearing gloves, though they were black lace ones with no fingertips, so she was pretty sure they were meant to be fashionable rather than warm.

"Maybe temperatures are cooler in The Seabreeze," Sandy said. The Seabreeze—East Dumpsford's most exclusive waterfront neighborhood—was where the Bentleys' large house was located.

"Right—not like sweltering, overpopulated India," Parm snapped.

"Dude, I didn't say anything about India!"

"Cool it, you guys," Gladys begged—but before she could say more, the car door flew open.

"*Hola!*" Charissa squealed. She dropped her huge gift on the floor, threw her arms around Gladys, and planted a lipsticky kiss on each of her cheeks. "*That's* how they say hello in Spain," she informed everyone as she climbed in. "And this is what they wear. Or what flamenco dancers wear, at least." She smoothed the skirt of her dress with one of her gloves. "Since we're going to a Spanish restaurant, I thought it would be the perfect outfit. I had Mommy order it specially for me from Madrid!"

"How thoughtful of you, Charissa!" Gladys's mother exclaimed. It was no secret that Gladys's mom liked Charissa the best of Gladys's friends, possibly even more than Gladys liked her. Charissa loved to be the center of attention and tell everyone what to do—traits that made her pretty much Gladys's opposite. But they had one important thing in common: They both loved good food, and could talk about it for hours on end. Gladys wasn't sure yet that she could trust Charissa with her restaurant-reviewing secret, but if she was going to a fancy restaurant, she knew she wanted Charissa with her.

As the station wagon merged onto the highway, Sandy gawked at Charissa's dress. Gladys couldn't blame him; it gleamed like fluorescent strawberry juice, even in the low light of the car.

Charissa eyed Sandy coolly. "You know it's rude to stare, right?"

"Sorry," he mumbled.

Charissa pursed her brightly colored lips, and Gladys felt sure that she was about to chew him out. But instead she said, "That's okay. You're Gladys's little friend—Sandy, right?" She shot him an indulgent smile. "I wouldn't expect someone *so* much younger than the rest of us to know about proper manners."

"I—what?" Sandy spluttered. "I'm only a year younger than you!"

"Yes," Charissa continued, "but boys are less mature than girls to start. So an eleven-year-old boy is really the equivalent of, like, an eight-year-old girl. Don't you think, Parm?"

"I'm staying out of this," Parm said.

Gladys had to jump in. "Sandy's very mature," she

assured Charissa. "Like an adult sometimes, really. You should see some of the computer games he's designed!"

Sandy gave Gladys a small smile of thanks.

"Well, Gladys," Charissa drawled, "it's your birthday, and he's your friend, so of course you're right. I'll say no more."

And she didn't. In fact, nobody did all the way into Manhattan—not even Gladys's mom, though in her case it may have been due to nerves. Unlike Gladys's dad, who took the train into Manhattan every day for work, her mom hardly ever ventured into New York City. She said that the tall buildings made her feel claustrophobic, and she worried about pickpockets. In fact, she had left her purse at home and insisted that Gladys's dad take only his driver's license and a single debit card on the birthday outing to help limit their losses in case of a violent holdup.

"This is completely unnecessary," her dad had grumbled as he emptied his wallet onto the kitchen table. But he'd given in to avoid starting the night off with a fight.

As everyone lined up in the entryway to Fusión Tapas, Gladys hoped that her friends wouldn't be fighting all night. She had a job to do, after all, and she was going to need them to work together to pull it off.

Sandy was standing closest to her, so she decided

to check in with him first. "Which three tapas will you be ordering again?" she whispered.

"The calamari, the potato omelet, and whatever special number two is," he whispered back. According to the restaurant's website, it always served two specials in addition to the regular menu, so Gladys had planned to order one of them and have Sandy—her least finicky friend—order the other. "Don't worry, Gatsby," he assured her. "I've got this."

She nodded; no matter what else happened, she knew she could rely on Sandy. Gladys turned to check in with Parm next, but found Charissa standing in her way.

"Gladys, do you know what you're going to get?" she asked excitedly. "I've been studying the menu online all week! I have to get the smoked almonds; that's a given."

Gladys had assumed this—since she knew how much Charissa liked nuts—so it was already filled in on the ordering chart. And as for the other two slots next to Charissa's name . . .

"How about the stuffed piquillo peppers," Gladys suggested, "and maybe the goose kebabs?"

Charissa's button nose wrinkled. "I don't know," she said. "Isn't goose really greasy? I wouldn't want to get stains on my dress."

"Right," Gladys said, doing some quick calculations in her head. Maybe *she* could order the goose and let

Charissa have the griddled polenta cakes that were next to her own name on the chart. "Well, how about the—"

Just then, something slammed into Gladys's shoulder—hard. It was Parm. "Stupid sandals," she muttered. "I never trip in my cleats."

"So, Parm," Charissa said, tossing her ponytail over her shoulder, "what are you going to order? I thought you didn't eat anything other than, like, plain spaghetti."

Gladys felt Parm's body stiffen and hoped her friend remembered the answer they had practiced in case this question came up. In truth, Parm was the pickiest eater Gladys knew; she ate a couple of things besides spaghetti, but not much, and certainly nothing that would be found on the menu of a Spanish restaurant.

"In honor of Gladys's birthday, I'm going to be adventurous," Parm recited. "I'm going to try some new dishes and hope to be pleasantly surprised."

Gladys gave Parm's pinkie a grateful squeeze. She felt confident now that Parm remembered her role, too: keep track of what everyone else orders, and then order whatever is left on the menu. Gladys knew Parm had no intention of putting even one morsel of tapas into her mouth, so it really didn't matter what she ordered in the end.

"Gladys Jane?" the maître d' called out. "Party of six?"

Gladys's hand shot into the air. "That's us!" Thankfully, her parents had allowed her to make the dinner reservations, and she'd been careful not to give the restaurant her last name, since she published her reviews under the byline "G. Gatsby." But as the maître d' swept them off to their table in the middle of the loud, mirror-paneled dining room, Gladys couldn't help but worry. There were still so many moving parts to her plan.

Soon they were all seated at a round table covered with a funky turquoise tablecloth. Ice clinked in their skinny water glasses as they perused the menu, and the waiter came by a few minutes later to recite the specials. "We have some lovely steamed lobsterrr claws today, serrrved with frrresh dill-infused butterrr sauce." He rolled his *r*'s so forcefully that, next to Gladys, Sandy giggled. "And, forrr a second special, we have the chef's homemade rrrabbit sausage, gently charrred and serrrrved atop a stew of fava beans."

Sandy stopped laughing, and Gladys immediately knew why. He had two pet rabbits at home, Edward and Dennis Hopper, and rabbit meat was possibly the only food on earth he wouldn't eat.

"Arrre we rrready to orrrderrr?" the waiter asked. "I hearrr we have a birrrthday girrrl?" He turned to Gladys, his grin wide beneath a pencil-thin mustache.

Gladys froze. Should she stick with the original plan and order the lobster, special number one? Or should she order the rabbit special for herself and hope that Sandy got the hint and switched with her? But would Sandy ever talk to her again if she ate rabbit right in front of him?

"Um . . . I . . ." Gladys looked frantically around the table, but that only added to her confusion. What was Charissa going to decide on—the goose or the polenta? And what about her parents?

"Perrrhaps you need anotherrr minute," the waiter trilled, and relief washed over Gladys as he backed away. It would be easier if she could place her order near the end.

"Well, I know what I'd like," Gladys's mother said, and the waiter turned eagerly back toward their table. "The beef-filled baguette—that's like a hamburger, right? I'll try that. And these olive-oil-crisped potato wedges—that sounds sort of like French fries. Oh, and the ham-wrapped roasted asparagus." She shot Gladys a wink. Gladys was pretty sure her mom had never tasted asparagus until the day Gladys had practically forced her to try a sample at Mr. Eng's Gourmet Grocery. But now that she knew she liked it, she ate it all the time. *Good job, Mom,* Gladys thought. *Maybe we'll try Brussels sprouts next.*

"Everything my wife mentioned sounds good," Gladys's dad said, shutting his menu with a decisive *clap!* "I'll have the same."

"No!" The word flew out of Gladys's mouth before

she could stop herself. In an instant, all the heads at her table—and several tables around them—swung in her direction.

*Fudge,* she thought. Rule number one of restaurant reviewing was *not* to make a spectacle of yourself. Staying unnoticed and anonymous was the best way to avoid exposing your identity.

But now everyone was staring at her, so she had to say something. "Remember how we talked about this, Dad?" she said. "About how we were all going to order different stuff tonight? That way, we can share and all get to try more new things!"

"That was a nice idea, Gladdy," her dad started, "but I'm afraid that there just aren't many other things on this menu that appeal—"

"*Excuse me.*" Charissa was now rising from her seat. "If Gladys wants everyone to order different things, then that's what we should do. A girl's birthday is *not* the time to say no to her. Is it, Mr. Gatsby?" Charissa flashed her teeth at him in a way that seemed to be half smiling, half threatening to eat him alive.

Gladys's dad's eyes widened, and for a second, it looked like he might tell Charissa that he could say no to his daughter anytime he darn well chose. But then his hands betrayed him by slipping the menu back open across his plate.

"Well, I . . . I guess I could try the fried eggplant . . .

and, um, the chorizo sausage . . . and the gazpacho. Please," he added meekly.

Charissa retook her seat, and Sandy leaned over toward Gladys's ear. "Okay," he whispered. "I guess I can see why you brought her."

Things got a little easier after that. Sandy placed his order, substituting the lobster special for the rabbit, and gave Gladys a look that made it clear that her ordering rabbit would *not* be okay with him. Charissa picked the polenta over the goose, so Gladys got the goose, the octopus, and the sliced pork loin. That meant that when Parm's turn came, there were only two items left on the regular menu that hadn't been mentioned yet. She dutifully ordered them from the waiter, then glanced over toward Gladys. "Should I get that other special, too?"

"No, that's okay," Gladys said—she would just have to leave the rabbit out of her review. She turned to the waiter again and said, "But would it be possible to get a small bowl of plain pasta for my friend, too? No sauce or anything—in fact, the clumpier the better."

The waiter said he would see what he could do, and Parm beamed. *Maybe it won't be such a bad dinner after all*, Gladys thought.

# Chapter 2

# DAD ON ICE

THE TAPAS BEGAN TO APPEAR WITHIN A few minutes: first, bowls of olives and smoked almonds, then more and more of the cooked dishes. Shifting her journal quietly out of her pocket and into her lap, Gladys unfolded the second chart Sandy had made her: one that listed every dish on the menu with a blank space for comments. Each time she tried a bite of something—creamy eggplant, salty potatoes, crunchy octopus legs—she made a quick note in her lap, thankful that her parents and Charissa were all on the other side of the table and couldn't see what she was doing.

"So, what are everyone's plans for the summer?" Gladys's dad asked.

Charissa, not surprisingly, piped up

first. "Camp Bentley, of course," she said. "My parents say it's going to be our best summer yet!" Charissa's parents owned the local day camp, and most of Gladys's classmates went there every summer. "This year, we're even getting a celebrity camper," she continued.

"A celebrity?" Gladys's mom exclaimed. "How exciting! Who is it?"

"Oh, I'm not allowed to tell," Charissa said. "Really, I shouldn't have even mentioned it." She giggled, and Parm rolled her eyes.

Gladys's mom looked a little disappointed, but she turned to Sandy next. "And what about you, Sandy?" she asked. "I think your mother mentioned you're going to camp as well?"

Sandy, who was busy trying to pick up an olive with a lobster claw, didn't respond, and Gladys had to nudge him under the table with the edge of her sandal.

"Huh?" He looked up, and the olive once again rolled out of his claw's grasp. "Oh, um, yeah—Mom's shipping me off to karate camp."

"Shipping you off?" Gladys's dad frowned. "That doesn't seem like a very nice way to put it. Sleepaway camp isn't exactly cheap."

"Yeah, I know," Sandy said. "I'm just not sure this place is gonna be worth it. My mom's been talking to the head of the camp, and I think he may be a little . . ."

Sandy twirled his lobster claw around next to his ear. "But I guess you'd *have* to be crazy to want to run a summer camp, huh?"

Charissa's expression turned absolutely murderous.

"And how about you, Parm?" Gladys's mom asked quickly. "Any exciting summer plans?"

"Just a trip to Arizona to visit my cousins," Parm said. "Though I'm not sure how long we'll stay there." She flicked her long braid over her shoulder and stabbed a clump of noodles with her fork. "I suppose it'll depend on how much weight I lose."

This was clearly not the response Gladys's parents had expected, and even Sandy and Charissa stared at Parm now in confusion. Sandy, though, was the only one brave enough to blurt out what the others were thinking. "But you don't need to lose any weight," he said.

Across the table, Charissa nodded. "He's right," she said, "and I should know. My mom always has me trying some stupid diet or another."

An exasperated noise escaped Parm's lips. "Of course I won't be *trying* to lose weight," she said. "It just tends to happen when my family travels. I don't enjoy the spicy flavors of Southwestern food."

Gladys sighed. She'd been working on Parm for weeks, pointing out some of the tamer regional specialties (fresh corn tortillas! cactus-flower honey!) that she could try in Arizona. But her campaign hadn't been successful. Parm only lamented that she and Gladys didn't look alike; otherwise, they could have pulled off a *Parent Trap*–style switcheroo, sending Gladys off to Arizona to eat in Parm's place.

But Gladys would be spending the summer at home in East Dumpsford like she did every year—and that was okay with her. Three months had passed since she'd paid off the damages from the crème brûlée–triggered fire she'd accidentally started at Christmas, so she'd had her kitchen privileges restored for a while. But between school, writing her first restaurant review, and planning the second, she'd hardly had time to cook anything lately. Now that school was out, she was looking forward to a long summer of trying new recipes, broken up only by bike rides to Mr. Eng's for more ingredients or the library for more cookbooks.

"You are a wrrriterrr?"

Gladys slapped her journal shut in her lap, but it was too late. The waiter, who was reaching over her shoulder, had seen it.

*Fudge!*

Gladys looked around the table, but her parents and Charissa were deeply absorbed in a conversation about Camp Bentley and apparently hadn't heard him.

"Oh, yeah," she said, thinking fast. "I want to be a poet when I grow up."

The waiter's lips curved into a weary smile. "Ah, so do I, *mi niña.*"

He strode away with the dishes, and Gladys exhaled. That had been close—too close. It would be better if she could go somewhere more private to finish taking her notes, where she could write even more without worrying about anyone noticing.

"I need to go to the ladies' room," she announced, pushing back her chair.

A minute later, she was locked safely in a stall. Leaning against the wall, she took her notebook out again, turned to a clean page, and began writing the full sentences her brain had been craving to get down all through dinner.

*While, at first bite, the potatoes may seem too crispy to some diners, once they're dunked in Fusión's homemade garlic aioli, the texture hits just the right note. And those who prefer their root vegetables in a creamier form will want to order the golden beet puree, which comes whipped into a mountain that is almost too perfectly sculpted to eat.*

*Less attractively presented, however, are the oily goose kebabs. These morsels might look more tempting if served on a bed of greens rather than directly on the plate, where their grease pools unappetizingly . . .*

Gladys had filled nearly a page with her observations when the door to the bathroom creaked open and voices spilled into the room.

"Chef's in a real tizzy," one voice said. "He's sure the *Standard*'s going to send a critic this month, and he doesn't think it's going to be that Gilbert Gadfly, either. Apparently, Gadfly's getting very picky about what restaurants he'll try these days. So Chef thinks they may send that new critic, Gatsby."

Gladys's pencil froze in the middle of a word.

"Okay," the second voice said. "So what do we know about Gatsby?"

"Almost nothing," said the first voice. "That's the problem!"

Gladys peeked through the crack in the stall's door. Two women in the restaurant's black-and-gold waitress uniforms stood fixing their hair in the mirrors over the sinks.

The owner of the first voice, whose blond hair was pulled back in a tight bun, continued. "For starters, we don't even know if it's a man or a woman. 'G. Gatsby' is what the byline said on the Classy Cakes review."

"At least it was a good review," said the second waitress, who was patting her thick, dark curls.

"Yeah, well, that hasn't put the chef at ease. He's been fussing so much over every plate that it's a wonder I can get anything out of the kitchen while it's still hot." The blond waitress pushed a loose tendril of hair behind her ear, then turned on the tap.

The dark-haired waitress groaned. "If he keeps that up, we'll start losing tips. People don't like cold food!"

"Well, it might be worth the loss in tips if you can ID the critic. Chef's posted a sign on the board: a thousand dollars to anyone who can find 'G. Gatsby.'"

Gladys's breath caught in her throat.

"A thousand dollars?" the dark-haired waitress squeaked. "But . . . what if you ID them at the end of the meal? Then it'll be too late for Chef to serve them something special!"

"True," said the blond waitress, "but it won't be too late for him to sell a description to other chefs around town. Apparently, some will pay plenty more than a grand for that kind of info."

Gladys could hardly believe it. She'd only published one review in the *Standard* so far, and already there was a bounty on her head?

The blond waitress continued as she pulled a paper towel off the stack on the sink. "We're pretty much out of luck, though, unless this Gatsby charges the meal on his or her own card."

Her friend sighed. "No critic for the *Standard* would be stupid enough to do that."

The bathroom door creaked again as the two waitresses exited . . . and the moment it clicked behind them, Gladys shot out of her stall. She didn't have a card, of course, but her dad did—a shiny plastic Super Dump-Mart rewards debit card with the name GATSBY plastered across it in raised letters! If their waiter was already on the lookout for a Gatsby, then that card might lead him to wonder whether the critic might be sitting at their table. And he had even seen her writing in her notebook!

Gladys burst out of the bathroom and set off across the dining room at a brisk pace. When she spotted her table, she was momentarily distracted by the sight of a burning candle sticking out of a small dish of flan— the waiter must have brought her a birthday dessert. But when she looked at her father, her fears were confirmed. The waiter had also brought the check, and her dad was examining it . . . reaching into his pocket . . . pulling out his debit card . . .

Gladys broke into a run, but before she could reach her table, a busboy cut in front of her carrying a full pitcher of ice water. She couldn't have stopped what happened next if she'd tried.

Time seemed to slow down as she barreled into him, sending the pitcher flying in an almost-perfect arc. An arc that landed right on her table, showering it with water and ice cubes and snuffing out Gladys's birthday candle.

"EEEE-YAH!" her dad shrieked, shoving his chair

back and leaping to his feet. The water poured onto the floor like a waterfall, and her dad's shocked fingers released their grip on the debit card.

"Oh, sir, I'm sorry—I'm so sorry!" the busboy cried. "I'll go get some towels from the kitchen." He hurried away, leaving the path between Gladys and the table clear.

Her friends—and much of the restaurant—were gaping at her, but for once Gladys didn't care. The "Don't make a spectacle of yourself" rule of restaurant reviewing had just gone out the window, having been replaced by a more important rule: "Don't let the servers see a debit card with your name on it!"

Still, she hadn't meant to turn her own father into a casualty. "Dad, are you okay?" she asked. "I'm sorry—that busboy just showed up out of nowhere!"

"It's all right, Gladdy," her dad said, gently swatting his wife away as she attempted to wring out his tie. "It's just water."

"That's a great attitude!" Gladys said brightly, sidling up close to the table. In one deft motion, she swept the fallen debit card off the tablecloth and onto the floor. "I'll help him clean up when he gets back with the towels. Oh, look, here he is."

The busboy had raced back with a pile of paper towels, and as he got to work mopping up the table, Gladys grabbed a towel and dropped down to work on the puddle on the floor.

Or so she made it seem. The moment she ducked under the table, she grabbed the debit card. But then a thought struck her. Her mother had specifically insisted that they not bring any cash into the city. If her dad couldn't use his card, then how were they going to pay for the meal? She needed a new plan.

Gladys crawled out from under the table and rose back to her feet. "There's still a lot of water down there," she said. "I'll go get some more towels from the bathroom." Then, before her parents could protest, Gladys took off across the dining room again.

She didn't head for the bathroom, though; she went straight for the cash machine she had spotted earlier in the restaurant's foyer. Shoving the debit card into the slot, Gladys thanked her lucky star fruits for all the times her parents had let her push the buttons at the East Dumpsford Credit Union ATM. Otherwise, she wouldn't have known the PIN or been able to operate the machine so quickly. But as it was, it only took a few seconds for her to withdraw three hundred dollars from her parents' bank account.

Gladys's mind raced as she stopped in the ladies' room to throw the receipt away and grab some extra towels. She had the money now, but how could she use it to pay the bill? Her parents knew she didn't have that kind of cash lying around.

"Let me prrrint you a new check," the waiter was saying when Gladys returned to her group. He peeled the sodden one up off the table in front of Gladys's dad. "With a bit of a discount for yourrr trrroubles."

"Why, thank you," Gladys's dad said. "How thoughtful."

"Sandy," Gladys said loudly once the waiter had wheeled away, "could you help me finish drying up, please?"

Sandy barely had time to say "Uh . . . okay" before Gladys had grabbed his arm and pulled him down to the floor.

"Dude," he said as she shoved him under the table, "it doesn't even really feel wet any—"

"Shhh!"

Gladys reached into her pocket, retrieved the wad of cash, and thrust it at Sandy.

His eyes grew wide. "Gatsby," he whispered. "What the heck is going on?"

"I need you to volunteer to pay for dinner," she said. "I'll explain later!"

When they crawled out from under the table, the waiter was just arriving with the new bill. As Gladys expected, her father couldn't find his debit card—and, as she predicted, this upset him.

"It was *right here*!" he insisted, pawing at the damp tablecloth. He crouched down to look under the table, but of course, it wasn't there, either.

"Thieves, George," Gladys's mom whimpered. "I knew this would happen if we came to New York City!"

Her breathing was growing shallow. "How on earth will we pay the bill?"

Gladys nudged Sandy.

"Uh, hey, Mr. Gatsby," Sandy said. "Just let me pay for dinner. You know, as an extra birthday present for Gladys." He held the bundle of cash out to Gladys's dad, who stared down at it in disbelief.

"Good gracious!" Gladys's mother exclaimed, still sounding fairly hysterical. "Sandy Anderson, why do you have that kind of money with you?"

Gladys quickly realized her mistake. She should have slipped the money to Charissa, who everyone at the table knew was rich, or at least to Parm, whose family Gladys's parents didn't know very well. But they knew that Mrs. Anderson was a single mother who worked two jobs to support herself and Sandy. Of course it was suspicious for him to offer to pay.

But Sandy didn't miss a beat. "My grandparents," he said with a shrug. "They're always giving me money. They actually pay for my private school, too."

Gladys could have kissed him. Her mom, meanwhile, blinked rapidly, and her dad harrumphed. "Well," he said, "I guess it's this or wash dishes all night. Thanks, Sandy—I'll pay you back as soon as the bank sends me a new card."

Gladys, trying not to grin too hard, shoved a bite of birthday flan into her mouth. (*A bit watery,* she thought, *though that isn't exactly the chef's fault.*)

Then she offered it around to her friends. Parm passed; Sandy cried, "It's alive!" and jiggled his forkful around for at least thirty seconds before eating it; and Charissa scarfed down far more than her fair portion before their change arrived.

*Happy birthday to me,* Gladys thought as they all left the restaurant. Her secret identity was intact, and her notebook was full of notes for her next review; she couldn't have asked for better birthday gifts. And as she climbed into the family station wagon, she made a mental note to give her parents a present, too: her dad's stolen debit card, returned to his wallet that night after he had gone to sleep.

# Chapter 3

# CAKE AND PRESENTS

BACK AT THE GATSBYS' HOUSE, EVERY-one piled into the kitchen to sing "Happy Birthday" and eat the cake Gladys had baked. It had a strawberry-puree-and-lime-juice-infused frosting that she'd invented herself, and she watched everyone's reactions carefully as they took their first bites.

"Wow, Gladys!" Charissa cried. "This is the best dessert I've had since Classy Cakes!" No one else in the room had been to Classy Cakes on Charissa's birthday outing, but Sandy and Gladys's parents nodded in agreement, anyway.

"Itsh sho good," Sandy said through a mouthful—and after he swallowed, "I'm sure my mom will want the recipe."

Even Parm tried a tiny bite of the cake, and although she shuddered as she put it in her mouth, she didn't spit it out, either. Gladys decided to take that as a compliment.

"Is it time for presents now?" Charissa cried the moment Gladys finished her last bite. "Mine is the most awesome present ever. You're going to have *so* much fun using it!" She glanced over at Sandy and Parm then, and lowered her voice. "But maybe you should open theirs first. You know, save the best for last."

"Yeah, presents!" Sandy cried, and everyone trooped into the living room where the gifts were waiting on the coffee table. Gladys's mom pulled out her camera and started snapping shots as Gladys reached for the ribbon-tied bag from Parm.

Inside was a large jar of cardamom pods: green on the outside, though Gladys knew that the fragrant little seeds inside the pods were black. Cardamom was one of the most expensive spices at Mr. Eng's shop, and Gladys had never bought any for herself. But with this much cardamom, she'd be set for at least a year. "Thank you, Parm!" she cried. "This is perfect!"

"Oh, good—I thought you'd like it," Parm said. "My dad's recipe for gajar ka halwa is in the bag, too, in case you want to make it."

Gajar ka halwa was a delicious Indian dessert with carrots, nuts, and plenty of cardamom that Mr. Singh had taught Gladys and Parm how to make. "I can't wait to try," Gladys said.

Sandy pushed his gift toward Gladys. "Here, open

mine next." She tore through the reindeer paper ("Sorry—it was all I had," he said) to find a small yellow notebook. Its spine creaked as she opened it, and the paper inside felt thicker than normal paper and slightly fuzzy.

"Ooh, a diary," Gladys's mom exclaimed. "What a thoughtful gift, Sandy."

Sandy scooted closer to Gladys as her mom took a photo of them with the book. "It's waterproof," he whispered. "So you don't have to worry about ruining it at the beach or the pool or"—he grinned—"at restaurants with clumsy busboys."

Gladys grinned back. She didn't have any big plans to go to a beach or pool this summer, but a waterproof journal could definitely come in handy in places where she needed to write—like restaurant bathrooms. "Thanks, Sandy," she said. It really was a thoughtful gift.

"Okay, time for mine, time for mine!" Charissa was bouncing up and down on the edge of the sofa, her shiny red skirt crinkling and crumpling with each little jump. Gladys set the journal aside and felt her heart speed up as she reached for the huge gold box Charissa had given her in the car. Parm's and Sandy's presents were terrific, but she couldn't deny that she was especially excited to open this one. Charissa loved to shop, and she seemed to share Gladys's appreciation of good food like no one else. Could her friend have bought her a new set of shiny copper pots—or maybe even a standing mixer?

These fantasies evaporated the moment Gladys picked up the box; it may have been huge, but it was way too light to hold any of the kitchen equipment she'd been thinking of. In fact, when she pried off the top, the box appeared to be completely empty . . . until she saw an envelope sitting at the bottom.

"Okay, I sort of tricked you with the big box," Charissa admitted (though, of course, she didn't apologize). "It's just that this present is *so huge and awesome* that it deserved a big package!"

Gladys's mind started racing all over again, this time with thoughts of what could be in the envelope. A gift certificate to one of Manhattan's best restaurants? A picture of the new, professional oven that Charissa was having delivered to her house tomorrow?

She opened the seal and pulled out a piece of paper.

Congratulations! it said in bold purple typeface. You have been awarded one free summer at East Dumpsford's favorite day camp: Camp Bentley!!!

Gladys's stomach dropped.

Your summer of fun begins this Monday, July 1, at 8:30 am. Please wear shorts and sneakers and bring a swimsuit for your initial swimming evaluation.

Yours truly,

Laura & Carl Bentley, cofounders & directors

and Charissa Bentley, counselor-in-training!! ♥☺♥☺

"We'll spend the *whole* summer together!" Charissa shrieked, leaping to her feet. "Is this the best present ever, or what? Camp Bentley has arts and crafts, and relay races, and there's swimming time *every* day . . ."

Gladys sat stone-stiff, trying to process the words on the paper. She got sunburned after about one minute outside, was a terrible swimmer, and hated being in big groups. Camp sounded like her own personal nightmare; in fact, she'd been refusing to go for years, even when her parents begged her to try it. For the last couple of summers, Gladys had appealed to her father's penny-pinching side and convinced him that it would be a huge waste of his money. But now that it was free . . .

Charissa was dancing around the shreds of wrapping paper on the floor, her arms opening wide for the big hug of gratitude she no doubt thought she deserved. Meanwhile, Gladys's dad leaned over her shoulder, reading the letter. "Jen, have a look at this," he said. "Charissa's family has given Gladdy a free summer at Camp Bentley!" He plucked the paper out of Gladys's hand and passed it to her mom.

"Oh, how generous!" she exclaimed. "Honey, what a great opportunity for you to make even more friends!"

But Gladys didn't want more friends. In fact, she wasn't sure she wanted to keep all the ones she had at the moment.

Charissa didn't see her expression, though—her arms were already around Gladys's torso, squeezing like a boa constrictor. "You're welcome," she said into Gladys's ear. "It's going to be the *funnest* summer of your life."

# Chapter 4

## THE CAMP CRITIC

"LOOK, I'VE BEEN THINKING ABOUT IT," Sandy said the next day as he ushered Gladys through the door of his room, "and . . . maybe Camp Bentley isn't such a bad idea for you."

"*What?*"

"Just hear me out."

He motioned for her to sit down on the floor—which was pretty much her only choice since every other surface in the room was covered with stuff he needed to pack for karate camp. White practice pants exploded out of the big gray duffel bag on his bed; his desk was covered with bottles of sunscreen and bug repellant; and his desk chair could barely be seen under a pile of socks and underwear.

"So," Sandy continued, "you're probably going to get assigned more reviews for the *Standard* this summer, right?"

"I hope so," Gladys said.

"And do you have a plan for how you're going to get into the city for the next one?"

She sighed. "Not yet."

Sandy pulled a pair of socks off the desk chair and began to ball them up. "Well, you can't use birthdays anymore—yours and Charissa's have already passed, and mine's not until October, plus me and Parm will both be away. So you probably won't be able to come up with an excuse to get someone's parents to take you."

Gladys ran a fingernail along the crack between the two nearest floorboards. "What are you saying?"

"I'm saying that you might need to sneak into the city on your own—take the train and just do the reviews yourself. And if that's the plan, well . . . camp may give you the perfect opportunity."

Gladys looked up from the floor. "I don't get it."

"Think about it this way," Sandy said. "If you're supposed to be home and your mom drops in to check on you, she'll freak out if you're missing. But if you're supposed to be at camp . . . well, there are so many kids at camp, they probably won't even notice that you're gone!"

*Hmm.* Gladys hadn't thought about it that way. "So

are you saying that camp could be, like . . . a cover?" she asked.

Sandy tossed his balled socks in the general direction of the duffel bag, but they landed short, rolling under his bed. He shrugged and reached for another pair from his chair. "Exactly," he said. "I mean, I wouldn't play hooky right away. I'd take a week or two to figure out the system—when they take attendance, when you could sneak away."

"Yeah, but . . . I don't *want* to go to camp, even for a couple of weeks!" Gladys could hear the whine in her voice, but she couldn't help it. "I thought summer was supposed to be fun—a time to do stuff you like but can't fit in during the school year. And for me, that's cooking!" She slumped back against the side of the bed. She expected her parents and Charissa to be all gung ho about the camp plan, but now Sandy, too? He was supposed to help her think of a way *out* of this mess.

"Well, my camp isn't gonna be so amazing, either," Sandy said.

"But you really like karate!"

"I like the karate classes I take *here*," he explained. "But I also really like my computer. And there aren't going to be any computers for the kids at camp! We're supposed to 'divorce ourselves from technology' or something—that's what the brochure said." He flung another pair of socks at the duffel bag—too hard this time, and they bounced off the wall behind it. "My camp is in the middle of the woods in New Hampshire. My mom says it'll be good for me—she thinks I'm addicted to my computer. But what's really unfair is that I *know* the adults are allowed to go online, 'cause my mom's been e-mailing with the camp director!"

"Ugh, that is unfair," Gladys said. "I hate it when there are different rules for adults and kids."

"Tell me about it." Sandy threw a third sock ball, but this time he didn't even seem to be aiming for the duffel; Gladys heard a crinkle as it ricocheted off the corner of his Nikola Tesla poster. "I mean, if you go to Camp Bentley, at least you'll be able to cook at night and on the weekends," he said. "But I won't be able to use screens at all."

This was true, and suddenly Gladys felt bad for discounting Sandy's plan. Really, using camp as a cover for sneaking into the city was a pretty good idea.

"I guess if you can handle a whole summer at a camp without computers, then I can *try* going to Camp Bentley," Gladys said. "I mean, we may not be together, but at least we'll both be miserable at the same time!"

A small smile crossed Sandy's face. "I don't plan to be miserable the *whole* time," he said. "I think the karate parts will still be fun."

"Well, you're never going to find out if you don't finish packing." Gladys stood up. "C'mon, I'll help."

She started on a circuit of the room, collecting stray balled-up socks and other clothes. The underwear, though, she left for Sandy.

In the end, they stuffed his duffel so full that Gladys had to sit on it while Sandy closed the zipper. Then they made their way down to the Rabbit Room, where Sandy let tiny black-and-white Edward and fat brown Dennis out of their hutch to hop around.

"Will you visit them while I'm away?" he asked Gladys. "I'm sure my mom will let you in whenever you want."

"Sure," Gladys said. She loved playing with the rabbits—though between camp, cooking, and reviewing restaurants, her summer schedule was starting to look very full.

"And, hey, if any of the other restaurants you review have rabbit on the menu . . ." Sandy started.

"Don't worry," Gladys said. "I won't order it."

"Or, well . . . just don't tell me if you do, okay?"

Gladys grinned. "Okay."

That evening, back at her house, Gladys surprised her parents by announcing that she was excited to give Camp Bentley a try.

"Well, good for you, Gladdy," her dad said as he stuck a cup of take-out wonton soup in the microwave. Gladys had spent so long helping Sandy pack that she hadn't had time to cook dinner. Her parents had recently given her permission to cook for them twice a week, though she wasn't supposed to light the stove burners unless one of her parents was with her.

"I really thought you'd fight us on this one," her dad continued, "but I'm glad you're opening yourself up to new experiences. That's very mature of you."

Gladys wasn't sure how making silly crafts and playing in a pool was a more mature choice than teaching herself advanced cooking techniques, but she kept her mouth shut.

Her mom stabbed at a wonton with her fork. "I should be able to drop you off at camp on my way to work in the mornings," she said. "And the website says that lunch is provided, so we won't have to worry about that."

*Ugh,* Gladys thought. Camp lunch was at the top of a long list of things that she *should* be worried about.

As she lay in bed that night, her tummy tossing lo mein noodles around like shoelaces in a clothes dryer, Gladys's eyes wandered toward the window that faced her best friend's house. She was staring down a summer of ridiculous activities, bad meals, and secret reviewing missions—and she was going to have to do it all without Sandy. If only there was some way they could communicate, even while he was out in the middle of nowhere! Maybe he could sneak into the camp director's office and use the computer. Or maybe . . .

Gladys bolted upright in her bed. She had an idea—

but she'd have to do it before Sandy left for camp first thing in the morning. She set her alarm for five a.m.

Gladys woke up suddenly, jarred out of a dream in which Charissa had grown shark teeth and kept trying to bite off Gladys's toes. After checking to make sure that all ten were still intact, she slipped out of bed and into shorts and a T-shirt. Then she grabbed another T-shirt from her drawer and wrapped her present for Sandy in it.

The light outside was pale gray, and Sandy and his mom looked like shadows as they loaded Sandy's duffel into their trunk. "I'll go get the snacks," Gladys heard Mrs. Anderson say as she headed back toward the house. Gladys's moment had arrived.

She stepped outside and dashed across the lawn. "Sandy!" she hissed.

He looked up, surprise brightening his blue eyes. "Hey, Gatsby! What are you doing up?"

"I brought you this!" she said, a little breathless.

"An 'I heart cupcakes' T-shirt? Uh, thanks."

"No! It's inside the T-shirt."

Sandy took the shirt out of her hands, then slid the corner of something hard and rectangular out through the neck hole. His mouth fell open. "Your tablet? I can't take this!"

"Yes, you can," Gladys insisted. "It's not like I use it that much, and anyway I've still got my parents' computer. This way, you can hunt for a Wi-Fi signal— there must be one if the adults are getting online, right? And then, if you can hack into the network, you can e-mail me."

"Wow," Sandy said softly.

Gladys grinned. "Stuff it into your bag, quick, before your mom comes back."

Sandy had just wedged the T-shirt-wrapped tablet into his duffel when Mrs. Anderson reappeared, carrying a cooler.

"Good morning, Gladys!" she said. "You're up early!"

"I just wanted to say good-bye," Gladys told her.

"How sweet of you," said Mrs. Anderson. "Well, make it quick, kids—it's a long drive up to New Hampshire."

As she started the car, Gladys and Sandy stood looking at each other.

"Thanks," Sandy said. "I'll e-mail you as soon as I can."

"And I'll keep you posted on what's going on here," Gladys replied.

"Excellent. Well, have a great summer."

"You too."

They stared at each other for another moment. *Should we hug?* Gladys thought. *Shake hands?* Sandy looked just as unsure as she felt. Finally, she gave him a dopey little wave, which he returned before climbing into the car. He waved again as they backed out of their driveway, and then they were gone.

Gladys trudged home and removed the last piece of her homemade birthday cake from the fridge. That seemed like a better breakfast choice than anything else in the house, at least until she got a chance to stock up on pancake ingredients from Mr. Eng's. She carried the cake upstairs and grabbed her reviewing notebook on the way into her parents' office. They liked to sleep in on Sundays, so she would have a few hours to work on her review of Fusión Tapas before they woke up.

Three hours later, the cake long gone, Gladys clicked "Send" on an e-mail to her editor, Fiona Inglethorpe. The e-mail contained her review, and Gladys was proud of herself for meeting her deadline; she knew that Fiona was going on vacation tomorrow afternoon, and this would give her enough time to edit the article and send it to the Production department before catching her flight.

The *New York Standard*'s Dining section was always published on Wednesday, so that was when Gladys expected her review to come out. She hoped that, like the first time she'd had a review published, Mr. Eng would save her a few copies of the paper at his store. The chances that he would have extras seemed good since almost no one in East Dumpsford read the *Standard*—least of all Gladys's parents, who were devotees of the local paper, the *Dumpsford Township Intelligencer*.

Gladys didn't have to worry about her parents seeing her byline in the newspaper—the much bigger threat to her secret was that the *New York Standard* would mail her another check. She shuddered as she remembered when the first one had arrived unexpectedly and her mother had opened it in front of the whole family. The envelope was addressed to "Gladys Gatsby," but the check itself was made out to "G. Gatsby," the name under which she published her reviews.

Gladys had had to think fast. Luckily, her dad's name, George, started with a *G*, too. "This check must be meant for you," she'd told him.

It was a stretch, but Gladys's dad was an IRS agent and had recently visited the *Standard* offices demanding payment of back taxes. Gladys knew this because she had been with him that day (and very narrowly avoided catastrophe when she ran into her editor in the lobby).

Thankfully, her dad had swallowed her explanation like a spoonful of silky banana pudding.

"What idiots," he'd muttered. "Don't those *New York Standard* accountants know they're supposed to send the check to my office?"

"And then to put your daughter's name on the envelope," Gladys's mom had added. "How confused can one department get?"

"It must be because I came to work with you that

day," Gladys had said quickly. "They probably mixed up our name tags or something."

Gladys's dad shook his head. "I'll have to have Silverstein file the paperwork for a misdirected tax payment. This could take months to sort out!"

So Gladys had watched her payment for reviewing Classy Cakes disappear into her father's briefcase. Losing the money hadn't felt like a big deal to her then, since she'd never expected to get paid in the first place. The much bigger problem was what would happen once the people at her father's office figured out that the check actually hadn't been meant for him. And now that Gladys had submitted a new review, a fresh check would be heading her way soon. A check that she'd have to intercept at the mailbox and destroy before her parents got a glimpse of it.

Just one more thing to worry about this summer.

# Chapter 5

## A TASTE OF CAMP

MONDAY MORNING DAWNED HOT AND sunny, and Gladys's mom insisted she pack an extra-large bottle of water in her lobster backpack. The bag was already stuffed with a swimsuit, a towel, a huge tube of sunblock, a Mets baseball cap, and of course, Gladys's new waterproof reviewing journal.

"Mom, I'm sure they have *water* there," she said.

"It's just that you're so fair," her mom replied, brushing Gladys's dark hair away from her pale face. "And, well . . . you haven't spent a lot of time playing outside. Sunburn and dehydration can sneak up on you a lot faster than you'd think!"

For a moment, Gladys considered telling her mom that she actually planned to spend as little time as possible in the sun. But if her parents knew Gladys was hoping to find a shady corner to hide out with her journal instead of doing lots of camp activities, they probably wouldn't be very happy.

"Fine," she grumbled and shoved the water bottle as deep into the lobster's stomach as it would go.

In the car, her mom listened to the radio, but Gladys could barely hear anything over the thumping of her own heart. She wasn't sure what made her more anxious: managing her secret reviewing assignments or talking to kids her own age.

As it turned out, the entrance to Camp Bentley was swarming with kids of *all* ages. Little kids, barely older than toddlers, clung to their parents' hands, while older kids squealed and screeched and hugged like they hadn't seen one another in ages, even though school had let out less than two weeks before. The one thing everyone had in common was their purple shirts, which read CAMP BENTLEY: THE *FUNNEST* CAMP EVER! in white letters. Gladys felt pretty sure that Charissa was responsible for both the color scheme and the wording.

Wiping moist palms on her own purple T-shirt (which Mr. Bentley had dropped off while picking Charissa up from her party), Gladys took a deep breath. *You can do this,* she told herself. *A writer for the world's most famous newspaper doesn't get intimidated by stuff like camp.* She kissed her mom on the cheek and slid out of the car.

She was almost through the camp's giant wooden arch when a hand pulled her shoulder backward. She spun around, and there was Charissa with her two best friends, Rolanda Royce and Marti Astin.

All three were scowling. This Gladys would have expected from Rolanda and Marti, but she thought that Charissa, at least, might have given her a warmer welcome.

"Gladys!" Charissa hissed. "You can't go in that way!"

"Um . . . okay," Gladys said. "Why not?"

Charissa's ponytail whipped over her shoulder as she gave her head an exasperated shake. "*Because* you haven't been oriented yet! New campers can't use the main gate until they've taken the Camp Bentley Oath of Loyalty. It's tradition!"

"Yeah, *Gladys*," Marti echoed. "It's *tradition*."

Charissa sighed. "Did you even read the pamphlet I e-mailed you?"

"Oh. Uh . . ."

Gladys hadn't read it. She'd tried to spend her last day of freedom thinking about camp as little as possible, and she'd figured the orientation pamphlet wasn't a big deal. But now she could see that Charissa was actually hurt.

"I mean, do you even want to be here?" Charissa asked, her voice growing smaller with every word.

"Of course I do!" Gladys lied. "I was just really busy yesterday finishing up some . . . stuff . . . so that once camp started, I could be totally committed."

This answer seemed to cheer Charissa up. "Well, good!" she said. "Because I think you're *really* going to love it. Oh, and before I forget, here's your CIT pin."

Charissa pulled a large button—white with purple writing that said *CIT*—out of her canvas bag. Gladys noticed that Charissa, Marti, and Rolanda were already wearing them.

"Cool," Gladys said, fumbling to pin the button onto her shirt. "What's a CIT?"

*"What's a CIT?"* Rolanda's eyes bugged out like she'd never heard such a stupid question in her life.

"Calm down, Ro—she's never been to camp before," Charissa said. "Gladys, a CIT is a counselor-in-training. You have to be at least twelve to be one."

"Yeah, and you're *supposed* to have at least four years of camp experience, too," Marti muttered.

"That's true," Charissa said. "But Gladys has other experience that's going to make her an awesome CIT." She grinned at Gladys, who smiled back tentatively, wondering what this experience might be. "Anyway, it basically means you get to help one of the counselors or staff members do their jobs. We do our CIT duties in the morning, then we have the afternoon free for swimming and crafts and stuff like that."

"What kinds of duties?" Gladys asked.

"Well, it depends on your skills," Charissa said. "Like, Marti's really good with kids, so she'll be helping with the Tiny Tots group. And *I'm* great at organization, so I'll help my parents in the front office."

"What about you, Rolanda?" Gladys asked, trying to be friendly.

Rolanda stared at her. "Swimming, duh."

"Ro's training to be a lifeguard," Charissa said, "so she's going to help Coach Mike teach swimming lessons."

"Swimming lessons?" Gladys gulped. "Do we all have to take swimming lessons?"

Rolanda laughed. "Only if you can't pass your swim test—which is, like, the easiest test ever. Just one length of the pool." She gave Gladys an appraising look. "You *can* swim that far, right?"

Gladys didn't answer. The closest she usually got to large amounts of water was boiling a pot of spaghetti. Her mom had been a champion swimmer when she was a kid, but Gladys was pretty sure that talent had gotten lost somewhere on the way to her own gene pool.

A bullhorn sounded from within the camp. "Ooh, the welcome ceremony's about to start!" Charissa cried. "You guys go ahead through the main gate. I'll take Gladys around to the new campers' entrance."

"We'll save you a spot," Marti said, and she and Rolanda joined the stream of kids bustling through the arch.

"I can't wait to see your face when you get your CIT assignment," Charissa said as she led Gladys along the white fence that enclosed the camp's property. Gladys almost had to jog to keep up. "It's *such* a perfect fit! Mommy and Daddy weren't sure that a first-time camper would be able to handle it, but I told them that you definitely could."

"Uh, thanks?" The focus of Gladys's anxiety switched from the swim test to the CIT thing all over again. What would she have to "handle"? For some reason, she pictured a cage full of snakes. "Camp Bentley doesn't have a zoo, does it?" she asked.

"A zoo?"

Gladys had never been so happy to be on the receiving end of Charissa's "You're talking like a crazy person" stare. So it wasn't snakes, then.

"Okay, here we are," Charissa announced. They were at a nondescript gate in the fence. "The other new campers must have already gone in, but if you hurry, you can catch up before the introductions. I'll see you after!" And with that, she took off running back the way they had come.

If Camp Bentley had so many rules—or, at least, traditions—just for how to walk in, then Gladys wasn't sure she'd be able to keep up. *I really should have read that pamphlet,* she thought.

Close-growing trees shaded the pathway she was walking down now, and the noisy crowd at the arch seemed miles away. Gladys was starting to feel almost calm when another bullhorn blast ripped through the air, sounding much closer than it had from the front entrance. Her path curved around a corner, and she spotted people ahead.

There were probably twenty kids in the camp uniform—most very small, though a few bigger ones were mixed in—all standing in a clump, glancing around nervously. Gladys saw steps that led up the side of a stage. Charissa's mom was standing on that stage in her purple camp shirt, though a huge oak tree blocked Gladys's view of what Mrs. Bentley was facing. But soon enough, she heard.

"Wellllcome to Camp Bentley!" Mrs. Bentley bleated into a microphone. "Who's ready to have the awesomest summer ever?!?"

An enormous cheer rose up from beyond the stage, and the sound actually sent Gladys stumbling back a few paces into the woods. Never before had she heard screaming, clapping, and whooping like that— definitely not at school assemblies, and not even at *Glossy Girl: The Musical,* the Broadway show she'd seen with Charissa and her parents.

Mrs. Bentley let the cheering die down before she continued. "We have an *amazing* summer planned for everyone this year! There will be swimming! There will be archery! And in August, we'll divide into two teams for an epic color war!"

The cheers rose up again, but at least this time Gladys was ready for it. She held her ground, then even took a few steps closer to the kids grouped by the stage steps. As Mrs. Bentley began to speak again, Gladys tapped the shoulder of a girl who was compulsively smoothing the front of her shorts. "Excuse me," Gladys asked, "but do you know why we're standing here?"

"'Cause Mrs. Bentley said to," the girl answered in a voice barely above a whisper. Her braces flashed in the sunlight as she spoke. "She said to wait here 'til she calls our names. *And* she said no talking."

"They're ridiculous, these rules," a louder voice said. "Stand here. Wear this shirt. Be quiet. Like we're *children.*"

Gladys turned around to see who had spoken and spotted a boy leaning against a tree trunk. She was surprised she hadn't noticed him there before, but standing under a leafy branch, he blended right into the shadows.

The fact that he was dressed in black from head to toe probably also helped him blend. He wore a black shirt, black pants, black boots, glasses with black frames, and a black brimmed hat that Gladys knew was called a fedora, since her dad sometimes wore one, too.

She smiled at him. *Here* was someone who understood! She was about to say that she agreed about the rules—and ask how he'd gotten out of wearing the camp shirt—when he pushed himself off the tree with one foot and continued.

"Of course, most of you *are* children—so you wouldn't know any better than to follow along."

Gladys felt her smile flatten out.

"She said *no talking!*" the girl with the braces hissed. "If you're talking, we won't be able to hear our names being called!"

*Oh, NO.* An image flashed into Gladys's mind: Charissa, in their sixth-grade classroom, announcing everyone's names as they came back from winter break. Gladys hadn't enjoyed the attention then, and her class only had twenty-two students. How many campers were there at Camp Bentley? Gladys edged up closer to peek carefully around the trunk of the big tree . . . but the moment she did, she wished she hadn't. The entire field beyond the stage was crammed with kids—there had to be at least two hundred sitting out there.

The boy, meanwhile, was ignoring Braces Girl's warning completely. "Oh, I'm used to hearing my name called over the sounds of cheers and shouts," he said, his chest puffing out slightly. "For example, at the Preteen Choice Awards—"

"*SHHH!*" Flecks of spit sprayed out of the girl's mouth. "It's starting!"

She was right—Mrs. Bentley's voice seemed to be getting louder. "Please welcome our newest class of campers," she cried. "The Flamingo Fives!"

Cheers erupted, and the cluster of tiny kids ran up the stage steps. One by one, they accepted pieces of paper from Mrs. Bentley as she called their names, then exited down the other side of the stage, where a counselor was waving a FLAMINGO FIVES sign.

"But the Flamingos aren't our only new campers this year!" Mrs. Bentley said into her microphone. "So let's please give a big old Camp Bentley welcome to our next new attendee, Sophie Appelbaum!"

Braces Girl sucked in a huge breath, smoothed her shorts one last time, and climbed the steps.

Mrs. Bentley's voice echoed around the field. "Sophie has transferred from West Dumpsford Day Camp," she said, "and she'll be joining the Ninja Nines group! Let's all give her a round of applause!"

Cheers rose from the audience again.

When Mrs. Bentley next introduced a boy named Ian DeBaun, Gladys realized that she was going in alphabetical order—and that the *G*'s couldn't be too far off. Gladys also noticed that Ian—who, it was announced, had just moved to town from Indiana—got significantly less applause than Sophie, who was a local.

Dread now clumped in Gladys's stomach like cold oatmeal. *Will anyone other than Charissa cheer for me?* she wondered.

She didn't have to wait long to find out.

"Our next new camper, joining us as a CIT, is Gladys Gatsby!"

Gladys's ears seemed to stop working properly, because she couldn't tell if the buzzing she heard was cheering or a malfunction in her brain. Her legs, at least, seemed okay; in fact, they must have carried her onto the stage of their own accord, because suddenly she was looking out at the enormous crowd but didn't remember how she'd gotten there.

Handing her a piece of paper, Mrs. Bentley nudged Gladys toward the far steps, which she managed to descend without tripping even though her limbs felt numb. Then she noticed Charissa beckoning to her from under a banner that said CITs, so she hurried over and sank down next to her on the grass.

*I did it!* Gladys thought. Her heart was still thundering, but slowly her hearing returned.

"There he is, next to the stage," Charissa whispered in Gladys's ear. "I've never seen an actual celebrity before, have you? I mean, I guess on Broadway, but that doesn't count. Wow, he's so tall in person!"

"He—what? Who?" Gladys asked.

Mrs. Bentley's echoing voice answered that question for her. "Campers, please give a warm welcome to our other brand-new CIT, who has just moved here from upstate New York: Hamilton Herbertson!"

The tall boy dressed in all black strolled casually onto the stage.

*Hamilton Herbertson,* Gladys thought as she stared up at him. *I've heard that name somewhere before.*

Up on the stage, Hamilton leaned in close to Mrs. Bentley's microphone. "Thanks, Mrs. Bentley," he said. "I've prepared a short speech to introduce myself. May I?"

"Oh, um . . . of course!" Mrs. Bentley seemed a bit flustered at this request, but stepped back from the microphone as Hamilton cleared his throat and puffed out his chest once again.

"Greetings, fellow campers," he began, his voice resonating across the field. "As some of you probably know, I've recently made a name for myself in the literary world." To Charissa's left, Marti let out a small, excited squeal (though Gladys was pretty sure she had no idea what the word *literary* even meant).

"Earlier this year, my essay about a zombie-ridden future won the *New York Standard* sixth-grade essay contest."

*That's it!* Gladys thought. That was why she knew his name. She had never actually read the essay, but her sixth-grade teacher, Ms. Quincy, had been annoyed on her behalf, since Gladys's own essay had lost to his zombie entry.

"After that essay was published, an editor at Future-Flame Publishing offered to publish the book I'd been working on. So just last month my novel, *Zombietown, U.S.A.*, was published, and now I'm officially a *New York Standard* number one best-selling author!"

A series of *ooh*s and *aah*s rippled through the crowd.

"I've heard that *Zombietown, U.S.A.* is *so* good!" Rolanda breathed.

"So," Hamilton said, "I know lots of celebrities say they just want to be treated like regular people"—he paused dramatically here, peering through his black-framed glasses at the crowd—"but I'm not like most celebrities."

The crowd hushed.

"I'm only attending this camp because my parents are forcing me," Hamilton went on. "But I will *not* be wearing the Camp Bentley uniform, and I will *not* be participating in any CIT duties. I'll be using my time at camp to work on my next book in that pavilion over there." He pointed to a covered patio, where rows of lunch tables were set up.

Mrs. Bentley stepped forward. "Now, Hamilton," she said, "while we're all very impressed with your accomplishments—"

But Hamilton wasn't finished. "However," he interrupted, "I'm not entirely without respect for my fans. I'll reserve one half hour every day for book signings. You can bring your copies of *Zombietown, U.S.A.* to my table between eleven thirty and noon for an autograph, though I request that no flash photographs be taken at that time." Hamilton then took a small bow and said, "Thank you for your attention. Over to you, Mrs. Bentley."

He stepped away then, leaving the microphone clear,

but at this point Mrs. Bentley's mouth was hanging so far open that it was pretty clear no words would be coming out of it for a while. The entire audience watched in near-silence as Hamilton vaulted himself off the front of the stage and loped across the field toward the lunch patio. There, true to his promise, he turned his back on the campers, pulled a notebook out of his black messenger bag, and sat down to write.

Charissa's face, meanwhile, had turned as red as the flamenco dress she'd worn on Gladys's birthday. "Who does that kid think he is?" she fumed. "No one gets out of CIT duties. Being a CIT is an *honor.*" She took a deep, shuddering breath. "And no one gets away with not wearing the uniform. I don't care if he *is* a celebrity—Mommy and Daddy will kick him out of this camp before lunchtime."

Gladys didn't always agree with Charissa's snap judgments, but in this case, she was pretty sure her friend had it right. Sure, Gladys herself had had similar thoughts about the purple T-shirts . . . and the CIT duties . . . and, okay, she may also have fantasized about slipping away to find a quiet place to write. But she would never have stood up in front of the whole camp and made such a braggy speech about it.

In her mind, Gladys added one more item to the short list of things she and Charissa had in common: They both thought Hamilton Herbertson was a jerk.

# Chapter 6

# SALTY MEAT ON WHITE BREAD

MORE NEW CAMPERS WERE INTRODUCED after Hamilton, but Gladys didn't pay attention to their names. She wasn't sure any of the other kids did, either, since their glances all kept trailing over toward the lunch patio. Even Mrs. Bentley seemed distracted, stumbling over one-syllable last names and running her hand repeatedly through her auburn bob. Finally, she wrapped up the announcements with a feeble "New campers . . . er . . . please kneel for the Oath of Loyalty, led by Counselor Jamie."

A perky-looking teenage girl with short black hair bounded up onto the stage to take the microphone. Gladys would have gladly stayed seated and skipped the oath, but Charissa elbowed her. "C'mon," she hissed, "this will make it official! The words are on that paper my mom gave you."

Reluctantly, Gladys pushed herself onto one knee and looked at the paper just as Counselor Jamie's squeaky voice began to lead the new campers through the words.

> *We new campers solemnly swear*
> *to brush our teeth and comb our hair*
> *each day before we climb the ramp*
> *to enter this most awesome camp!*
>
> *We'll mind our manners, won't throw punches,*
> *won't complain about our lunches,*
> *will not fret, or squeal, or bawl,*
> *and won't start any fights at all!*
>
> *And so we make this oath today*
> *to fill our summers up with play*
> *and rise like new-anointed knights*
> *as fully fledged Camp Bentleyites!*

The entire camp burst into applause yet again—well, everyone except Hamilton Herbertson. Under the awning, he scribbled away as if nothing was happening on the neighboring field.

Mrs. Bentley retook the microphone. "Counselors," she said, "please take charge of your groups, and, um . . . Charissa, honey, will you give out the CIT assignments? Happy camping, everyone." Then, still looking slightly lost, she shuffled offstage toward the camp office.

"I'm sure she's going to call that idiot's parents this second," Charissa said, shooting a death glance over her shoulder at Hamilton. Then, in a much louder voice, she cried, "CITs! Attention, CITs! Please line up here to get your assignments!"

Out of her bag, Charissa pulled a set of cards. "Rolanda, Marti, you already know yours," she said, handing them their cards first. "Please report to your supervising staff member or counselor. Next I've got Jake Wheeler. Jake! Where's Jake?"

"Here I am," the dark-haired boy said, pushing to the front of the line.

Charissa glanced down at the card. "You're on music duty. Report to Counselor Linda in the Melody Tent."

Jake left whistling.

"Owen Green and Ethan Slezak?" Charissa called.

Owen strode forward, and Gladys wondered if it was possible that he'd grown another inch since school let out. "Am I helping on the basketball court?" he asked.

Charissa's eyes narrowed. "You wish. You'll be at the front gate with Counselor Dave on security detail. You too, Ethan," she told the shorter boy.

"Sweet!" Owen cried. "Do we get guns?"

"*No*, you don't get *guns*," Charissa snapped. "And

now I wonder if I need to switch you with someone else. I'm not sure you're smart enough to learn security. Anyone have a pen?"

"That Herbertson jerk does," Mira Winters said.

"Want me to go steal it from him, Charissa?" Ethan asked, pushing his floppy red hair out of his eyes. "I've got the moves!" He karate-chopped the air to demonstrate, coming within millimeters of whacking Charissa on the nose.

"You're gonna have janitor duty in a minute," she snarled.

"Okay, okay, we'll go," Owen said, snatching the card out of Charissa's hand. He and Ethan took off for the front gate, glancing over their shoulders to make sure she wasn't coming after them.

Charissa went on handing out assignments and sending kids to the far corners of the camp. Finally, only she and Gladys were left.

"I saved yours for last on purpose," she said with a grin, "because it's so awesome. Anticipation is just the best feeling ever, don't you think?"

Gladys, who wanted to shake Charissa by her purple-clad shoulders, didn't think that at all, but she managed just to give her friend a tiny nod.

"Okay, your CIT assignment is . . . kitchen assistant! See, I knew you'd love it!"

Gladys hadn't even had time to react, but for once she could admit that Charissa was right—that did sound like the perfect assignment for her. "Wow, thanks," Gladys said, taking her card.

"Now, I have to warn you: Our camp cook can be a little . . . prickly," Charissa said. "Like, she insists that we call her 'Mrs. Spinelli,' even though all the other counselors go by their first names. And, well"—Charissa glanced toward the kitchen, then lowered her voice—"her last couple of CITs haven't exactly worked out."

"Oh," Gladys said.

"But you have *so* much more cooking experience than they did," Charissa continued, "so I'm sure she'll love working with you. And who knows, maybe you can even teach her a couple of new recipes! I mean, our food is *fine*," she added quickly. "Camp Bentley would never serve anything horrible. But there's definitely room for improvement, and I think you're just the CIT to do it."

Gladys grinned. "Challenge accepted." She couldn't wait to see the camp's kitchen. If it fed two hundred campers a day—plus the counselors and staff—it had to be much bigger and better than her kitchen at home. Gladys pictured gleaming stainless-steel appliances, counters covered with thick cutting boards, an assortment of razor-edged knives.

And she was pretty sure she'd be able to handle this Mrs. Spinelli—after all, she'd seen every episode of *Purgatory Pantry,* the cooking competition show on Planet Food. No one could be meaner than Head Chef Rory Graham, who was famous for making contestants cry—usually with her sharp tongue, though sometimes with actual sharp kitchen utensils, which had a tendency to slip out of her hands when she got angry.

"The kitchen is right next to the lunch patio," Charissa said, pointing to a small building near where Hamilton was writing. "Ugh, you'll have to walk past *him*—but I'm sure he'll be gone by the time lunch is served. I'll catch up with you then, okay? I need to get to the office."

After waving good-bye, Charissa took off across the field at a jog, and Gladys made her way to the lunch patio. Hamilton didn't even look up as she passed.

She let herself into the kitchen through a screen door and found a much smaller space than she'd imagined—just one counter by the window and an island in the center. The room smelled a lot more like bleach than food, and the appliances on the counter were older and less gleamy than Gladys had hoped. In fact, the only thing that really appeared to be gleaming was the sweaty forehead of the sunken-cheeked woman who stood next to the island, ripping open bags of white bread and laying the slices out in an enormous grid-like pattern.

The door creaked shut behind Gladys, and the woman looked up.

"Hi!" Gladys said as cheerfully as she could. "I'm Gladys, your CIT."

The slice of bread in the woman's hand fell to the countertop. "You have *got* to be kidding me," she said in a voice that seemed way too big for her skinny body. "I asked them for a boy! A big, strapping boy who could haul fifty-pound bags of French fries out of the walk-in freezer. And this is what they send me—some little shrimp who can't even reach the top shelf?" The woman's hands moved to her aproned hips as she looked Gladys up and down. "How tall are you, girlie, three foot two?"

"I'm—I'm four foot nine," Gladys sputtered.

A curly, graying lock fell out of the cook's hairnet as she shook her head. "That won't cut the mustard in this kitchen," she said. "Now, you march right on over to that front office and tell 'em that Mrs. Spinelli says thanks, but no thanks. What I need is an experienced prep cook, not some scrawny little camper whose momma's gonna yell down the phone at me every time I send her home with a few boiling-oil burns."

Gladys opened her mouth to respond but didn't even know where to begin. Should she tell Mrs. Spinelli that she *was* an experienced cook? Or that if she burned herself in the kitchen, her mother was the last person she would tell?

"Well, what are you waiting for?" Mrs. Spinelli reached again for the bread. "And tell 'em to send your replacement on the double. These sandwiches aren't gonna make themselves."

"What kind of sandwiches are they?" Gladys asked.

Mrs. Spinelli gave an irritated snort. "You sure like wasting time, don't you, girlie?"

Gladys bristled. She was many things, but a time waster wasn't one of them. She turned away from Mrs. Spinelli only to catch a glimpse of Hamilton Herbertson through the window. *He wouldn't take this,* she thought. *He would stand up for himself, and make an obnoxious speech, and get what he wanted.*

She puffed out her chest. "Actually, I *hate* wasting time," she told Mrs. Spinelli. "So that's why I'm going to wash my hands while you tell me what kind of sandwiches we're making." She shrugged off her lobster backpack, stepped over to the sink, and turned it on.

Mrs. Spinelli gaped at her. "What kind *we're* . . . ? You've got some kind of moxie!"

Gladys soaped her hands silently, hoping that the lather might hide the fact that they were shaking.

"Now, let's get one thing straight," the cook said. "A kitchen is like a country, and not the democratic kind, either. In this kitchen, *I'm* the queen, and what *I* say goes."

Gladys turned off the sink, took a deep breath, and drew upon her final reserve of courage.

"Then all you have to do is tell me where to start,"

she said. "And what I don't already know how to do, I'll learn."

The cook gave Gladys another once-over, then let out a bark of laughter. "All right," she said. "You'll do exactly what I tell you, *when* I tell you, with no back talk. And if you mess things up, it's three strikes and you're out. Is that clear?"

"Yes, ma'am," Gladys said.

"Then go find an apron in the closet and get a hairnet and gloves from those boxes over there. And don't dally."

Gladys raced to the closet at the back of the kitchen and threw on the first apron she found. It happened to be adult-size, so its hem brushed the floor, but she didn't stop to look for another one. Somehow she suspected that Mrs. Spinelli cared more about her assistant being quick than having the right accessories. Next she shoved her hair under a tight hairnet and yanked on a pair of latex gloves.

"Today's sandwich choices are going to be ham and cheese or bologna and cheese," Mrs. Spinelli announced when Gladys returned to the counter. "I've got the bread laid out already. Go to the walk-in refrigerator and bring me the other ingredients."

Gladys waited a moment longer to see whether Mrs. Spinelli would specify what ingredients those were, but when she said nothing more, Gladys scurried off. She was a professional restaurant critic—surely she could figure out what went into those sandwiches herself. She wondered what her cheese choices would be, and whether the kitchen stocked different kinds of lettuce or just one. Meat and cheese wasn't the most exciting sandwich combination, but with some fresh mozzarella, a ripe tomato slice, and a zingy green like arugula, even a bologna sandwich could be saved.

Arctic air from the walk-in refrigerator blasted Gladys's face when she pulled open the heavy door, and a light blinked on automatically when she stepped inside. But rather than containing an explosion of colorful produce, the shelves around her held dull brown cardboard boxes. One box simply read HAM. Another read BOLOGNA. Gladys scanned the boxes for cheese names, but the only one she came across was AMERICAN, which barely counted as cheese at all.

The results were even worse when she started looking for vegetables. There were no tomatoes, and she had to shift several heavy boxes out of the way on the bottom shelf before she revealed a small one labeled ICEBERG. Pulling open the flaps, she found a single soccer-ball-shaped head of the pale, tasteless lettuce, its leaves already brown around the edges. Still, it seemed to be her only option, so she added it to the pile of boxes she was amassing by the door.

The sandwiches probably also needed a condiment, and Gladys advanced farther into the fridge to search for one. She found industrial-size jars of peanut butter, grape jelly, and mayonnaise before she spotted an enormous carton of butter on a high shelf. A vision of sandwiches sizzling in a pan came to her: boring white bread crisping up, bright orange American cheese melting slowly over the edges. She could save the sandwiches from mediocrity by grilling them! Standing on her tiptoes, Gladys stretched toward the butter and was just edging the carton off the shelf when—

"What do you think you're doing?"

Mrs. Spinelli stood in the refrigerator doorway, her left hand on her hip and her right gripping a long wooden spoon. Then she charged into the refrigerator, holding the spoon like a sword, and for a moment Gladys was sure the cook was going to whack her with it. But she stepped around Gladys at the last second, reached up, and used the spoon to shove the butter carton back into its place on the shelf.

"Butter?!" she bellowed. "Haven't you ever made a lunch-meat sandwich before, girlie?" She turned back toward the door and noticed the small box on the top of Gladys's pile. "And what on earth is this?"

Gladys rushed over. "I'm sorry," she said. "I looked and looked, but that was the only lettuce I could find in the whole refrigerator."

"Lettuce!" Mrs. Spinelli spat the word like it was poisoned. "Why would I want to put lettuce on my sandwiches? Just so I could watch the campers pull them apart and throw the green stuff away? No thanks! I'm not in the business of wasting this camp's money on food that kids don't eat."

"But," Gladys said, "maybe if you used a better-tasting green, like red leaf lettuce or arugula . . ." Her voice trailed off under the cook's stare.

"Back talk," Mrs. Spinelli said simply. "That's strike one." She tucked her wooden spoon into a loop on her apron. "Now, you grab that mayonnaise and meet me in the kitchen."

"Yes, ma'am," Gladys mumbled. She took two steps back toward the condiments and slid the enormous mayonnaise jar off the shelf while Mrs. Spinelli shoved the box of iceberg into a corner with her heel.

"I know what the kids like," the cook murmured half to herself as Gladys followed her out of the refrigerator. "Been feeding 'em for decades, and oh, I know. Bologna sandwiches. Hot dogs and French fries. And sloppy joes on Tuesdays for variety. Salty meat on white bread and nothing too fancy, that's what the kids go for. I know."

# Chapter 7

# THE "HAM HERB"

GLADYS SPENT THE REST OF THE MORN-ing keeping her mouth shut and doing whatever Mrs. Spinelli told her to do. Spreading mayonnaise carefully onto two hundred and twenty pieces of bread took almost an hour. Layering three slices of meat and one slice of cheese onto them took almost another. And of course, Mrs. Spinelli saved the only fun part—chopping the sandwiches in half with the biggest knife Gladys had ever seen—for herself.

By the time eleven o'clock rolled around, Gladys was already sick of kitchen duty. Her hands were moist inside their gloves, bits of meat and cheese were stuck to her arms, and she could feel sweaty strands of hair plastered to her scalp under her hairnet. But the sandwiches still had to be plated, and Mrs. Spinelli was wheeling a barrel toward the sink.

"Apples!" she announced cheerily, and Gladys looked over in surprise. Apples didn't seem to fit into Mrs. Spinelli's "salty meat on white bread" lunch plan, but Gladys stopped herself from saying anything before she got another strike for sass.

"I'll plate the sandwiches," the cook told her. "You wash these apples, then wrap each one individually." She patted a large box of aluminum foil.

Gladys was too surprised to stop herself from saying something this time. "Wrap them? Why?"

Mrs. Spinelli looked down at Gladys like her brain was smaller than a fruit fly's. "Don't you know anything, girlie? Kids like unwrapping stuff. You can trick 'em into eating fruit if they think it's a present." Shaking her head, she moved toward the cupboards to get plates.

Gladys sighed as she reached into the barrel. These apples were Red Delicious, her least favorite kind, and based on how mushy they felt, they weren't exactly fresh, either. "Maybe kids would eat more fruit if it wasn't *going bad*," she muttered under her breath.

The sink was right under an open window that looked out onto the cafeteria patio, and as Gladys rinsed the apples, movement outside caught her eye. Hamilton was standing and stretching his arms over his head, his writing notebook open on the table in front of him. So he was still here, scrawling stories to his heart's content while she followed orders like a scullery maid. Resentment boiled inside Gladys like someone had turned a burner on beneath her.

She glanced up again several apple washings later, expecting to see Hamilton hunched over his notebook, but this time the book was closed and he was staring off into the distance. Then he glanced at his watch. Was he waiting for somebody? Gladys checked the clock on the kitchen wall and saw that it was eleven thirty. Oh, yes—this was the half hour that Hamilton set aside for book signings.

After rinsing the apples, Gladys moved to the counter, where she started ripping off sheets of foil to mold around the fruits. Of every job she had done this morning this one seemed like the most ridiculous use of her time, so to take her mind off it she kept watching Hamilton out the open window. Eleven thirty-five came and went, then eleven forty. At 11:43, the boy tossed his fedora onto the table, stood up, and started to pace.

At 11:47, someone finally arrived. "Oh, hello," Gladys heard Hamilton say. "Have you come to have a book signed?"

Gladys craned her neck and saw a portly figure approaching the patio: Charissa's dad, who was handing something to Hamilton. It wasn't a copy of *Zombietown, U.S.A.*, though. It was a phone.

"Hamilton, I have your father on the line," Mr. Bentley said. "He'd like to speak with you."

Hamilton's back was to Gladys, so she couldn't see his face, but the boy took the phone from Mr. Bentley with a grunt.

"Hullo, Dad," he said. His voice already sounded much less boisterous than it had a moment ago. "Uh-huh. Uh-huh. But, Dad . . ." There was a long pause. Then, in an even quieter voice, Hamilton said, "Yes, I can compromise. I know that's something adults do." He said good-bye and returned the phone to Mr. Bentley.

"So we're all settled, then, Hamilton?" Mr. Bentley's voice had none of the warmth with which his wife had introduced the boy just a few hours earlier. "You'll write in the mornings, but then participate in all regularly scheduled camp activities in the afternoons? And take whatever level of swimming lessons your test places you in?"

"Yes, of course!" Hamilton's voice, by contrast, had grown warm and hearty. Too hearty. "I'm *so* glad we could come to this understanding. We're all grown-ups here, after all." He patted Mr. Bentley on the arm.

Mr. Bentley shook his head and turned back toward the office.

Mrs. Spinelli's voice called Gladys's attention back to the kitchen. "How many apples are left, girlie? Lunch starts in ten minutes!"

CIT duty was supposed to end at noon so that the CITs could eat lunch with the other campers, but when Gladys started to untie her apron, Mrs. Spinelli balked. "Where do you think you're going? Who's going to help me serve?"

"I . . ." Gladys started, but then she thought better of it. If she complained about staying late, Mrs. Spinelli might decide to get rid of her—and as bad as this kitchen job was, Gladys wasn't sure there were any other CIT duties she would be better at.

So she took the spot next to Mrs. Spinelli at the serving window as the first kids lined up with their trays. "Ham or bologna?" Mrs. Spinelli asked each one, then passed them a plate. Gladys was in charge of handing out the apples, so at least she didn't need to say anything to anybody, and the kids helped themselves to drinks from a cooler on the patio.

Charissa showed up at the window about halfway through the lunch rush. "Hey, Gladys!" she cried. "How was your first morning in the kitchen?"

"Oh, um—"

"No talking!" Mrs. Spinelli barked. "You're holding up the line!"

Charissa rolled her eyes but accepted her apple from Gladys and moved on.

Ten minutes later, the lunch supplies were running low, and the line had thinned out. Gladys was bending over to scoop one of the last wrapped apples out of her barrel when she heard a voice respond to Mrs. Spinelli's "Ham or bologna?" question with "Excuse me, but have you got any herbs handy?"

"Any *what*?"

Gladys straightened up to see Mrs. Spinelli's incredulous stare beaming through the window at Hamilton Herbertson.

Hamilton smiled. "Herbs. You know, those green things that people use for seasoning. Maybe some basil, or oregano? Even arugula would work."

Mrs. Spinelli swung her gaze from Hamilton to Gladys. "Arugula? *You* put him up to this, didn't you?"

"What?" Gladys asked.

"Oh, I see what you're up to," the cook said. "You think I won't listen to you about the lettuce, so you got one of your friends to ask me for it instead!"

Gladys was outraged. "I did not!" she cried. "And he's not my friend!"

But Mrs. Spinelli wouldn't listen. "Your tricks won't work on me," she muttered. "That's strike two for attempted sabotage. You're on thin ice now, girlie." She turned back to Hamilton. "And you—you'll eat the lunch you're given, or nothing at all." She shoved a ham sandwich at him and stepped away from the window. "You can serve the rest of the lunches yourself," she told Gladys. "I'm taking my break."

Gladys's mouth opened and closed wordlessly as she watched Mrs. Spinelli disappear through the screen door. Then she turned back to the window where, to her annoyance, Hamilton was still standing.

"I didn't get my apple," he said.

Gladys thought about throwing it at him. "What was that all about?" she demanded. "You just got me in a lot of trouble—and for something I didn't even *do*!"

Hamilton looked flustered. "Well, I'm sorry about that," he said, his tone not unkind. "It's just that I always like to have herbs on my ham sandwiches."

Gladys's fury ebbed a tiny bit. "I guess I understand," she said. "I mean, they're pretty disgusting otherwise."

"Oh, no, it's not that," Hamilton said. "It's just that ham with herbs is my signature sandwich. 'Ham Herb'—short for Hamilton Herbertson. Get it?"

"Huh?" Gladys had definitely not expected this explanation.

"There's a bar in Manhattan called the Tipsy Typist, where writers hang out," Hamilton explained. "The bartenders name cocktails after famous customers. But since I'm too young to drink alcohol, they invented a sandwich for me instead: the 'Ham Herb'! So now, whenever I eat it, I'm reminded of how many people love my book."

He gave Gladys a toothy smile, but her teeth were clenched way too tight to return it. Why did everything about this boy have to come back to how famous and special he was? "Well, sorry," she said finally, "but there are no herbs here. I've checked."

Hamilton sighed. "I guess I shouldn't have expected that a kitchen like this would be up on the latest culinary trends," he said. "I'll just bring my own herbs tomorrow." Then, after snatching the forgotten apple out of Gladys's hand, he turned away from the window and headed for an empty table in the corner.

# Chapter 8

# SABOTAGE
# (ON A SESAME SEED BUN)

WHEN THE FINAL CAMPER HAD BEEN served, Gladys made herself a tray. A sandwich was really the last thing she wanted after hours of smelling lunch meat and cheese—but at the same time, she *was* hungry, and still had an afternoon of camp to survive before she could make something better at home.

The moment she stepped out of the kitchen, though, Gladys knew she had made a mistake. The patio was crammed with kids laughing, shouting, and flinging bits of food at one another, and she couldn't spot a single open seat except at the farthest table. It was empty except for Hamilton, who sat hunched over a fat book, reading.

*Probably his own book,* Gladys thought.

*To remind himself what a good writer he is.* No way was she sitting there.

"Gladys!" Charissa waved at her from two tables away. "Over here!"

Gladys could have wept with relief. She hurried over and settled into the spot her friend had saved, murmuring "Thanks." Charissa grinned, but nobody else at the table looked particularly happy that Gladys had joined them. Mira Winters scowled openly, and Rolanda and Marti leaned in to each other to whisper. Gladys's face grew warm as she picked up her sandwich.

"Hey, Gladys," Leah Klein called from farther down the table. Leah had always been nice to Gladys, and Gladys knew that she played soccer with Parm. "Charissa said you're the kitchen CIT now?"

Gladys swallowed her first bite quickly. "Yeah!" she called back.

"So does that mean you made these?" Leah asked. "They're good!" She shot Gladys a sweet smile.

One seat closer to Gladys, Mira's head snapped to attention. *"You* made these?" she asked in a much less complimentary tone. She glanced at Leah, then back at Gladys. "Yeah, they're great," she said, her voice oozing sarcasm. "Really gourmet."

Rolanda and Marti snickered, and Gladys gulped. How could she explain that she had no control over the menu?

Charissa beat her to it. "Chill, you guys," she commanded, and the snickers died. "It's only Gladys's first day on the job. Trust me, she'll have the entire lunch program overhauled before you know it. She's an amazing cook!" Under the table, she squeezed Gladys's knee. "In fact," she went on, "on Wednesday, she's coming over to *my* house after camp, and we're gonna spend the whole afternoon cooking, just the two of us. Right, Gladys?"

That was the first Gladys had heard of this plan, but it sounded good to her. "Yep," she said.

Around the table, eyes narrowed. Clearly, the other girls had all hoped to get the first invitation of the summer to Charissa's.

"Girlie!" Mrs. Spinelli's voice boomed so loudly in Gladys's ear that she almost spat her boring sandwich back out onto her plate. She turned around to see the cook waving a piece of paper in the air. "Take this order form down to the camp office, and tell Mrs. Bentley to fax it to Foodstuffs, Inc. before the end of the day. Otherwise, we won't get our ingredients in time for next week."

Shoving one last bite of sandwich into her mouth, Gladys pushed herself out of her seat and slung her lobster backpack over her shoulder. She was happy for an excuse to get away from the table of death stares, but would her CIT duties never end?

As she crossed the field toward the camp office, she

looked over the form. It listed hundreds of food items in alphabetical order, and Mrs. Spinelli had checked off the ones she wanted and written in quantities next to them. Five hundred sesame seed buns. Ten bags of frozen chicken pieces. Three cases of prepackaged lemon bars.

In short, the makings of hundreds more mediocre lunches. And the sad thing was that Foodstuffs, Inc. seemed to sell plenty of interesting and delicious ingredients.

A wild idea struck Gladys. All the markings on the form were made in pencil—they'd be so easy to change. But did she dare? Mrs. Spinelli would be livid if the wrong ingredients got delivered, and would surely blame Gladys.

Then again, Charissa had pretty much promised everyone that Gladys was going to reform the camp's lunch program, and Gladys didn't want to let her down. Plus, if she got caught, she could say that she was technically acting on the Bentleys' (or, at least, *a* Bentley's) orders.

Gladys ducked behind a tree and rummaged for a pencil in her backpack. A few minutes of furious erasing and scribbling later, the task was done.

After she dropped off the revised form at the office, she saw Charissa beckoning to her from where she stood with the other CIT girls, who were now all in their swimsuits. They must have changed after lunch.

Rolanda's braids still looked damp after her morning with the swim coach, and muscles rippled under the deep-brown skin of her bare arms and legs. Gladys's limbs, by contrast, looked like floppy white worms.

"Quick, go get changed and meet us by the pool," Charissa told Gladys. "Once we've all passed our swim tests, we can have Free Swim time! It's the *best* way to spend the afternoon."

The bites of sandwich in Gladys's stomach turned over. She'd completely forgotten about the swim test.

Charissa pointed Gladys toward the changing room next to the kitchen building, and Gladys plodded inside on heavy legs. She couldn't disappear on the very first day of camp, could she? No, everyone would notice if she didn't turn up at the pool. Besides, she really needed to save her hooky playing for days when she had to go into the city, and she hadn't gotten a new assignment yet.

Once she'd changed into her plain blue swimsuit, Gladys made her way toward the pool area. It had a huge twisty waterslide on one side, but all the action seemed to be taking place at the other end of the pool, which was roped off into lanes. A bald, stocky man in swim trunks and a Camp Bentley T-shirt was hunched over the side of the pool, alternately blasting his whistle and shouting, and Rolanda was perched beside him, taking frantic notes on a clipboard.

"Stein, lane three, you've got a lazy arm on that crawl stroke!" the man bellowed. "Rolanda, stick him in Intermediate! And Percheski, lane one, don't bend those knees so much when you kick! Rolanda, it's Advanced Beginners for her!"

Gladys couldn't believe how nervous she'd been just to walk across the stage that morning. This was going to be so much worse.

Charissa spotted her. "C'mon, Gladys," she called. "CITs are up next!"

The smell of chlorine wafted up from the pool as Gladys moved closer, making her feel even more nauseous than she did already. She must have looked sick, too, because Charissa hurried over and put an arm around her. "Don't worry," she said. "Coach Mike is a lot harder on the younger kids. I'm sure you'll pass!"

"Charissa," Gladys started, "I've never actually—"

But a sharp whistle cut her off. "Squirrel Sixes, out of the pool!" the coach shouted. "CIT group, line up!"

The kids around Gladys scurried to the edge of the pool, and she could do nothing but follow. There were six lanes and—Gladys counted quickly—nineteen CITs who needed to be tested, so they would have to take turns. She knew that she didn't want to go in the first group, but she also realized that three rounds of swimming would cover eighteen kids, so one kid was going to have to swim on his or her own. She *definitely* didn't want to be that kid, so she made sure to join a line that only had two swimmers in it.

She ended up behind Rolanda and Charissa. The coach's whistle blew again, and the first wave of kids jumped into the pool. Gladys watched as Rolanda's limbs cut a graceful line through the water; in fact, she made it to the other end of the pool and pulled herself out before most of the other swimmers had even reached the halfway point. Barely stopping to towel herself off, Rolanda retook her place at Coach Mike's side and started taking notes about her peers on the clipboard.

"Wheeler, lane six, square those shoulders! Don't make me knock you back to Intro Lifeguarding!" the coach cried. Over in lane six, Jake's torso immediately straightened.

Before Gladys knew it, the first round of swimmers had finished. "Congratulations!" Coach Mike shouted. "You can all enjoy Free Swim! Next group!" He blew his whistle again, and a new row of kids jumped into the pool.

Charissa's strokes weren't quite as graceful as Rolanda's, but her form was strong enough that she made it across without any trouble. Gladys observed her friend as closely as she could, trying to figure out how she propelled herself down the lane so easily, but by the time Charissa climbed out on the other side,

Gladys still didn't have an answer. Her heart felt like it was beating in her mouth.

"You all pass!" Coach Mike shouted. "Group three, you're up!"

Next to Gladys, Ethan Slezak stepped forward, curling his feet over the lip of the pool. Gladys did the same, and when the cold water touched her toes, a shiver spasmed through her whole body. She glanced up and saw Charissa and everyone else who had already passed watching her group from across the pool.

The whistle sounded.

Gladys tried to jump in feetfirst, but somehow her body got tilted on its way into the pool, and she landed on her belly with a *smack*! Pain radiated through her midsection, and chlorinated water flooded her nose. Groping for the surface with her arms and legs, Gladys felt her throat and nasal passages burn. It was like she'd just jumped into a pool of fire, not water.

Her head finally broke the surface, and she gasped for air, managing to get in one good lungful before she sank again. Flailing her arms and legs, she tried to make her body obey her brain's commands. *Stretch out!* she told herself. *Straighten those elbows and knees! No lazy arms!*

But it was no use. Gladys had never learned how to swim, and as good as she was at picking up cooking techniques by watching other people, that skill didn't seem to extend to the pool.

Terror gripped her now as she bobbed in and out of the water, and she barely caught snatches of the coach's shouts. "Lane tw—" "Gats—" "Oh my—" Then she sank under again, deeper this time, and everything went quiet.

A moment later, she felt a strong arm wrap around her waist and drag her upward. Then her head was above the surface, and Rolanda was towing her coughing, spluttering self backward toward Coach Mike's end of the pool. Gladys glanced around—somehow she'd made it almost halfway across on her own, though she doubted that would count for anything.

All the other CITs were standing at the pool's edge, staring down at Gladys and Rolanda. "The rest of you pass," the coach told them, "but Gatsby . . . well." He looked into the pool at her. "It'll be Basic Beginners for you."

Gladys pulled herself out of the water quietly, too mortified now to look anyone in the face. Her worst fear about the swim test had come true—she'd failed spectacularly, humiliating herself in front of almost everyone she knew. The only saving grace, she supposed, was that she hadn't actually died.

"Okay, fourth group!" Coach Mike called. "Ready?" He tooted on the whistle one more time, and a splash sounded three lanes away as the final swimmer jumped into the pool.

Gladys turned to find out who was taking the test

last and saw the long, lanky form of Hamilton Herbertson in the water. Of *course* Hamilton would have the confidence to take the test alone. He wore sleek black swim trunks and a black swimming cap—but when Gladys looked more closely, she realized that his movements were anything but sleek. He thrashed around in the water, hardly making any progress toward their side of the pool. In fact, if she didn't already know that she was the worst swimmer in the group, Gladys might have suspected that . . .

"Holy Toledo!" Coach Mike cried. "This one's going under, too!"

It only took Rolanda a few seconds to dive back into the pool and reach Hamilton. Gripping him around the midriff, Rolanda hauled him to safety, just like she had done for Gladys. When he climbed out of the pool, Gladys observed that Hamilton's limbs were just about as pale and unmuscled as her own, though his face was flushed with effort.

"Do I pass?" he asked breathlessly.

The coach barreled over, nearly as red in the face as Hamilton was. "I would *hope*," he barked, "that after *just* seeing a girl almost drown, you might think twice about jumping into a pool with such an appalling lack of swimming skills. Have you ever been swimming before, Herbertson?"

All eyes were on Hamilton now, but that didn't seem to bother him. "I've been too busy developing my writing skills to learn things like swimming," he said. "But I figured that it couldn't be too hard if all these other kids could do it."

Gladys cringed. It sounded incredibly stuck-up coming out of Hamilton's mouth—but hadn't she hoped almost the same exact thing herself?

The coach let out a squeak of rage, then finally managed to say, "It's Basic Beginners, Herbertson, for you and Gatsby both."

Hamilton shrugged, seemingly not bothered by this turn of events. But Gladys felt like sinking back to the bottom of the pool. The only thing worse than being stuck in beginner swimming lessons had to be having the most annoying person at camp condemned to them right along with her.

# Chapter 9

# CAT EATS MOUSE

FIFTY MILES AWAY IN NEW YORK CITY, Fiona Inglethorpe was stuck with one of her least favorite people, too.

The editor sat in her office chair as her head restaurant critic, Gilbert Gadfly, paced and fumed in front of her. "It's not that I'm *jealous* of this Gatsby person," he said, pausing to lean on the edge of her desk. "It's just that, well, because our last names are so similar, some readers think that *I* wrote that Classy Cakes review! And a man like me has more important things to do with his time than read fan mail about how much people liked something that was written by someone else."

*Better things to do like barging in here,* Fiona thought. These days, she pretty much knew what to expect when she saw

Gilbert's bulky form shadowing her doorway. It was never good.

"In any case, I don't see why you would have sent *Gatsby* to review Fusión Tapas instead of me," he concluded, plopping himself down into her guest chair with a *creak*.

"Because, Gilbert, you told me specifically that you were not interested in reviewing tapas restaurants anymore," Fiona said. "In fact, I believe I have it right here in an e-mail you sent me." She turned to her computer, and with a few quick keystrokes had performed a search of her e-mails. "Ah, yes—here it is, in a message dated May third. 'INGLETHORPE, I HAVE ALREADY COVERED SIX TAPAS RESTAURANTS IN THE PAST NINE MONTHS. I HAVE TAPAS COMING OUT OF MY EARS. PLEASE REFRAIN FROM ASSIGNING ME TO REVIEW ANY MORE OF THEM.'"

Across the desk, Gilbert hemmed and hawed. "Well," he finally managed to say, "I didn't necessarily mean forever . . ."

Fiona shook her head. Nothing she did ever seemed to please this man. Yes, he was an excellent writer and an eater of wide experience, but this wasn't the first time she'd found herself wondering if his best days as a critic might be behind him.

"I can tell what you're thinking," Gadfly said.

Fiona let out a small sigh. "Can you?"

"Of course," he said. "You're thinking that it's not too late to pull that review of Fusión Tapas, cancel Gatsby's contract, and send me off to review the place instead."

"I will do *nothing* of the sort!" Fiona replied. "Gilbert, that review is written and edited and set to be published this Wednesday. By which time, I hope you remember, I will be far away from here, enjoying my first vacation in . . ." How long was it since she'd taken any time off? It felt like years. "In quite a while."

"Yes, yes," Gilbert grumbled, "your well-earned break. I don't know how you managed to convince the publishers to let you take more than a month off. That's unheard of in this business."

It was rather unorthodox, Fiona knew—but then again, she'd been working at the *Standard* for a long time now, and she had amassed quite a backlog of vacation days. What's more, she had made sure to line up five weeks' worth of assignments for all her staff members so that plenty of stories would still get written while she was gone. In fact, she had been in the process of sending off her very last set of assignments when Gilbert had burst in.

"Well, unheard of or not, everything should be perfectly under control while I'm gone," Fiona said. "That is, if I ever get to finish my last few tasks today. My flight leaves at four thirty." She glanced meaningfully over at her wall clock, hoping that Gilbert would get the hint. It was one forty now, and she really needed to leave for the airport no later than two.

But contrary to her hopes, Gilbert relaxed even more deeply into his chair. "Ahhh, Inglethorpe," he intoned. "I just can't imagine you relaxing on a beach somewhere, a pink drink in your hand. Well, the drink, yes. But the rest of it doesn't seem to fit."

"Who said I was taking a beach vacation?" Fiona asked, though she immediately regretted it. She'd really rather not reveal to Gilbert where she was heading. The whole idea of this vacation was to get *away* from work. She'd already told the publishers that she was not planning to turn her phone on the entire time she was gone, and that any Dining crisis could more than ably be handled by her deputy editor, Jackson Stone.

Thankfully, Gilbert didn't press any harder about her vacation destination. "We'll miss you while you're gone," he said. "You know . . ."

Fiona stopped listening. If she wanted to get out of here on time, she was going to have to multitask. Turning back to her computer, she finished typing her e-mail to Gladys Gatsby, assigning her two new restaurants to review: a ravioli bar in Midtown and a West African café in Greenwich Village. Fiona remembered from Gladys's original cover letter that she was a fan of Ethiopian food, so she was curious to see what her newest critic would make of a restaurant focusing on cuisine from the other side of Africa.

She was just clicking "Send" when she felt a puff of hot breath on her neck.

"Gilbert!" she cried, whirling around in her swivel chair. Her knees knocked into the large man's stomach and he stumbled back, nearly toppling the orchid she kept in the window. "What are you *doing*? Are you reading over my shoulder?"

"Don't be preposterous," he snorted. "I was just . . . taking a look at this lovely flower. It's actually looking thirsty, if you ask me. Don't you think you should water it before you go?"

Drat—the orchid *was* looking peaked. Fiona hated it when Gilbert was right.

"I suppose so," she admitted, "unless you'd like to volunteer to do it?" The nearest sink was clear on the other side of the fourteenth floor.

"Oh, you've wasted enough of my afternoon already," Gilbert chortled. "I really need to get back to work. But I'll walk you out."

*At least that'll get rid of him,* Fiona thought, and she rose to her feet and grabbed her pitcher. Just fifteen minutes until she'd be out of here and free of Gilbert Gadfly for a whole month—that was enough to put a little spring in her step. At the doorway, Fiona turned left to head for the restrooms and Gilbert turned right toward his cubicle.

What Fiona didn't see was that Gilbert kept turning until he'd spun a full one hundred eighty degrees and stepped right back into her office, gently sliding the door closed behind him.

She didn't see him scurry over to her computer and open up her Sent folder. She didn't see him compose a second e-mail to Gladys Gatsby with the subject line "New assignment—disregard my last message!"

She didn't see what he typed in the body of the e-mail before he clicked "Send" and slipped back out of her office, grinning like a cat who'd just eaten a mouse.

But two and a half hours later, Gladys did.

# Chapter 10

# A WATCHED INBOX
# NEVER BOILS

GLADYS OPENED HER NEW JOURNAL the moment she got home. Her pencil dug into the paper so hard that it nearly punched a hole through the page.

*Hamilton Herbertson is the worst!!! He is ickier than Pathetti's goopy-crusted pizzas, slimier than the gravy from Fred's Fried Fowl, and has a head bigger than the giant plastic burger outside of Sticky's. Who cares if he's written a book? I'm a published writer, too, and I don't go around asking for special treatment or bragging about my "signature sandwich." Ugh!!*

*And now I'm going to have to take*

*swimming lessons with him every single day. I wish Rolanda had just let me drown.*

*No stars! (completely irredeemable)*

She slammed the journal shut and flung it across her room. Reviewing usually calmed her down, but she was feeling just as agitated now as when she had walked into the house. Maybe it didn't work so well when you reviewed a person instead of food.

It was four thirty; Gladys's mom had dropped her at home after camp and then returned to work. How would Gladys fill the time until her parents came home for good? Tonight wasn't one of her nights to prepare dinner, and after all those hours in the camp kitchen, she didn't really want to touch more food, anyway. This was a strange new feeling, and she didn't like it.

Instead, she headed for her parents' home office and turned on the computer.

Gladys logged into her DumpMail account, and there in her inbox sat two new e-mails, both from her editor at the *New York Standard*. Hurrah! She clicked to the first one.

Dear Gladys,

Thanks again for your terrific review of Fusión Tapas!

Look for it in Wednesday's issue. I'm impressed with just how much of their menu you were able to cover.

As I've mentioned before, I'll be on vacation for the remainder of July, but there are two restaurants that I'd like you to review in the meantime: Café Accra is a brand-new West African eatery in Greenwich Village, and Ristorante Massimo is a small ravioli bar in Midtown that opened last year that we haven't gotten around to visiting yet. I'd like to see reviews of both of these establishments upon my return to work on August 5.

The addresses of the restaurants are below. Have a terrific July!

Cheers,
Fiona

*Two* new assignments! Her editor must have really liked the work she'd done so far. And both of these restaurants sounded great! How many flavors of ravioli would Gladys get to sample at Ristorante Massimo? What would the cuisine of Western Africa taste like? She'd have to experiment with some recipes at home before venturing to Café Accra.

Opening up a new tab in her browser, Gladys immediately began researching West African food. She had just bookmarked a recipe for a tasty-sounding Ghanaian dish called red-red (beans and tomatoes and ginger, oh my!) when she remembered that there had been a second e-mail in her inbox. Clicking back over, Gladys opened it up.

Gatsby,

Please disregard my last message—those reviews are canceled. I have a different assignment for you instead: Find the best hot dog in New York City.

Leave no street corner unvisited, and no dog untasted!

Your deadline remains August 5.

Cheers,
Fiona

P.S. Don't bother responding to this e-mail—I'm on vacation.

Gladys stared at the screen.
*Hot dogs??*
She felt like the message had reached out of the computer and slapped her across the face. It wasn't just what it said, but the way it was written—so harsh and commanding! Her editor was usually so much nicer over e-mail.

But even if Fiona had written it in her usual friendly way, there would be nothing nice about this message. In one fell swoop, Gladys's exciting summer filled with delicate pastas and boldly flavored stews had been ripped away and replaced with . . . salty meat on white bread.

Gladys clicked to the first e-mail; it had only been sent five minutes before the second. What had happened in those five minutes to change Fiona's mind? Why would her editor think this crazy hot dog assignment was a better fit for her?

She thought back to those forms she had filled out for the *Standard* a few months back, including her address and social security number. Could someone at her dad's office have already figured out that the check she'd received wasn't a mistake, and that the *New York Standard* had a twelve-year-old on its payroll? Had they told Fiona? And had Fiona decided to sentence Gladys to a summer of reviewing hot dogs because that was the kind of food a twelve-year-old would eat?

*Stop thinking crazy,* Gladys told herself. *Fiona Inglethorpe isn't Mrs. Spinelli.* And anyway, if her editor found out that Gladys was only twelve, she wouldn't waste time cooking up a ridiculous assignment to punish her.

She would just fire her.

Gladys didn't want to get fired. Being a restaurant critic had been her life's dream ever since she'd found out that such a job existed. *You'll just have to write the review,* she told herself. That's what professionals did—accepted assignments without questions or complaints. And with her boss on vacation, it wasn't like she could ask questions now even if she wanted to.

Still . . . find the best hot dog in New York City? Where should she even begin? She thought back to the day she'd spent with her dad in March, traipsing around Manhattan collecting taxes. There had been hot dog carts on almost every corner. And that was in just one of the five boroughs! What about Queens, and Brooklyn, and Staten Island, and the Bronx? There had to be thousands of street corners with hot dog vendors on them. How on earth was she supposed to get to them all?

She needed Sandy's help. Opening a new message, Gladys began to type furiously.

Dear Sandy,

Hi! If you're reading this, you've found the Wi-Fi. (Good job!)

Camp Bentley is just about as bad as I imagined, but I doubt I'll be spending much time there after today. The reason is my new assignment: I'm supposed to find the best hot dog in New York City. Gaaaah!

There are so many street carts selling hot dogs, I don't even know where to start. Any ideas? Maybe you could put together some kind of grid or matrix to help me figure out how many different places I need to try and how to organize them?

Sorry to be so demanding in my very first e-mail of the summer.

Miss you lots,
Gladys

She clicked "Send," then sat at the computer for almost fifteen minutes watching her inbox. Maybe Sandy was combing the woods right now, holding her tablet above his head in search of a signal. Maybe now was the moment that he was breaking into the camp director's network. Or . . . *now!*

But no message came through. *I guess a watched pot really never does boil,* Gladys thought—and with a heart that felt as flat and heavy as a cast-iron skillet, she reluctantly turned off the computer.

# Chapter 11

# BOBBING LIKE A HOT DOG

DAY TWO AT CAMP BENTLEY STARTED OFF much like day one, except this time Gladys was allowed to come through the front gate with the rest of the campers. Everyone gathered in the field for the morning announcements, and Gladys couldn't help but glance around for Hamilton Herbertson. Was he wearing his purple shirt today, or still protesting against the camp's dress code?

*Not like I care what he wears,* she told herself. *It's just that it's rude to Charissa and her family if he won't wear the uniform.*

She finally spotted him and, like yesterday, he was clad in black from head to toe. Charissa was going to have a fit. Gladys turned to ask if her friend had seen him yet, but then Mr. Bentley's voice came booming out of the speakers.

"The swimming lesson schedules have been posted on the pool bulletin board, so if you're not sure what time your lesson is, please check there. Just like last year, the day will start with the least advanced class and progress to the most advanced right before lunch. So Basic Beginners will meet at nine o'clock, Advanced Beginners at nine thirty, et cetera. And, of course, today is also the start of Free Swim in the afternoons for anyone who has passed their lap-swimming test."

Gladys tore a blade of grass out of the ground in front of her. She'd thought that she would at least have until the afternoon to mentally prepare for her first swimming lesson, but now she had less than fifteen minutes.

The announcements ended with a "Go get 'em, Camp Bentley!" and all the campers rose to their feet. Gladys quickly headed to the kitchen to try to catch Mrs. Spinelli and explain her new schedule before her lesson started.

As she passed through the covered cafeteria patio, she noticed that Hamilton was already in his usual seat, scribbling away in his notebook. Turning her nose up at him, she marched to the screen door and popped her head in.

Just like yesterday, Mrs. Spinelli stood behind the counter, though this time she was laying out rows of burger buns instead of bread slices. At the squeak of the screen door, she looked up.

"Hot lunch today, girlie!" she announced in lieu of a greeting. "Head on back to the pantry and grab me twelve of those jumbo cans of baked beans. Unless you're too puny to carry 'em, that is."

"Um . . . I . . ." Gladys felt pulled in too many directions. Part of her wanted to march to the pantry and prove that she was *not* too puny, and part of her wanted to inform Mrs. Spinelli that homemade baked beans, seasoned with bacon and maple syrup, were far superior to canned ones. But the part of her that didn't want to be screamed at by Coach Mike for being late won out.

"I actually came to tell you that I can't start my CIT work at nine o'clock anymore," Gladys said.

"Giving up already?" Mrs. Spinelli nodded to herself. "I guess I shouldn't be surprised. The moment I laid eyes on you, I knew you weren't cut out for it. It's not for the weak of spirit, this work."

"I'm not weak of spirit!" Gladys cried. "It's just that my swimming lessons start at nine, so I'll have to come in a little later."

Mrs. Spinelli slowly set down the bun she was holding, and Gladys gulped, sure that she was about to get a final strike for sass. But to her surprise, the skinny cook chuckled.

"Weak of swimming skills, then, is it? Well, you'd

better get to work on that. We can't have you bobbing around in the pool like a hot dog on the boil, can we?" She waved the back of a latex-gloved hand toward the door, dismissing Gladys. "And you tell that Coach Mike that Yolanda Spinelli sends her regards. I saw him put away six of my hamburgers at last year's end-of-summer cookout. He's an impressive man, that one."

Mrs. Spinelli looked quickly back down at her array of buns. Was she . . . blushing? Gladys stared for what was probably a moment too long, then turned and raced out the door before the cook gave her a strike for cheekiness.

She hurried to the changing rooms, and when she emerged, the camp's central clock said five minutes to nine. She was about to head over to the pool when a rustle sounded behind her: Hamilton turning to a fresh page in his notebook. He had not changed into his swimsuit, and he didn't seem to have any intention of going to the pool at all.

*Forget about him,* she told herself. *Who cares if he gets into trouble?* But she couldn't help thinking that if *she* was about to miss her lesson accidentally, she'd appreciate being warned.

"Hey!" she said in the sharpest voice she could muster. She might be helping Hamilton, but that didn't mean she had to be nice about it. "We're supposed to go to the pool for our swim lesson."

Hamilton glanced up, but his eyes looked vague

and unfocused behind their black-framed spectacles.

"It's almost nine!" Gladys pointed to the camp clock. Hamilton looked, then sat up straighter.

"Oh," he said. "I'm sorry, but I'm only signing books between eleven thirty and noon. So if you wouldn't mind coming back—"

"I don't want you to *sign a book*." Gladys was trying to keep her cool, but he wasn't making it easy. "I was just pointing out that your swimming lesson starts in three minutes."

"My swimming—oh!" He jumped to his feet. "That's right—I promised. I have to get dressed. Will you watch this for me?" And without waiting for an answer, he shot around the corner toward the changing rooms, leaving his notebook on the table in front of Gladys.

"Hey!" she cried after him, but he'd already disappeared.

*Fudge.*

Gladys glared down at the notebook that was now going to make her late. For a moment, she considered just leaving it there and running to the pool, but she understood how important a notebook was. She would hate it if she asked someone to keep an eye on her reviewing journal and they just disappeared. Then again, Hamilton had just assumed that she would be happy to watch it for him—probably because he was a "celebrity." *Ugh,* she thought. *After we make it to the pool, I'm never speaking to him again.*

Hamilton ran back a minute later in his swim trunks, stuffing his other clothes into his bag and grabbing his notebook. "Come on!" he said impatiently—as though *Gladys* was the one making *him* late! More annoyed than ever, she followed.

Hamilton walked quickly, and given that his legs were longer than Gladys's, she had to scurry to keep up. The camp clock struck nine with a *bong!* when they were halfway across the field. "Maybe we'll just be able to slip into the group unnoticed," Gladys panted.

"Sure," Hamilton said, but a second later, as if by unspoken agreement, they both broke into a run.

They reached the pool in less than a minute, but any hopes of quietly joining the class were shot the moment they skidded to a stop on the concrete.

"Late!!!" screamed a high-pitched voice. "Coach! Coach! The big kids are *late!*"

The source of the scream was a little girl with bright red pigtails and freckles on pretty much every bit of skin not covered by her frilly pink bikini. She was pointing a finger at Gladys and Hamilton and nearly jumping up and down with excitement. Next to her, an even smaller boy with dark skin and closely shaved hair was shaking his head like he'd never been more disappointed.

"Late, *late*, LATE!" the pigtailed girl sang, and around her, more and more of her peers joined in.

Gladys had hoped that the Basic Beginners group

might have a couple more older campers in it—maybe a poor swimmer from the Elephant Elevens or the Tarantula Tens—but not one of the kids looked to be over the age of six. In fact, she was pretty sure she saw a swim diaper poking out of the littlest boy's trunks.

"Silence!" roared Coach Mike. From behind her clipboard, Rolanda smirked.

The coach paced back and forth along the pool's edge. "This is Basic Beginners—which means that none of you little varmints has the foggiest idea how to swim. You are one false move away from drowning. And the only people who stand between you and a miserable death are me and my assistant, Rolanda. So you'd better listen up and do exactly what we say, or when the time comes . . ."

The coach just let those words hang in the air, but he didn't have to finish the sentence. All the little kids were staring at him now, several of them trembling as they no doubt imagined their watery demises.

"Well, that's a bunch of baloney."

Gladys had been thinking the same thing, but at least she'd been smart enough not to say it out loud. Now every head in the group (including Coach Mike's and Rolanda's) turned toward Hamilton, whose ghost-pale chest was puffed out, Gladys realized, in preparation for another speech.

"You may be able to scare these children with your

threats, Coach Mike," he began, "but I am your intellectual peer. I know that you're legally required to save every one of us, no matter how badly we listen to you or how little we obey. If you let a child drown, this camp will be shut down and you'll lose your job—and probably be sued. So you can request that I do you the favor of listening, but empty threats against my life will get you nowhere."

Now the little kids were gawking at Hamilton.

"Herbertson," the coach growled. "My office. Rolanda, start them on the drills."

Hamilton's spine was straight as he marched past the other kids and followed Coach Mike into the office at the edge of the pool area, and Gladys honestly wasn't sure who to root for. Resolving to forget about both of them if she could, she turned her attention to Rolanda, who was now demonstrating the arm movements and breathing patterns for a basic crawl stroke.

It turned out that Gladys needn't have changed into her swimsuit for this lesson, since they never even went into the pool. After the demo, Rolanda moved in and out of the rows, straightening elbows and adjusting heads. Five minutes before the end of the lesson, Hamilton and the coach finally returned to the group.

In spite of herself, Gladys craned her neck along with everyone else, trying to read Hamilton's expression. Had he been punished? Or had he managed to

maneuver his way into yet another set of special circumstances? Unfortunately, just as he came into her
sight line, Rolanda reached out and jerked Gladys's
head back in the opposite direction.

"You breathe at regular intervals," she hissed into
Gladys's ear, "or you drown."

By the time Gladys was able to peek up again, Hamilton had disappeared into one of the rows behind her.

The moment she got home from camp that day,
Gladys made a beeline for the computer. *Please have
found Wi-Fi, please have found Wi-Fi,* she thought
desperately. But when she logged in to her DumpMail
account, there was no message from Sandy.

She shoved the keyboard away in frustration. She
needed to get started on this crazy hot dog assignment—but, more importantly, she just really wanted
to talk to her friend. In the week after school had finished, she and Sandy had hung out constantly. Gladys
could hardly even remember what they'd talked about
in all that time. All she knew was that now she was
bursting to tell someone about Mrs. Spinelli, and
swimming, and Hamilton, but Sandy wasn't around
to listen.

At least tomorrow would be Gladys's last day of
camp for the week; Thursday was July 4, and Camp
Bentley was shutting down for the long weekend. So
Gladys would be off from camp on Thursday and Fri-

day, even though her parents only had Thursday off from work.

Gladys's dad had grumbled about this all through dinner the previous night. "No rest for government employees," he'd said between bites of a drumstick off the chicken Gladys had helped her mom roast. "When am I supposed to spend time with my family? Here's my daughter, growing up before my eyes, and I'm barely home to see it. How tall are you now, Gladdy, five seven?"

It was the best wrong estimate of her height that Gladys had heard all day.

Just for that, Gladys was planning to surprise her dad tonight with a key lime pie, his favorite dessert. *I'd better get started if I want it to have enough time to chill before dinner,* she thought, and shut down the computer.

The rest of the afternoon flew by as Gladys separated eggs, zested limes, and smashed graham crackers into bits for the crust. The harder she worked, the lighter her worries became, until they floated away like the steam that rose off her pie when she finally took it out of the oven.

On the menu for dinner that night was leftover chicken and microwaved frozen vegetables. Gladys settled in at the kitchen table with her plate, and her dad started up again about having to work on Friday.

"It wouldn't be so bad," he said, "if all week long on

the train I didn't have to listen to everyone *else* talk about where they're going with their families. Robbins is taking his kids to the Jersey Shore!"

Gladys's mom raised an eyebrow. "You're jealous of someone who's going to New Jersey?"

"I—no—look, it's the principle of the thing!" he spluttered. "On Friday, he'll be strolling down the boardwalk with his boys, playing arcade games and eating junk food, and where will I be? Schlepping around the city as usual." He sighed, then turned to Gladys. "Have you got any fun plans for Friday, Gladdy?"

She was just about to say "Nope" when an idea struck her. She was off from camp on Friday . . . her dad wanted to spend more time with her . . . and she needed to get to New York City to start working on her review. It wasn't a boardwalk, but why couldn't they stroll around together eating hot dogs in Manhattan?

"Um," she said, "actually, yeah. But first, I have a surprise for you, Dad!" And she hurried off to get the pie from the fridge.

Three slices later, her dad was like lime-flavored putty in her hands. He agreed to her plan immediately, and everything was all set: On Friday, Gladys would once again head into the city with her dad. Operation Top Dog was a go.

Chapter 12

# THE RIGHT BALANCE

WHEN GLADYS MET CHARISSA AT THE end of camp the next day, her high ponytail was still wet from the pool. "Man," Charissa said, "it is *such* a bummer that you can't do Free Swim with us. What have you been doing with your afternoons?"

"Oh," Gladys said. "I've been going to the archery range."

Despite her determination not to like anything about Camp Bentley, Gladys had to admit that the archery range wasn't bad. For starters, no kids under ten were allowed, so it tended to be pretty quiet. Plus the archery counselor, a college student named Lanie, was really nice. Just today, she'd advised Gladys to imagine the faces of her least favorite people on the targets—and once Gladys began picturing Hamilton, Coach Mike, and Mrs. Spinelli, her aim improved quite a bit.

"See?" Charissa said. "I told you you'd love camp! Oh, look, there's Daddy." She waved to her father. "Come on, Daddy, let's go!"

Mr. Bentley strode toward them, his purple Camp Bentley T-shirt stretched tight across his ample midriff. "Where to, cupcake?"

"First to Mr. Eng's," Charissa said, "and then straight home. Gladys and I are going to make—what are they called again, Gladys?"

"Tatale," Gladys said. "They're pancakes made with plantains, ginger, and cornmeal." It was a recipe that Gladys had found while researching West African cuisine, and even though she didn't have to do the Café Accra review anymore, she still wanted to try making them. Luckily, Charissa said she had a nice big griddle, which would certainly make the cooking easier.

Gladys had also purposely selected a recipe that Charissa wouldn't have all the ingredients for. That way, they would have to make a stop at Mr. Eng's, where Gladys could look at a copy of the *New York Standard*. Her review of Fusión Tapas had been published today, and while she'd already sneaked a peek at it online before camp, there was nothing quite like seeing her words in the physical paper.

Charissa had the door open almost before the car

was parked in front of Mr. Eng's. "Come on!" she cried, and Gladys scrambled to follow her. Moments later, Charissa was tearing down the aisles like a cornmeal-seeking missile.

Gladys stepped inside more quietly, though she was just as excited as Charissa to be visiting her favorite spot in East Dumpsford. The Gourmet Grocery was filled with ingredients for any kind of cooking project you could imagine: fresh local produce, fancy meats and cheeses, and imported delicacies that changed on a weekly basis, meaning there was always something new to discover.

Mr. Eng, the owner, was standing at the check-out counter, and a smile split his wrinkled face when Gladys gave him a wave.

"Gladys!" he said. "I was wondering whether I'd see you today." Then, lowering his voice, he informed her, "I have five copies of the *Standard* saved here for you behind the counter. Do you want them now?"

Gladys glanced over her shoulder, and saw Mr. Bentley with a shopping basket weighing down his arm. "Keep up, Daddy!" Charissa demanded as she finished loading the basket with heavy plantains and moved on to the ginger bin.

"Um, better not," Gladys said. "Charissa can be a little nosy. I wouldn't want to have to hide the papers from her."

Mr. Eng nodded knowingly. "Are you sure I can't

tempt you with a peek right now, though?" he asked.

"Well, maybe just a little one."

Mr. Eng passed one of the papers to Gladys, then stepped out from behind his counter. "Miss Bentley! Mr. Bentley!" he called. "Why don't you come back to the storeroom with me for a moment? I've just received a shipment of premium Brazil nuts, and would be pleased to offer you a sample." He left Gladys with a wink as he led the Bentleys away.

Grateful for the moment of privacy, Gladys flipped to the Dining section to examine her second-ever published review. "Tradition and Creativity Collide at Fusión Tapas," read the headline, and under that was "by G. Gatsby" in slightly smaller print. Gladys couldn't help but run a finger across the smudgy ink that spelled out her name.

Thanks to her thoroughness and attention to detail, now diners would have an idea of what to order if they visited Fusión Tapas. And the chef there might even get some ideas for how to improve his less successful dishes. Overall, Gladys was very pleased with her work on this review. And she'd thought Fiona was, too—at least until the editor had sent her that awful hot dog assignment.

Gladys heard the storeroom door squeak open and hurriedly closed the paper. There was no use dwelling on her new assignment now—not when there were plantain pancakes to cook!

Gladys had never been in Charissa's house before, and it turned out to be just as impressive inside as it was on the outside. In the living room, pristine white couches sat atop white carpeting. The dining room was paneled in gleaming dark wood, and the breezes wafting through floor-to-ceiling windows brought in smells of the nearby ocean. There was no hint of the stench of Mount Dumpsford, the local landfill that made Gladys's part of town smell icky on hot summer days.

But nothing compared to the kitchen. Everything was state of the art, from the giant super-cold freezer to the double-decker oven. The stovetop featured six burners instead of the usual four, plus a built-in griddle. Copper pans hung from the ceiling like shiny mobiles, gleaming knives clung to a magnetic strip on the wall, and the countertop held the thickest wooden cutting board Gladys had ever seen.

"Okay," she said, heading for the knives. "The first step will be to peel the plantains and mash them. Where do you keep the mixing bowls?"

Gladys didn't even realize how much she was bossing Charissa around until the first set of pancakes were sizzling on the griddle. But if Charissa minded being the sous-chef in her own kitchen, she didn't say so. In fact, even with her clothes dusted with yellow cornmeal and bits of sticky plantain goo in her hair,

Charissa looked more relaxed and happy than Gladys had ever seen her at school or camp. Gladys hadn't thought about it much before, but being the person everyone always looked to for leadership was probably exhausting. She remembered the few weeks when her classmates had all badgered her for cooking advice at recess; she hadn't liked it one bit.

As the girls flipped the pancakes (of course, the Bentleys had *two* no-slip, easy-grip spatulas), Charissa asked Gladys what it was like taking swimming lessons with Hamilton.

"Oh, well, you know . . ." Gladys said, "it's not like we really talk much."

*Or at all,* she added mentally. Today, Hamilton hadn't needed any reminding to show up on time, and after their lesson, he had beelined back to his writing spot on the patio. Which, of course, was just fine by Gladys.

"Well, you're not missing out," Charissa said, poking at a freshly flipped pancake. "From what I can tell, he's, like, a first-class jerkface. I begged Mommy to just kick him out after his outburst on Monday, but apparently his parents paid a boatload of extra fees so he could register at the last minute and stay all summer." She leaned in closer to Gladys. "And then, when my dad called his parents and said he was refusing to do the morning activities and stuff? They just offered to pay *more*! 'Whatever it takes to keep him in camp,' they said." She shook her head. "He must be as annoying at home as he is to us."

Gladys nodded—Hamilton certainly was annoying—but even as she did, she felt the tiniest pang in her gut for him. Her own parents hadn't always supported her passions, but at least they'd never *forced* her to go to camp.

"Oh," Charissa said, "and I almost forgot. Rolanda heard him talking about you!"

"About me?" Gladys almost dropped a pancake onto the griddle wrong-side down. "What did he say?"

"He was asking one of the little kids about you before swim class—Marti's sister, Kyra."

"The red-headed girl?" Gladys hadn't realized that that was Marti's sister, but it made sense. The two of them shared the same shrill voice and frequently nasty expression.

Charissa nodded. "Rolanda said he wanted to know the name of the girl who worked in the kitchen and never smiled."

"What?" Gladys blurted. "I do smile! I just . . . concentrate hard in swim class and in the kitchen! I—"

"Whoa, Gladys, calm down," Charissa said. "I told you, he's a jerkface. Everyone says so. Well, I mean, I'm the one who said it first, but by now everyone else is saying it, too." She grinned. "So don't worry. Look, if I hear that he's said anything else about you, I'll make sure he pays. I've got your back, okay?"

"Okay." Gladys took a deep breath to steady herself—and noticed a charred smell. "Fudge!" She'd gotten so caught up in the Hamilton drama that she'd let the first batch of pancakes burn. "Quick, grab that platter," she instructed Charissa, and a moment later they were scraping pancakes off the griddle.

"We'll get it right on the next batch," Gladys insisted. "And if not, then the one after that." There was plenty of batter—Charissa had bought a *lot* of plantains.

Batch number three turned out perfectly, with just the right balance of savory and sweet, crispy and chewy, in each pancake. Gladys grabbed a bottle of hot sauce, and she and Charissa brought their plates upstairs to Charissa's very purple bedroom. They settled in together on the canopy bed and gorged themselves while watching a marathon of *Purgatory Pantry*, which Charissa had recently started recording at Gladys's suggestion. Gladys had already seen all the episodes, but she didn't mind viewing them again—she loved to watch her favorite contestant, BeBe Watkins, show off her knife skills.

Charissa, though, seemed much more enamored with the host, Rory Graham. "Wow," she commented during the third episode. "Everyone is so afraid of her! I need to study her techniques." Somehow, Gladys didn't think Charissa was talking about Rory's cooking skills.

Eventually, Charissa put on an album by a pop

singer named Sasha McRay, whom Gladys was careful not to admit she'd never heard of. The music was fun and upbeat, though, and the two girls bounced around Charissa's room dancing until their tatale-stuffed stomachs couldn't take it anymore. Finally, Gladys's mom arrived to take her home, but Charissa made Gladys promise to come back soon.

It only took Gladys half a second to agree. Spending time at Charissa's had been a lot more fun than she'd expected.

The next day was decidedly less fun, as Gladys's parents insisted on heading to Dumpy Beach for the Fourth of July.

Gladys wasn't surprised—her family did this every year. Her parents would spend their day off from work swimming and playing Frisbee while Gladys sat under a large umbrella, reading a book about techniques for cooking fish. She didn't expect this year's beach outing to be any different and brought along a large volume called *Ocean to Mouth: A Fish Lover's Guide.* She had just finished a particularly interesting section about searing and closed her eyes to imagine how, one day, she might lay a fillet of cod in a panful of sizzling butter when her mom's voice broke into her daydream.

"You know," she said, "you might actually get to see some fish if you put that book down and came in the water."

Gladys opened her eyes and looked at her mom skeptically. "I don't know," she said. "I'm not a very good swimmer."

"But haven't you started lessons at camp?" her mom asked. "Come on, you can show me what you've learned." She grabbed Gladys's hand and hoisted her to her feet. Apparently, Gladys didn't have a choice about this.

At the water's edge, the surf rushed in over her toes. It was freezing, and she gave an involuntary yelp.

Her mom laughed. "It's not that bad once you start moving," she said. "Let's go!" Then, before Gladys could protest, her mom pulled on her hand and ran into the icy Atlantic.

In seconds, Gladys's lower body was numb. Salty water sprayed her in the face, stinging her eyes, and they only felt worse when she stupidly rubbed them with her salt-coated hands. Her mom was out ahead of her now, her arms and legs propelling her quickly through the surf with form that was even better than Rolanda's.

Gladys knew that she should follow, but her body was paralyzed with cold and fear; in fact, she felt seconds away from a full-on panic attack. She was about to take a step back toward the shore when her mom resurfaced by her side.

"Let me give you a few pointers," she said.

Gladys's teeth chattered. "O-o . . . k-kay . . ."

First, Gladys's mom told her that salt water would actually keep her more buoyant than pool water, making it easier to stay afloat. Gladys was skeptical, but then her mom explained it in a different way.

"Remember that day when you showed us how to boil water for pasta?" her mom asked. Gladys managed a shivery nod. "Well, you had us add salt to the water."

"For seasoning," Gladys said. "And to make it boil faster."

"Yes, well, you may not have noticed," her mom said, "but the salt also made the pasta float in the water more easily." She laughed. "Listen to me, trying to teach *you* something about cooking! I should just stick to what I know, huh?"

"No, Mom—that actually helps," Gladys said.

And her mom was right. Once Gladys got used to the waves, she was able to float on her back much more easily than she had during Wednesday's lesson at camp. And with her mom by her side, Gladys even grew brave enough to flip over and try floating on her stomach, with her face in the water for seconds at a time.

Gladys could hardly believe it, but on the car ride home she realized that her fish book had sat unread on her towel all afternoon.

# Chapter 13

# NEW YORK CITY'S
# NEXT TOP HOT DOG

ON FRIDAY MORNING, THE PLATFORM AT the East Dumpsford train station was far less crowded than it had been the last time Gladys went to the office with her dad. Apparently, he hadn't been exaggerating when he'd grumbled about being the only person working on July fifth.

The ride to New York City took about an hour. At each stop, just a handful of commuters climbed aboard, looking sunburned and bleary as they collapsed into their seats. Most snoozed or played on their phones, but Gladys noticed that a few pulled fat black books out of their bags to read. When she looked closely, she saw the title: *Zombietown, U.S.A.*

*Great*, she thought. Even when she wasn't at camp, she still couldn't get away from Hamilton.

Gladys pulled out her reviewing journal so she'd have something to look at that wasn't his stupid book. She had tried to write down some criteria the night before that would help guide her through the day's tastings.

*Meat: all-beef or mixed? kosher?*
*Bun: white or whole-grain? freshness? toasted?*
*Condiments: quality? best combination?*

Honestly, though, it wasn't much. She would just have to taste as many samples as she could find.

From Penn Station, Gladys and her dad took a subway downtown to his office on Wall Street. When they exited onto the sidewalk, the first thing Gladys noticed was a huge red-and-white umbrella near the corner. They got a few steps closer, and her suspicions were confirmed: It was a hot dog stand!

"Hey, Dad, can I get a hot dog?" Gladys asked.

Her dad stared at her. "*Now*, Gladdy? It's eight thirty in the morning!"

"I didn't really eat much breakfast," she said, which was true. She'd been saving space for Operation Top Dog.

"Well, a hot dog's not really breakfast," her dad replied. "But there's a good bagel shop around the corner. How about we stop in for a couple of bialys and schmear?"

Gladys's mouth watered at the suggestion. A fresh-baked bialy, all warm and chewy and covered with browned bits of onion, sounded divine—but she had to stick to her assignment. "I'd much rather have a hot dog," she forced herself to say. "And hey, people eat sausages for breakfast."

"I guess that's true," her dad said. "All right, I suppose that just this once it won't hurt."

He stepped up to the vendor—a middle-aged man in a Yankees cap—and ordered a hot dog for Gladys. "What do you want on it, Gladdy?" he asked.

"Oh—just whatever people usually get."

The vendor fished a long pinkish dog out of his vat of boiling water, placed it on a white bun, and squiggled yellow mustard and bright red ketchup on it. As her dad paid, Gladys snuck out her journal and speedily noted down the name of the stand, the corner it stood on, and the type of hot dogs it served ("Hungry Cow, all-beef"). She barely managed to drop the journal back into her bag before her father turned to hand her the hot dog.

"Well?" he asked after she'd taken her first bite. "How is it?"

"Er," Gladys said with a swallow. "It's great, Dad."

But it wasn't. The wet hot dog had immediately turned the bun soggy, and the ketchup was separating before her eyes into juicy liquid and a tomatoey clot. The meat itself didn't have much taste, but what it was lacking in flavor it made up for in gristly bits.

*Hungry Cow,* she thought, *you are out of the running to become New York's City's Next Top Hot Dog.*

As they entered her dad's building, Gladys looked around for a trash can. "You'd better finish that up, Gladdy," her dad said. "There's a strict no-food policy in the elevators here."

"Oh, okay," Gladys said. "I'll just throw it out, then."

But as soon as those words were out of her mouth, her dad's jaw stiffened, and she knew she'd be doing no such thing.

"Throw it *away*?" he squeaked through clenched teeth. "That is not how I raised you, Gladys Gatsby! Do you know how much a hot dog costs in this city?"

Already lamenting the wasted stomach space, Gladys forced herself to take as big a bite as she could; she might as well get it over with quickly. But once the bite was in her mouth, she knew that that had been the wrong strategy. What she should have done was taken a tiny bite, and then another, eating so slowly that her dad got fed up and either let her throw it out or finished it himself. Why hadn't she thought of that before she'd filled her mouth with the nasty stuff?

Meanwhile, Gladys's dad's pocket was vibrating, and as she swallowed her second bite, he pulled out his phone. "Text from Robbins," he muttered, swiping at the screen. "'Give my regards to Wall Street!' What nerve. And look, a picture of him and his sons at the Cape May arcade."

"Sorry, Dad," Gladys said.

"Are you done eating that thing yet?" he snapped.

Sheepishly, Gladys took another enormous bite.

Two minutes later, the last piece of hot dog had finally disappeared down Gladys's gullet, and she and her dad were on their way up to the twenty-eighth floor. "I've got a meeting at nine o'clock," he said. "Do you want to come?"

"No thanks, Dad—I wouldn't want to be a distraction," Gladys told him. "I can just hang out at your cubicle 'til you get back."

"All right, it shouldn't take too long—half an hour, tops, unless Silverstein goes off on another one of his rants about spreadsheet formulas." He sighed. "Some accountants need to get a life."

Gladys's dad got her situated in his cubicle, which was far from the elevator but close to a window. The July sun beat in, warming the desktop.

"All right, I'm off—the conference room is just down that hallway if you need me," he said, pointing to the right. "You can use the Internet if you want, but don't mess with my files, okay?"

"Okay, Dad! Have a good meeting!"

When he left, Gladys scanned the hubbub out the window twenty-eight floors below. People dotted the sidewalk and yellow taxis zoomed down the street, and at the end of the block stood a large blue-and-green umbrella. Another hot dog stand!

After making sure her dad had disappeared around the corner of a neighboring cubicle, Gladys took off in the opposite direction, walking as quickly as she could back toward the elevators.

In less than five minutes, she was downstairs and out on the street. Half an hour should be plenty of time to get to the corner and back. She looked to the left, expecting to see the blue-and-green umbrella on the corner, but there was nothing but a subway entrance. Confused, she looked to the right, but there was no hot dog stand there, either.

*Fudge!* Her dad's window must not have faced the same direction that the front of the building did. Which way was it oriented? She knew that Wall Street was close to the southern tip of Manhattan Island, but she didn't remember seeing a lot of water from her dad's office. So that window probably faced north.

But which way was she facing now?

*Just ask someone,* said a voice in her head. But it was a small, quiet voice—just like Gladys's voice in real life. She hated talking to strangers, and the people flitting past her on this street, conversing with each other or shouting into cell phones, looked particularly intimidating.

She'd just have to figure it out herself.

Gladys thought back to the hours she and Sandy

had spent studying an online map of Manhattan before her foray to Classy Cakes in the spring. City blocks were rectangular. So all she needed to do was pick one direction and start walking. If she followed the block all the way around, she'd find the hot dog stand and make it back to the front door of her dad's building, no problem! Feeling more confident now, Gladys turned left and made for the corner.

Once she got there she turned left again, onto a louder, busier street. Scaffolding shadowed the side-walk and cut off a good portion of the walking area, forcing people to crowd into a tunnel-like space as they moved down to the next corner. Gladys found herself buffeted on all sides by sweaty, fast-walking men and women, the corners of their bags and brief-cases jabbing painfully at her bare arms. She tried to look around for a blue-and-green umbrella, but all she could see were people.

As she turned onto the next street, Gladys glanced down at her watch. Thirteen minutes had passed since her dad left for his meeting, and she still didn't have her hot dog!

*One more block,* she told herself, *then left again.* She repeated the directions to herself like a mantra as she hurried toward the next intersection.

The sun slipped behind a tall building as she turned the corner, throwing the entire block into a murky dimness. Gladys was tempted to pull out her journal and make a note about the atmosphere—*A twilight-esque ambience blankets the Financial District's hot dog stands*—but she needed to keep moving, so she tried to commit the description to memory.

It wasn't until Gladys had walked half a block up the third side of her square that she remembered to actually look around for the hot dog stand she'd seen from the window. She should be getting close to her dad's building again—where was that umbrella? If she didn't get a hot dog, this whole expedition had been for nothing!

Her watch read 9:24 when she finally spotted a silver cart near the upcoming corner. Yes! And there wasn't even anyone else in line. Reaching down into her pocket for money, Gladys dashed up to the vendor, whose bald pate shone in the sun. "One hot dog, please!" she gasped. "With all the regular toppings!"

The vendor assembled a hot dog for her without comment. Gladys thanked him and took off down the street. She hadn't had time to take notes on the name and location of the stand, but she figured that once she was back up in her dad's office, she could get that information by looking out the window again.

Turning the corner, she finally paused to take a bite of her hot dog—and a series of unfortunately familiar sensations coursed through her mouth.

Soggy bun. Gristly meat. Weirdly clumpy ketchup.

Gladys looked back at the stand where she'd just

bought her hot dog. The umbrella hanging over it was red and white. And just then, the vendor pulled a Yankees hat out of his apron pocket and set it back on top of his bald head.

Gladys couldn't believe it. She'd bought a hot dog from the *same cart* she'd already tried that morning!

She looked around desperately but could spot no sign of the blue-and-green umbrella she'd seen from the window above—and according to her watch, it was now 9:28. Her time was up.

Rage quickened her steps as she tore up the street, breaking into a run when she finally spotted her dad's brown building. At least this time she was able to do what she'd wanted to do with her first hot dog of the day; she hurled it into a black trash can outside the entrance. Then she burst into the lobby and, after flashing her guest pass at the security desk, dashed toward the elevator bank. On the ride up, she caught her breath and used the elevator's reflective wall like a mirror to smooth her hair. It was 9:32 now, so she could only hope that Silverstein had indeed gotten going about those spreadsheets.

The elevator jerked to a halt at floor 28, and Gladys stepped toward the door. *Just act calm and normal,* she told herself. *You have nothing to worry about.*

But then the doors opened to reveal her dad's face, and he didn't look calm at all.

Chapter 14

# A (HOT) DOG DAY OF SUMMER

"GLADYS!" HE CRIED. "WHERE HAVE YOU been?"

A bevy of potential explanations swirled through Gladys's brain:

*I wanted to see the rest of your building.*

*Another accountant asked me to deliver some papers.*

*Your desk smells bad, so I went looking for some air freshener.*

But what came out of her mouth was "Bathroom! I needed to go to the bathroom."

Her dad's face scrunched up in puzzlement. "On another floor?"

"Well, I looked on this floor," Gladys said, "but I couldn't find it, so I had to go downstairs."

"You couldn't find it?" Gladys followed her dad's gaze and saw, with a sinking heart, a perfectly large and clear sign that read REST-ROOMS and pointed down the hallway next to the elevator bank.

"Oh," was all that she could think to say.

But it didn't seem to matter to her dad—he grabbed her and pulled her into a tight hug. "I'm just glad you're okay," he whispered. "But please don't go running off anymore without telling someone where you're going! I got back to my cubicle, and you weren't there, and no one remembered seeing you for a long time . . ."

"I, um, had some indigestion," Gladys said.

Her dad released her quickly from the hug. "Hmm," he said. "Maybe hot dogs don't make the best breakfast after all, huh?"

"No, no—I don't think it was the hot dog." Seriously, how many dumb things could come out of her mouth in one morning? If her dad thought hot dogs were making her sick, then he definitely wouldn't eat one with her for lunch . . . and forget about that mid-morning hot dog snack . . .

"Well, it's time to head out for a few meetings around the city," he said. "Are you feeling well enough to go?"

"Yes!" Gladys assured him—and thankfully, he believed her.

Ten minutes later, they were back in the subway, on their way to the Upper East Side. Gladys had never been to that neighborhood before, but when they got off the train, she quickly determined that it was a fancier part of town; posh boutiques lined one side of Fifth Avenue, and the green trees of Central Park beckoned from the other side of the street. *Do the people in this neighborhood even eat hot dogs?* she wondered.

Just then, she spotted a vendor by one of the gates leading into Central Park. "Hey, Dad, how about a hot dog?" Gladys asked.

"Another one?" her dad said. "It's not even lunchtime yet! Let's wait until after this meeting, at least." And he kept walking.

She scurried after him. "But, Dad . . ." She was pretty sure he wasn't going to let her out of his sight for the rest of the day, and there would be other vendors to try later. What would convince him to let her have another hot dog right now? "All this walking is making me hungry!"

"All this walking? Gladdy, we've gone maybe half a block from the subway exit."

"Yeah, but I'm shorter than you," Gladys pointed out. "So on my legs, it's like ten blocks!"

This got a laugh out of her dad, but it didn't stop him from continuing. The hot dog stand was now almost half a block behind them. It was time for desperate measures.

"Hey," she said. "Mr. Robbins and his sons are probably eating hot dogs right now at the Jersey Shore! I bet *they* don't care that it's still morning."

That stopped her dad in his tracks. "I bet you're

right," he murmured. "And why should they have all the fun?"

"Exactly!" Gladys cried. "And look, there's a stand right by the park. Let's get some hot dogs and text *him* a picture."

"Good idea!"

A minute later, they were taking a selfie in front of the vendor's stand. Gladys checked the picture after and was pleased to see that it had captured both the name of the stand (Yiddish Countrywide) and the intersection.

From then on, Gladys's dad was happy to stop for hot dogs as often as Gladys wanted—just as long as they took a picture and sent it to Mr. Robbins. The only problem was that she actually had to *eat* the dogs—as in finish them, every single time.

After Yiddish Countrywide, she ate an all-pork hot dog in Washington Heights, a mixed-meat hot dog on the Upper West Side, and even a vegetarian dog from a cute-looking cart in Greenwich Village. The dogs came slathered with mustards and ketchups, relishes and onions . . . but none of them blew her away. In fact, the more hot dogs she ate, the less she could taste them. Were the fat and salt in the meat dulling her taste buds? And if they could do that to her mouth, what were they doing to her insides?

By the time they got in line for a hot dog near Rockefeller Center that afternoon, Gladys's stomach was swelling painfully. "Hey, Dad," she said, "wanna just split this one?"

"What, and have Robbins think that I'm too cheap to buy my daughter her own hot dog?" Gladys's dad shook his head. "Oh, no, Gladdy. It's nothing but the best for my girl."

And so Gladys found herself staring down a full-size hot dog for the seventh time that day. This one was decidedly gray in color, and the gelatinous globs of snot-green relish that decorated it didn't improve her appetite.

Gladys forced herself to take a bite. Nope—it didn't taste any better than it looked.

When he finished paying, Gladys's dad beckoned her over to pose for their self-portrait. "C'mon—let's make sure to get Radio City Music Hall in the background," he said. "By the end of the day, Robbins's kids'll be begging to go on a hot dog tour of New York City!"

Gladys plastered a smile on for the camera, but deep down she knew she was as far from finding the best hot dog as she had been at the beginning of the day. She and her dad would have to keep eating, and eating, and eating, if she had any chance of finding a winner for her review.

And so they did. As they walked down Sixth Avenue toward Gladys's dad's next appointment, they stopped in Bryant Park for more hot dogs (*meat shriveled, bun stale,* Gladys scribbled in her notebook). Then after that meeting, they found another vendor near Grand Central Terminal (*nothing grand about these lukewarm dogs!*).

"Look at the time," her dad said as he glanced up at the ornate clock that hung over Grand Central's entrance. "Our train leaves from Penn Station in thirty minutes! We're going to have to walk fast if we want to make it."

He strode toward the intersection, but when Gladys tried to follow him, her legs didn't seem to be working right. They trembled underneath her, and the simple movement of taking a step made her feel incredibly queasy.

"Dad!" she called.

He hurried back over. "What's the matter?"

"I—I don't feel so good. I don't think I can walk to Penn Station."

"Okay," he said. "We can just take the subway."

But even walking down to the subway entrance was a trial for Gladys, who felt worse with every step. It seemed like her stomach had taken over her whole body. As she stepped onto a subway train beside her dad, she couldn't help imagining meat and buns and condiments shooting out of her ears and eyes and splattering all over the shiny plastic seats.

*Think about something else,* she told herself as the train lurched out of the station. *Anything else!*

So she closed her eyes and imagined Sandy, hundreds of miles away at karate camp. What was he doing right now? Practicing his roundhouse kicks? Hiking with his group in the woods? She wondered whether he had to wear his white karategi at all times; was it a camp uniform, like the purple shirts at Camp Bentley? She had so many questions to ask him when he wrote her back—if he ever wrote her back.

The train slowed to a stop, and Gladys opened her eyes. She'd made it all the way across town without getting sick!

"C'mon, Gladdy, we have to transfer," her dad said, grabbing her hand. "Let's hope a downtown train comes quickly."

She did her best to keep pace with her dad as they crossed the station at Times Square and hurried up another set of stairs. The platform was packed with people, heat seeming to rise off them in waves. Gladys's dad fanned himself with his fedora, and Gladys was tempted to pull out her journal and do the same. But the risk of dropping it was too great, so she just sweat quietly and took deep breaths, trying to keep her nausea under control.

There was a mad rush to board when a train finally pulled up to the platform, and Gladys and her dad barely fit inside. "Stand clear of the closing doors!" a recording pleaded again and again over the train's loudspeaker. Finally, the doors squeezed shut, and the train jerked out of the station.

Gladys's dad's back was flat against the door; Gladys's back was flat against his stomach. And less than an inch away from Gladys's stomach bobbed another person's stomach—a large, round one encased in a brown sport coat. With every lurch of the train, it bounced a little closer to her.

*Please don't bump into me,* Gladys prayed silently.

Another wave of nausea washed over her, and she looked around for something to focus on. Since the car was so crowded, she couldn't see much, so she stared at the man in front of her. The button that strained to hold his jacket closed had two letters embossed on it in gold: GG.

The man had one arm wrapped around a subway pole, and in his other hand he held a small black notebook, about the same size as Gladys's reviewing journal. He was flipping through the pages as best he could with the one hand, but when the train made a sudden jolt, the book tumbled out of his hand and landed at Gladys's feet.

"Pick that up for me, would you, little girl?" the man said in a gravelly voice.

Gladys didn't enjoy being called "little girl," or being asked to do this man a favor without so much as a "please"—but she could see that she was the only person who even had a chance of reaching the book in this packed car. Slowly, with her stomach protesting every inch of the way, she bent her knees and lowered herself to the subway's sticky floor.

When her head was level with the large man's knees, she was able to reach over and grasp the book. It had landed cover-side up but splayed open, and when Gladys flipped it over, the writing on the open page caught her eye.

*Reviewing notes for Ristorante Massimo,* it said.

Gladys gasped—she couldn't help it. Ristorante Massimo was one of the restaurants *she* was supposed to review for the *New York Standard* before her assignment got switched!

*Could this GG be . . .*

Unable to stop herself, Gladys flipped back through several more pages. There were notes on Brendler's Barbecue, and Steakhouse 57, and Café Cacao—all subjects of past reviews by the *Standard's* head restaurant critic. And then, one more page caught her eye. Its heading said *Classy Cakes & Fusión Tapas,* and the note underneath it was simple: *Assigned to Gatsby. Don't let Fiona make* that *mistake again.*

"Little girl!" the man's voice boomed from above. "What's taking so long down there?"

Gladys snapped the notebook shut and stood up as quickly as she could. On top of the nausea and dizziness, her brain was now swimming with questions. The man snatched the notebook out of her hand and shoved it into his pocket just as the train began to slow.

"This stop is Penn Station," the recording announced, and the train doors peeled open with a *whoosh*. Gladys's dad stepped off quickly, and she was just about to follow him when something slammed into her.

"Move it, kid," Gilbert Gadfly grumbled. "I have a reservation." His huge belly shoved her aside, and the hard, gold-embossed button on his jacket dug right into a soft spot in her stomach.

She threw up all over his shoes.

# Chapter 15

# ZOMBIE BREAKFAST

AS IT TURNS OUT, NOTHING CLEARS A packed subway car faster than someone tossing their cookies.

"Eurgh!"

"Blech!"

"Quick, before she does it again!"

People jumped, dived, and sidestepped to get past the puddle by the doorway and the large man who stood in the middle of it, his face turning redder by the second.

"These shoes are real alligator!" he roared. "Who is responsible for this girl? Someone must pay! Someone—"

But Gladys didn't stick around to hear any more. With her stomach finally emptied, she was feeling pretty good again, and capable of fleeing. Which, after grabbing hold of her bewildered dad's hand, was exactly what she did.

"Gladdy—wait—no!" her dad huffed as she dragged him toward the nearest staircase. "You have to go back and apologize to that man! We don't just barf and run in this family!"

"Dad," she cried, "do you have any idea how much alligator-leather shoes cost?"

His expression hardened. "Good point. And he pushed you, didn't he? Let's go."

Together they tore down the stairs and across Penn Station's vast underground lobby, dodging columns and commuters as they made their way to their track.

"Last call for the five twenty to East Dumpsford," an announcement declared. They raced down one last set of steps and leapt onto their train as the beeping doors started to close.

Slumping against the Plexiglas divider in the entryway, Gladys and her dad gasped for breath as the train trundled out of the station. Then, at the same moment, they both began to laugh.

"Did you—see—his face?" Gladys's dad squeezed out between guffaws. "It was as red as a fresh-boiled lobster—covered in marinara sauce—with a side of beets!"

"Perfect description," Gladys said between giggles. Her dad had recently started watching *Purgatory Pantry* with her; she had thought he only liked it for the yelling, but it sounded like he was learning something about food, too. "Anyway," she continued, "I think he

deserved what he got for shoving me out of his way."
She left out the part where she had also seen his comment about her in his book. She was going to have to think more about that later.

Gladys and her dad spent the rest of the train ride rehashing the day's events and flipping through his cell phone pictures of their hot dog–eating adventures. Gladys asked him if he'd had a favorite, hoping that he might help her pick a front-runner in her Top Dog quest, but he wasn't much use in that department. "They all tasted pretty much the same, to be honest," he said. "A hot dog's a hot dog."

Gladys was discouraged to admit that she agreed completely.

In bed that night, she looked over the notes in her journal. They'd been written in short spurts while she tried to keep out of sight of her dad, but Gladys didn't need to read them to know that she had not found the best hot dog in New York today—not even close. She was going to have to get back into the city, armed with a better plan.

But something even bigger was bothering her. Why had Gilbert Gadfly written in his notebook that Gladys's two published reviews had been "mistakes"? She had been a fan of his writing since she had learned how to read, but he clearly didn't feel the same about her.

Did Fiona agree with him? Was that why she had taken back the Ristorante Massimo assignment, sending Gladys on this crazy hot dog quest instead?

She wished she could just ask her editor, but Fiona would be unreachable for three more weeks. And she wished she could talk to Sandy about it, but he seemed to be just as far off the grid.

It looked like Operation Top Dog was still very much a solo project.

The next morning, Gladys tackled her stress the best way she knew how: by cooking. While her parents slept in, she baked cardamom-almond muffins; simmered a potful of plums with sugar to make jam; and layered berries, yogurt, and granola into pretty parfaits. By the time her parents stumbled downstairs in their bathrobes, Gladys was feeling calmer, and the jam was just about cool enough to serve.

"Please have a seat in the dining room," Gladys told them, "and I'll bring out your first course!"

She came into the dining room a minute later, her attention focused on the tray of parfaits balancing in her hands. Her dad let out a low whistle. "Well, look at this!" he said.

"*Very* impressive!" her mom agreed.

Gladys smiled and glanced up over the rims of the parfait glasses—but then realized that her parents hadn't been talking about her culinary creations at all. In fact, they hadn't even seen them! Her dad was hunched over an open copy of the newspaper, and her mom was perched on the arm of his chair, reading over his shoulder.

Gladys cleared her throat as she lowered the tray to the table, but they were both so engrossed in whatever they were reading that they didn't even look up. Annoyed now, she *thunk*ed a parfait glass down in front of each of her parents. Her dad reached over and picked his up mechanically, digging a spoon in and taking a bite without shifting his attention away from the paper.

Gladys's mom's parfait remained untouched. "Truly remarkable," she breathed.

"*What*," Gladys snapped, "is so interesting?"

"Gladdy!" Her dad finally looked up. "Look at this. Did you know that we have a famous author in our midst, right here in East Dumpsford?"

Gladys's heart froze in her chest. What newspaper were they looking at? Was it the *New York Standard*? Could it be Wednesday's *Standard*—with her review of Fusión Tapas in it?

Trembling, Gladys took a step closer . . . but when she saw the article they were looking at, a mixture of relief and exasperation flooded through her. The newspaper was, of course, the *Dumpsford Township*

*Intelligencer*—and right there, splashed across page two, was Hamilton Herbertson's face.

He wore his black fedora and black-rimmed glasses, and he wasn't smiling, exactly; in fact, he looked kind of bored. But that boredom clearly hadn't translated to Gladys's parents.

"He's only twelve!" Gladys's dad exclaimed. "Your age, Gladdy, and he's written an entire best-selling book! Have you ever heard of anything so extraordinary?"

Now Gladys tasted bile rising in the back of her throat. She understood that most people would find Hamilton's accomplishment impressive, but she wouldn't have expected her own parents to feel that way. They were always pushing her to "have more fun" and "enjoy being a kid."

"Well," she said, "he must not have much time for being a regular kid if he's busy writing novels."

"Oh, but he does!" Gladys's mom replied. "Look, it says right here that he's enrolled for the summer at Camp Bentley, where he enjoys 'playing in the pool and socializing with other children his own age.'"

*Socializing? In the pool?* Gladys thought. *Ha!*

"Do you know this boy?" Gladys's mom continued. "From camp? His name is Hamilton Herbertson."

"I've seen him around," Gladys mumbled.

"Ooh, I have a great idea!" her mom said. "We can run out right after breakfast and pick up a copy of his book. Then on Monday, maybe you could take it with you to camp and get it signed!"

"Wait until Robbins gets a load of *that*," Gladys's dad said excitedly. "A signed copy of *Zombietown, U.S.A.*, with a story about how *my* daughter is friends with the author. That'll put him in his place once and for all!"

"We're not *friends*—" Gladys started, but neither of her parents were listening. They had gone back to exclaiming about details of Hamilton's impressive life.

"One of the youngest number one best sellers ever!"

"A million copies in print!"

And when they ran out of impressive details, they even got excited over the less impressive ones.

"A Sagittarius!"

"Born in Syracuse!"

Gladys's parents wolfed down their parfaits and hardly seemed to taste their second course of muffins and jam. Then, after getting dressed with a speed usually reserved for weekday mornings, they hustled Gladys into the car for a trip to East Dumpsford's local bookstore.

It had been a while since Gladys had visited The Book Dump—she usually found all the reading material she wanted at the library. But the store looked very different from how she remembered it. In the past, the front window had displayed all different kinds of books. Now, one whole window was taken up with a poster of Hamilton (LOCAL AUTHOR! the tagline cried), and every remaining inch displayed copy upon copy of *Zombietown, U.S.A.*

Inside the store, things weren't any better. The black jacket of *Zombietown, U.S.A.* was the only one on the "New Fiction" table, and apparently Hamilton's book was also a Mystery, and a Travel Guide, and a Romance. Even the Children's Corner, which Gladys remembered as having a giant comfy chair and plenty of picture books, was almost completely given over to copies of *Zombietown* (WRITTEN BY A TWELVE-YEAR-OLD! the sign proclaimed). Seated in the old comfy chair was a life-size plastic zombie with the book in his hands and fake blood drooling out of his mouth as he "read."

Gladys's mom gazed around. "Isn't this delightful? Just look at how the store is supporting one of our own!" She and Gladys's dad shuffled around for a while, like they were possessed with a zombie virus themselves. Finally, they picked up two copies of the book.

"I think we'll each need one so we don't fight over it," Gladys's dad said. "Do you want your own copy, too, Gladdy?"

"No!" Gladys was truly getting fed up. She couldn't remember the last time her dad had read something other than the newspaper, and her mom's bookshelf held at least three times as many real estate–selling manuals as novels. Now they were going to buy *two* copies of Hamilton's book?

Gladys's outburst woke her mom from her zombie-like trance. "Now, honey," she said, "there's no need to be jealous of this Hamilton boy. Just because he's had a book published doesn't mean you're not a very good writer, too. That essay your teacher read us over the phone was very impressive!"

Gladys couldn't help but let a tiny smile cross her face. That *had* been a good essay—and Fiona Ingle-thorpe had thought so, too.

"Life isn't a race, you know," Gladys's mom contin-ued. "There's no prize for being the first kid to be a published writer."

"Actually, there is!" Gladys's dad pointed to a shiny silver sticker on the cover of *Zombietown, U.S.A.* "Finalist for Best Kid Author at the Kids Rock Awards!" he read.

Gladys groaned. As if Hamilton wasn't already in-sufferable enough, now his book had gotten him nom-inated for a big award.

The Gatsbys made their way to the checkout counter, which was festooned with *Zombietown, U.S.A.* book-marks and pencils. Gladys's dad pulled out his beloved Super Dump-Mart rewards card, and her mom picked out a black pencil with a hideous zombie-shaped eraser. "This'll fit in perfectly with my collection!" she exclaimed. The computer desk at home was already covered with her fuzzy, pink monster pens.

As they walked to the car, Gladys imagined the monster pens coming to life in the night and ganging up on the zombie, obliterating him in a storm of fluffy pastel feathers.

# Chapter 16

# OIL AND WATER(CRESS)

GLADYS'S PARENTS WERE SO ENgrossed in Hamilton's book that they hardly left the house the rest of the weekend. In fact, if Gladys hadn't brought them meals, they probably would have forgotten to eat. But at least the distraction meant that Gladys could get onto the computer as often as she wanted. She checked her e-mail on Saturday afternoon, and Saturday night, and again on Sunday morning—but there was still no word from Sandy.

By Sunday night, she couldn't wait any longer; it was time to take matters into her own hands. Clearly, there was no way she could visit every hot dog cart in New York. But how could she narrow the offerings down to a more manageable list of places?

Gladys thought back to her first-ever trip to New York City with her aunt Lydia, when she was seven. They hadn't eaten any hot dogs that day, but they had visited an Ethiopian restaurant, a kosher restaurant, and a Chinese restaurant. "If there's a specialty cuisine from somewhere in the world," her aunt had told her, "then there's a place in New York City that serves it."

Maybe narrowing things down wasn't the way to go at all, Gladys thought. Maybe she needed to expand her search instead.

She closed her DumpMail window and opened up a search engine. So far, Gladys had purposely avoided doing a web search for "New York's best hot dog." She knew there had to be lists and articles out there, but reading someone else's rankings would be cheating. She wanted to design her own quest, and maybe even discover a hot dog that no New York food writer had tried before. So Gladys quickly typed in *world's best hot dogs* instead. If she could figure out what kinds of amazing hot dogs existed in the world, then maybe she'd be able to find them for sale in the city!

Gladys only had to scroll through a few pages of search results to realize there were way too many for her to follow up on. She would have to go about this a different way. Who did she know who traveled extensively, and tried lots of foreign cuisines? There was her aunt Lydia, of course, who lived in Paris, and Gladys knew that Sandy's mom had traveled a lot when she was younger, too. Mr. Eng knew a lot about foreign food, so she should probably ask him . . . and Parm was the best-traveled of her friends, since she went to India every winter with her family.

It might not amount to much, but talking to these people would at least give Gladys a place to start.

When she walked into the camp kitchen after her swimming lesson the next morning, Mrs. Spinelli was standing over a large cardboard box with an apoplectic look on her face.

"This is *not* what I ordered." Her gray bun whipped from side to side in its hairnet as she shook her head. "Not what I ordered at all!"

Gladys's ingredients had come in.

*Play it cool,* she told herself. "What's the matter, Mrs. Spinelli?"

"The food supply company messed up my order, that's what," the cook growled. "I specifically requested seven bags of sesame seed buns, and look what they sent me!" She held up a plastic bag. "Sesame *seeds*! Ridiculous! What do they expect me to do, stick them to the buns myself?"

Gladys could have said something about the joy of baking your own fresh buns, but quickly decided against it. She needed to approach this situation cautiously—and for now, the best response to Mrs. Spinelli was to sympathize. "That *is* ridiculous," she said. "I can't believe they messed it up!"

"I know," the cook said, "but that's not even the half of it! I asked for five hundred mini bags for holding fruit slices. Look what they sent instead!" This time, she held up an armful of small, crusty-looking loaves of bread.

"Mini . . . baguettes?" Gladys asked.

"Exactly! French bread!"

"Geez," Gladys made herself say. "Don't they know this is America?"

Mrs. Spinelli let out a "Hmpf!" of agreement as she dumped the baguettes back into the box. "That's a good one, girlie. That's exactly what I'm going to say when I get these jokers on the phone. And look—look at this!"

Instead of frozen chicken pieces, they had sent chick*peas*. Instead of garlic salamis, there were heads of garlic and thick wheels of a fancy Argentinean cheese called Sardo. There were fresh lemons instead of prepackaged lemon bars. And instead of bottled water, the company had sent several packages of one of Gladys's favorite leafy greens: watercress. Gladys had made sure to choose substitute ingredients that were close to Mrs. Spinelli's choices alphabetically, so it might actually look like the company just made a series of mistakes.

"That's the last time I order from these bozos," Mrs. Spinelli concluded. But then she slumped against the counter. "What am I going to serve for lunch today, though?"

Gladys's big moment had come. "Mrs. Spinelli," she said. "I think I could come up with something."

The cook paused at rubbing her temples and gave Gladys an incredulous look. "You?"

Gladys took a deep breath. "Yes, me. I'm actually familiar with a lot of these ingredients, and I think I could make something that everyone will like."

Gladys waited. Would the cook agree and give her the run of the kitchen—or chase her out with the wooden spoon for even proposing such a crazy plan? They seemed like equally likely outcomes.

Mrs. Spinelli stared at Gladys for what felt like long enough to turn a barrel of fresh milk into finely aged cheddar. At last, she said, "All right. It's too late to send everything back, so what choice do we have?"

Gladys's heart pogo-bounced in her chest, but she did her best to look calm on the outside. "Thank you for this opportunity, Mrs. Spinelli," she said. "I won't let the camp down!"

"Oh, I expect you will," Mrs. Spinelli said. "I know what kids like, and it ain't nothing in that box. But you go ahead, girlie, and give it your best shot. I'm off to talk to the Bentleys about changing food-supply companies." She removed her hairnet, tossed it into the nearest garbage can, and stalked out of the kitchen.

For a moment Gladys felt bad for Foodstuffs, Inc., which really hadn't done anything wrong and was probably about to lose the camp's account. That is, unless they'd kept a copy of her doctored order form, in which case she'd be the one in trouble. *But,* she told herself, *if I can make this work, maybe the Bentleys will let me keep cooking and keep ordering from Foodstuffs.* Everything now depended on her lunch.

There wasn't a moment to lose. Stuffing her hair into a net and yanking on a pair of gloves, Gladys grabbed several bags of sesame seeds out of the cardboard box and poured the contents onto baking sheets. Her sandwiches would be spread with fresh hummus instead of Mrs. Spinelli's gloppy mayonnaise. But to make hummus, she needed a sesame paste called tahini, and to make tahini, first she needed to toast a huge amount of sesame seeds.

When the oven was heated, Gladys placed the sheets on all three racks and set the timer for ten minutes. Her next task would be to blend the toasted seeds with oil in the huge food processor.

Unfortunately, the only oil within easy reach in the pantry was a giant plastic container labeled FRYING OIL. Gladys searched high and low for an alternative, and finally spotted a small bottle of olive oil on the topmost shelf—but there was no stepladder.

She returned to the kitchen, grabbed Mrs. Spinelli's longest spoon, and hurried back to the shelf, hoping she could use it to nudge the bottle toward her. But even when she leapt in the air, she could barely tap it. *Fudge.* Now Mrs. Spinelli's complaints about Gladys not being a tall, strapping boy were starting to make sense.

But wait—there *was* a tall boy nearby! As much as Gladys didn't want to ask Hamilton for help, she couldn't stand the idea of her entire lunch failing just because she couldn't reach some oil. She raced out to the covered patio.

"Hamilton," she said. "Could you reach something for me in the pantry?"

Hamilton looked up from writing, and for a moment, Gladys thought he might shout at her for interrupting. But a smile spread across his face instead.

"Gladys Gatsby!" he said. "What a pleasure. You know, not every author gets a visit from his muse during a writing session."

"His . . . what?" she said.

"Muse! It's from the Ancient Greek. Muses are goddesses who inspire great artists in their work."

"O-kay," Gladys said. Hamilton was being as weird as ever, but she'd better not be too mean to him since she needed a favor.

Hamilton continued. "The other day, when you saved me from missing our first swimming lesson, you inspired me to add a new character to my sequel to *Zombietown, U.S.A.*," he explained. "She's based on you!"

Suddenly, the oil on the top shelf was the furthest thing from Gladys's mind. "You're basing a character in your new book on . . . me?"

"Yes," Hamilton said. "But don't worry—I've changed your name for privacy purposes. The drudge in my book is named Glynnis, not Gladys."

Gladys's brain felt like it had stalled. "I'm sorry," she said, "but what was that word you just used to describe me?"

Hamilton's expression shifted from beaming to slightly frustrated. "*Muse*, Gladys. I just gave you a definition, but if you want it again—"

"Not that one," she snapped. "The other one. *Drudge*?"

"Ah, yes, drudge," Hamilton said. "It means 'menial worker.' A drudge is a person who does dull work." Before Gladys could react, he went on. "From my spot out here on the patio, I've been watching you work in the kitchen. I've seen you lugging supplies around, spreading condiments, and doling lunches out to un-appreciative campers. If that's not drudgery, I don't know what is.

"So, my new character, Glynnis—she's a drudge, too. The only difference is that she works as a zombie slayer rather than as a kitchen assistant. But the idea is the same. Day after day, she kills zombies. And does anybody thank her for the hard work she's doing?"

Gladys stared at Hamilton, not sure whether she was supposed to be impressed or insulted by what he was telling her.

Just then, the *bong* of the camp clock reverberated over the field. It was ten thirty—only an hour and a half before lunch, and unless Gladys planned on serving plates of toasted sesame seeds, she needed to get a move on.

"Time for my hourly stretch," Hamilton said. He stood up and started to reach his long arms into the air when Gladys grabbed one.

"Come on—I know a better place where you can stretch," she said, and yanked him toward the kitchen.

"This is highly unusual," Hamilton protested. "The muse usually visits the artist's place of work, not the other way around."

"Yeah, well, this muse thinks you'll be more inspired if you can see how she works up close." With her free hand, Gladys pulled open the pantry door.

Hamilton followed her inside. "Hey," Gladys said, trying to keep her voice casual, "as long as you're in here, would you grab me that olive oil?"

Reaching overhead like it was the easiest thing in the world, Hamilton brought down the bottle. "You see, it's the repetitive nature of your work, and the lack of skills or education required, that's given me insight into—"

"Thanks," Gladys said, cutting him off as she took the bottle out of his hands. "Now, you'd better get back to work."

For a split second, Hamilton looked shocked at being interrupted, but then he brought his hand up to his fedora in salute. "As you command, Madame Muse!" he cried. Then he marched back out to his patio table.

"Good gravy," Gladys muttered. But at least she had her oil now, and she was pretty sure she wouldn't need any more supplies off the top shelf today.

# Chapter 17

# BEIGE GLOP ON BUTT-BREAD

THE NEXT HALF HOUR SAW GLADYS blending the oil and seeds into a great vat of tahini, then blending that tahini with chickpeas, fresh-squeezed lemon juice, cloves of garlic, and salt. Some water and a little more oil thinned out the mixture, and finally Gladys was able to taste her hummus. Not bad! She pulled the bowl off the food processor, threw it into the refrigerator, and turned to the next items on her mental list.

There were two hundred twenty mini baguettes to slice in half, and two six-pound wheels of Sardo to cut into one hundred ten wedges each. The watercress was prewashed, so at least she wouldn't have to worry about how to clean such a large volume of greens. After forty minutes of work with Mrs. Spinelli's knives,

Gladys's arm felt like it was going to fall off, but the cutting was done. All she had left to do was spread the hummus onto the baguette slices and assemble her sandwiches.

In twenty minutes. That was eleven sandwiches a minute. Could she do it?

As Gladys hauled the hummus out of the refrigerator and set to work, she wondered what was taking Mrs. Spinelli so long. At first she'd been happy to have the kitchen to herself, but now that it was crunch time, she could really use the extra set of hands. Had the cook spent the last hour yelling at Foodstuffs? Or had she quickly canceled their account and spent the rest of the time placing rush orders with somebody else? Gladys hoped Charissa would have the scoop that afternoon. Maybe she should even tell her friend what she'd done. After all, it was Charissa who had encouraged Gladys to teach Mrs. Spinelli some new recipes.

Gladys glanced at the kitchen clock: 11:57. Her arms whipping like crazed eggbeaters, she upped her sandwich-making speed. Schmear of hummus, hunk of Sardo, handful of watercress, close the sandwich. Schmear of hummus . . .

Outside, she could hear the first campers arriving for lunch, and the unmistakable, high-pitched whine of Kyra Astin told her that it was the Flamingo Fives. "I'm huuuuuungry," Kyra moaned. "Why isn't lunch reaaaaaady yet?"

"Yeah!" called another voice. "It had better be burgers today!"

"No *way*!" shouted a third voice. "Monday is always bologna day!"

"I want sloppy joes!" squealed another voice.

A louder, deeper voice inserted itself into the lunch debate. "I, for one, hope that today's menu includes ham. I brought the herbs to construct a Ham Herb."

Gladys couldn't help but smile as all the little voices quieted. "What's a Ham Herb?" one of the kids asked.

As Hamilton launched into his story about his signature sandwich, Gladys took a final glance over her handiwork. The last few sandwiches were a little messy, but overall, she was proud of them. This was going to be the best lunch of these campers' lives.

When Gladys finally eased the serving window open, twenty heads swiveled in her direction.

"LUNCH!" one of the kids screamed, and in seconds, the window was mobbed.

"One at a time!" Gladys shouted. "Line up, or you won't get any lunch at all!"

The kids finally formed some semblance of a line, and Gladys passed a plate out to the first set of little hands.

"Where's my dessert?" the boy demanded.

*Dessert!* Gladys had totally forgotten that camp lunch always included a dessert, even if it was just an apple or an orange. Today's dessert was supposed to be lemon bars, but of course Gladys had swapped them out for real lemons. She couldn't very well give out lemons for dessert, even if she had any left after squeezing juice for her hummus.

"Um . . . sorry, but there's no dessert today," Gladys said.

This set off a chain reaction down the line of five-year-olds.

"No dessert?"

"WHAT?"

"Boooo!"

"I want dessert!"

Then the boy in front of her opened up his sandwich and looked inside. "What is this stuff?" he asked.

"It's hummus with Sardo cheese and fresh watercress," Gladys said. "It's really good, I promise."

The boy just shrugged, turned away, and headed for a nearby table.

But the next girl wasn't so easy. "There's beige glop in my sandwich!" she shrieked.

"That's not glop; it's hummus," Gladys explained as patiently as she could. "It's a Middle Eastern staple that people have enjoyed for hundreds of years. Just try it."

With every kid, the reaction got worse.

"What's the matter with this cheese? It's hard!"

"Ugh, why's the lettuce so stringy?"

"The crust on my bread feels like it's made of wood!"

Gladys kept trying to explain the different components of the meal, but her patience quickly wore out. She finally gave up, and when someone asked, "What is this?" she answered, "It's a cheese sandwich."

The Squirrel Sixes and Scorpion Sevens were just as whiny about their sandwiches as the Flamingo Fives. Gladys hoped that the Emu Eights would act more mature, but if anything, they were worse.

"What did you do with the normal bread?" one boy asked Gladys accusingly. "This bread looks like a butt!"

The mini baguette looked nothing like a butt, but once the words were out of his mouth, there was no stopping them from spreading around the patio.

"Butt-bread, butt-bread!" a group of Ninja Nines chanted as they waited in line. And when they got to the window, things went downhill even faster.

"Ewwwwww—my butt-bread's got poop in it!" cried a skinny boy with curly brown hair. With his fingers, he scraped out a glob of Gladys's homemade hummus and flung it onto the patio.

That did it.

Gladys lunged through the window at the boy. Her fingers grazed the sleeve of his purple camp shirt, but the boy managed to back out of her reach just in time.

"Hey!" he shouted. "The crazy lunch CIT's trying to kill me!"

Heads whipped toward her, but Gladys was beyond

caring. How did Mrs. Spinelli deal with these monsters every summer? Right now, it was all she could do not to storm out to the lunch patio and find that kid. She envisioned knocking him to the ground and forcing him to lick up the hummus he'd thrown.

She was in the midst of taking a deep breath, trying to get hold of herself, when the high-pitched squeal of a microphone sounded.

"You children should be ashamed of yourselves!" a booming voice scolded.

Gladys peered through the serving window. On the other side of the patio, up on the platform that Mrs. Bentley sometimes used for lunchtime announcements, stood Hamilton. He had the microphone in one hand, and one of her sandwiches in the other—which was odd, because she didn't remember serving him.

"I just found this sandwich *in the trash can,*" he announced, answering Gladys's unasked question. "With not even *one* bite taken!" He held the sandwich high overhead for everyone to see. "Yes, the ingredients are a little strange. No, it's probably not as tasty as, say, a ham sandwich with herbs. But you should at least *try* it. That's the mature thing to do."

The lunch patio fell silent as Hamilton pointed at the kitchen. "That drudge in there worked very hard to make these for you—I watched her do it myself. So pull yourselves together. Rise above your childlike instincts for once, and eat your darn lunches."

Hamilton clicked off the microphone just as a gasp rose from the crowd. "He said a bad word!" one of the little kids cried.

But still—for one glittering moment—it looked as though his speech really might have gotten through to them. Most of the kids were like statues in their seats, and at a nearby table, one girl's hand was raising her sandwich to her mouth as though she was hypnotized. But then it passed her mouth unbitten and arched back over her shoulder before sailing through the air, raining watercress leaves on the heads of the Flamingo Fives and Scorpion Sevens. The sandwich slammed directly into Hamilton's chest.

He staggered back, his black T-shirt now streaked with pale hummus. A moment later, a hunk of mini baguette from a different hurler caught him on the arm.

Mrs. Bentley finally rushed up onto the platform, calling for order as Hamilton slunk off toward the bathroom. Gladys, meanwhile, spotted Charissa standing with Rolanda and Marti at the end of the lunch line. Her arms were crossed over her chest, and she was glaring at Hamilton's retreating back—probably remembering the first time he had grabbed the microphone to make a speech insulting the other campers.

But this time was different. Yes, Hamilton had once again shown off his pompous side—but he had done it to defend Gladys.

She felt her own rage softening like a pat of butter in a frying pan . . . but as it melted away, it left a film of confusion. The morning hadn't gone at all like she'd expected. There really was something to Mrs. Spinelli's assertions that she knew what kids liked to eat, and that it was salty meat on white bread. Maybe the camp cook was a tiny bit more knowledgeable in that culinary area than Gladys was.

And maybe Hamilton wasn't quite as horrible as she had originally thought.

# Chapter 18

## CARROTS AND CUPCAKES

SHORTLY AFTER HAMILTON'S SPEECH, Mrs. Spinelli burst into the kitchen. Mrs. Bentley followed close behind.

"She's just a child, Yolanda!" Mrs. Bentley cried. "What were you thinking, leaving her in charge of lunch?"

Gladys jumped in before the cook could say a word. "Please don't yell at Mrs. Spinelli," she begged Charissa's mom. "This was my idea, and I promised her I could handle it."

She glanced over at the cook, whose angular face now wore an expression of surprise. Clearly, she hadn't expected Gladys to stand up for her, but she was happy to play along. "That's right," she huffed. "It was all the girl's idea."

Looking exceptionally weary, Mrs. Bentley sank into a battered old kitchen chair and grabbed a sandwich off the serving line. She took a bite—and her droopy features perked up.

"This is what you made for the campers?" she asked Gladys.

Gladys nodded, and Mrs. Bentley swallowed.

"Well, I can see why kids might not go for it," Mrs. Bentley said, "but I think it's delicious! Here, try one, Yolanda."

Mrs. Spinelli lifted a sandwich to her dried-up lips and took a tiny bite. "Hmpf," was all she said after chewing and swallowing.

*Some review,* Gladys thought.

Mrs. Bentley took another bite of her own sandwich and looked Gladys over while she chewed. "You know," she said, "some of the staff and counselors have been complaining about having to eat the same lunches as the kids. I wonder . . . well, Yolanda, how would you feel about putting Gladys in charge of the staff lunches?" She turned to Gladys. "That would only be about twenty meals you'd be responsible for, rather than two hundred. Well, maybe a few more if the CITs decide they want the grown-up lunches, too—I'll have Charissa do a survey."

"But," Mrs. Spinelli said, "who will help me with the rest of the food?"

Mrs. Bentley licked a dollop of hummus off her finger. "Gladys can still assist you with the campers' lunches," she said. "But if she takes the staff lunches off your hands, that will decrease your workload, too."

Mrs. Spinelli looked over at Gladys, who was trying to look as disappointed as possible. She had a feeling that if the cook saw how much she wanted this job, she'd say no.

"Well," Mrs. Spinelli said finally, "if you think that's for the best, Laura, then I won't question your decision."

"Good, it's settled, then. Gladys, come on down to my office before the end of the day so you can fill out an order form for the ingredients you'll need. That is, if this plan sounds all right to you?"

Of course, it sounded more than all right to Gladys. Maybe it wasn't the camp-wide lunchtime revolution she had hoped for, but in a way, this was even better. She'd be able to completely control her own small menu every day—it would be almost like having her own restaurant!

"I'd be happy to prepare the staff lunches," she said.

Mrs. Bentley left—sandwich in hand—and once the door swung shut behind her, Mrs. Spinelli gazed around the messy kitchen. Dirty utensils were scattered all around, and bread crumbs, hummus smears, stray watercress leaves, and cheese bits coated almost every available surface.

"You've still got a lot to learn about kitchen management, girlie," the cook said with a chuckle. "But, well . . . you could have done worse." And then, to Gladys's utter astonishment, she took a second bite of her sandwich. "Yep," she repeated, "could've done worse. Now, start cleaning."

"Yes, ma'am," Gladys said. Then she made a quick show of hanging her head—which helped hide her smile.

The sky grew dark and drizzly after lunch, forcing all the usual poolgoers to do inside activities, and Charissa roped Gladys into joining her group in the Arts & Crafts Tent.

As Gladys had suspected, her friend was livid over Hamilton's display at lunch. "I can't believe the nerve of that kid, making *another* speech. I mean, he's not even an active CIT. If anyone was going to defend Gladys's sandwiches, it should've been me!" Charissa flung her ponytail over her shoulder, almost whacking a passing Emu Eight in the face. "He thinks he's *so* high and mighty," she continued, "because of that idiotic book."

"My mom's reading it right now," Leah said, reaching across the table for a piece of papier-mâché.

"Mine, too," said Marti as she pressed a wet strip onto her blob in progress. Everyone's projects looked like blobs to Gladys, including her own attempt at a pear.

"My parents bought two copies this past weekend," Gladys admitted, "so neither would have to wait to read it." She left out the fact that they'd also asked her to get Hamilton's autograph—a request she'd avoided, for today at least, by "accidentally" leaving the books at home.

"Well, I've told Mommy and Daddy that I'd better not catch them with their noses in it," Charissa said with a huff. "And I'm certainly not reading it, either. I don't think any of the CITs should!"

The other girls at the art table fell over one another to agree, though that didn't surprise Gladys—she was used to seeing everyone follow Charissa's lead. The question was whether *she* wanted to follow, too. Hamilton had stood up for her in front of the entire camp, and taken a sandwich to the chest for his troubles. That had to count for something, right?

As soon as she got home that day, Gladys opened her journal and looked at her list.

> *Step One: Ask people about the best hot dogs they've ever had.*
> *-Aunt Lydia*
> *-Mrs. Anderson*
> *-Mr. Eng*
> *-Parm*

Paris, where Aunt Lydia lived, was six hours ahead of New York, meaning it was ten thirty p.m. there. Gladys knew that her aunt worked the late shift at the local café on Monday nights, so calling her right now was out. Instead, she decided to start closer to home, and five minutes later, she was knocking on the Andersons' front door.

"Gladys, what a nice surprise!" Mrs. Anderson cried. She was holding her laptop under one arm, and a streak of flour ran down the front of her leggings. She always seemed a bit frazzled, juggling both of her jobs and her passion for baking, and it didn't look like sending Sandy off to camp had slowed her down at all.

"Are you baking something?" Gladys asked. She thought she smelled a hint of vanilla in the air.

"Oh, just cupcakes," Mrs. Anderson said. "It's Tallie's birthday down at the yoga studio, so I thought I'd surprise her. But she's vegan and doesn't eat gluten or white sugar, so I had to get creative."

"I'm sure they'll be delicious," Gladys said.

"Well, thank you, sweetie." Mrs. Anderson moved aside so Gladys could step into the foyer. "You can go straight on back, and grab a carrot from the fridge if you'd like."

"Sorry?" Gladys supposed it was nice of Mrs. Anderson to offer her a snack, though she would have preferred to wait for one of the cupcakes.

"Sandy said he told you to come by to play with the rabbits?"

"Oh!" Gladys had completely forgotten about that conversation. "Right!"

"I'll come back and get you when the cupcakes have

cooled, and maybe you can taste test one for me," Mrs. Anderson said. "How about that?"

"Sounds great."

Passing through the kitchen, Gladys helped herself to a carrot from the refrigerator and headed back to the Rabbit Room. After closing the door so they wouldn't get out into the hallway, she liberated tiny black-and-white Edward and fat brown Dennis from their hutch. Then she dropped to sit on the floor and let the Hoppers fight each other for the carrot in her hand. Edward, friendly and fearless, quickly climbed into her lap for better access, while skittish Dennis danced around her elbow, taking one hop back for every two hops he dared to take forward.

"Hey, have you guys ever eaten a hot dog?" she asked. "Probably not. I'm pretty sure rabbits are supposed to be vegetarians. Maybe a veggie dog?"

Edward was now balancing in her lap on his hind legs, stretching taller and taller to reach the carrot Gladys dangled high above him. Dennis, meanwhile, seemed to have gotten over his fear of Gladys and was now head-butting her other arm with the flat part of his face. Gladys finally gave in, broke the carrot in half, and let both animals go to town. If only feeding the kids at camp had been this easy!

A few minutes later, Mrs. Anderson arrived with a frosted cupcake on a small plate. "It's maple-flavored," she said as she set it down on Sandy's computer desk, out of jumping range of the hungry rabbits. "I had to use maple syrup to sweeten it, so I figured I might as well embrace the flavor. I hope Tallie likes them."

Leaving the Hoppers to their carrot, Gladys popped into the bathroom next door to wash her hands, then returned to try the cupcake. The icing was wonderfully creamy, and the cake itself was moist and sweet with a tiny but pleasant hint of coffeelike bitterness.

"Mmmm," Gladys said.

"You like it?"

"I really do. Thank you, Mrs. Anderson!"

From the depths of the beanbag chair she had settled into, Sandy's mom smiled.

Gladys quickly swallowed her cupcake bite. As much as she wanted to go on eating it, she had come over for a reason.

"Mrs. Anderson, I was wondering . . ." she started, "if you've ever had a really, really good hot dog."

Gladys couldn't blame Sandy's mom for shooting her a perplexed look. The question *was* coming out of nowhere.

"I mean, in all your travels," Gladys added quickly. "You mentioned once that you backpacked all around Asia, so I just wondered if, um . . . maybe they have hot dogs there?"

As soon as the words were out of her mouth, Gladys realized how dumb they sounded. Even at Palace of Wong, East Dumpsford's very Americanized Chinese take-out joint, Gladys had never seen a hot dog on the menu.

But Mrs. Anderson was nodding. "Actually," she said, "I *do* remember being surprised by all the hot dog vendors I saw on the streets in Thailand!"

"Really?" Gladys asked.

"I know—who thinks of Thailand and hot dogs? But they were a very popular snack. People don't eat them on buns like we do here, though—usually they come on sticks. Sometimes the vendors carve the dogs up with fancy patterns. And actually, the one I remember being the best was fried!"

"Like a corn dog?" Gladys asked.

"No, not really," Mrs. Anderson answered. "The coating was more like a Japanese tempura batter—do you know what that is?"

Gladys nodded. She had cooked tempura vegetables once, carefully coating chunks of different veggies in a delicate floury batter before frying them.

"Then you know that it's very light and crispy. Ha, I haven't thought about that hot dog in years." She smiled. "Why do you ask?"

"Oh, I was just curious," Gladys said. Then she added, "The lunch lady I'm assisting at camp really likes hot dogs, and I was wondering if there might be a more interesting way to cook them than how she does it."

Mrs. Anderson's eyes lit up. "I think there are a lot

of interesting ways if you look to other countries! Marisol, at my yoga studio? She's from Chile, and when she had a cookout last summer, she served us these great hot dogs called completo Italiano."

"Completo Italiano?" Gladys repeated. Who knew that Mrs. Anderson would be such a trove of hot dog information? "Are they Italian-style or something?"

Mrs. Anderson shook her head. "No, the name actually comes from the colors of the toppings, because they look like the stripes on an Italian flag! There's a layer of red tomatoes, then white mayonnaise, and finally chopped-up green avocado."

When Mrs. Anderson excused herself to frost the rest of the cupcakes, Gladys pulled her reviewing notebook out of her pocket. *Thai deep-fried hot dog on a stick,* she wrote. *Chilean completo Italiano.* She would have to get online later to do more research—and hopefully find some vendors in New York City who sold them.

# Chapter 19

# RICE THIS AND BEANS THAT

AFTER GLADYS'S VISIT NEXT DOOR, there was still enough time for her to bike over to Mr. Eng's before her parents got home. When she entered the shop, Mr. Eng was kneeling in the packaged-goods aisle, taking inventory of a shelf of gourmet pickles.

"Gladys!" he cried. "Welcome!"

"Hi, Mr. Eng," Gladys said. She hurried over and knelt beside him. "Here, let me help you count those."

"Oh, thank goodness." Using the middle shelf for support, he pulled himself to his feet. "These knees are getting too old for crouching. In fact, Gladys, if you want an after-school job when you're a little older . . . ah, but I forget that you already have one."

He shook his head, but for a moment,

Gladys imagined being a stock girl at Mr. Eng's instead of a restaurant critic. Getting to work would be a lot easier, for one thing—and she'd probably get to keep her paychecks!

"Anyway," he continued, "I've still got five copies of the paper on hold for you. We didn't really get to talk about your excellent review—there were some types of pork on that tapas restaurant's menu that even I hadn't heard of!"

"Thanks," Gladys said quietly. It was nice to hear that Mr. Eng thought she'd done a good job, even if Gilbert Gadfly didn't. "I had to do some serious research beforehand."

"Well, it paid off," Mr. Eng assured her. "I can't wait to see what you write about next."

"Oh," Gladys started, "I—"

"No, no, don't tell me." He waved a hand in the air. "I prefer to be surprised. And anyway, I go into the city to try new places myself sometimes. If I've already been to the restaurant you're reviewing, I wouldn't want to influence you with my opinion."

Somehow, Gladys doubted that Mr. Eng had been to any of the "restaurants" she'd be visiting for her next review; the closest thing to a hot dog he carried at his meat counter was an organic German knockwurst that sold for nineteen dollars a pound. But she still had to ask.

"So, Mr. Eng," Gladys said as she inventoried, "this

is kind of a random question, but . . . do you like hot dogs?"

Mr. Eng looked taken aback by this question, and Gladys was worried that she'd offended him. But then he said, "It's been a long time since I had a hot dog. But when I was a boy in Flushing . . . well, that's a different story."

"Will you tell me?"

Mr. Eng nodded slowly. "My family didn't have much money, and trips out of our neighborhood were rare. But one time, on a hot summer day . . . my father must have come into some extra cash, because he took me and all my brothers to Coney Island.

"We rode the Cyclone and the Wonder Wheel and played in the ocean—and when it came time for dinner, my father bought each of us a hot dog from that famous stand on the boardwalk, Nathan's. I'll never forget sitting on the pier, watching the waves, and eating that hot dog. It was the first time that I really felt like . . . well"—his voice cracked slightly—"like a real American."

*Huh.* This wasn't the kind of story Gladys had been expecting, but she could certainly use it. She slipped her notebook and pencil out of her pocket and scribbled *Nathan's at Coney Island—the true taste of America?* onto a blank page. Then she looked up to thank Mr. Eng and saw that, behind his glasses, his eyes were shining with tears.

He slid his hands into his apron pockets and glanced toward the produce section; she could tell he was embarrassed. Finally, not sure what else to say, she asked, "Would you like me to count up these jars of beets down here, too?"

That seemed to be just what Mr. Eng needed to hear. He cleared his throat and turned back to Gladys, the crinkles around his eyes deepening as he smiled. "The beets, yes—that would be such a help. Thank you, Gladys."

The next day, as soon as she got home from camp, Gladys called her aunt Lydia in Paris. Other than Mr. Eng, Gladys's aunt was the only adult who knew about her secret work for the *Standard*.

"*Bonsoir*, my Gladiola!" Aunt Lydia cried. "How are you? Have you been getting much use out of that garlic press I sent? They only make them like that here in France, you know."

"It's been great," Gladys said. In fact, she had thrown the press into her lobster backpack just that morning so she could use it in the camp kitchen. Once her new supplies came in, she had visions of making a pasta salad with garlicky pesto for one of her staff lunches. Today, however, she'd simply repeated yesterday's sandwiches. They'd received rave reviews from her fellow CITs, though that was probably just because Charissa had instantly proclaimed hummus,

Sardo, and watercress to be her favorite sandwich combination ever.

"Well, my Gladysanthemum," Aunt Lydia said, "what brings your lovely voice down my phone line today? Does it have to do with your job doing you-know-what for you-know-who?"

"Jeez, Aunt Lydia—you make it sound like I work for Voldemort!" Gladys laughed. "But, yeah, it does. My editor assigned me to review hot dogs. So I was wondering if maybe there's some amazing French variety that I don't know about."

"French hot dogs, no . . ." her aunt said, "at least, not that I know of. But guess which European country does have a surprising affinity for hot dogs? Iceland!"

"Iceland?"

"Indeed!" Aunt Lydia cried. "I was in Reykjavík on my holiday last year, and the food in Iceland can be very expensive. So for people on a tight budget—like *moi*—hot dogs are the cheapest food to eat. But they're not like American hot dogs at all! They're made mostly of lamb, and the lamb in Iceland is some of the best in the world. And they come with a very specific set of toppings, too: brown mustard, ketchup, raw *and* fried onions, and this delicious rémoulade made of mayonnaise mixed with relish."

Gladys scribbled frantically in her notebook. Special Icelandic lamb hot dogs—who would have thought? "Do you remember what they're called?" she asked.

Aunt Lydia chuckled. "As if your auntie ever forgot the name of a food she liked! They're called pylsur." She spelled the word for Gladys, who hoped once again that she'd be able to find a restaurant in the city that served them.

As soon as she hung up with her aunt, Gladys pulled out her birthday card from Parm. "Call me sometime!" said the note inside, and underneath it was her cousins' home number in Arizona. She dialed.

"Gladys! It's so good to hear from you!" Parm said once her uncle handed her the phone.

She asked Gladys about camp, and whether Charissa was any less bossy there than at school; Gladys asked Parm about Arizona, and whether she was any more adventurous in her eating there than she was at home. The answer to both questions was no.

"Honestly, I can't even find spaghetti on most of the menus here," Parm complained. "Everything is rice this and beans that."

"I guess you're pretty close to the Mexican border, huh?" Gladys asked.

"I guess," Parm said, "but trust me, there are some places here that really go overboard. I mean, does a hot dog really need to have beans on it?"

Gladys sat up straighter in her swivel chair. "Did you say hot dog?" She had planned to ask Parm if there were any special hot dogs in India, but this might be even better.

"Yeah," Parm said. "Everyone in Tucson is obsessed with them. The most popular ones are these hot dogs wrapped in bacon and covered with beans and . . . I don't know, a bunch of other stuff. They look vile to me, but my brother and my cousins *love* them."

"Do you remember what they're called?" Gladys asked.

"Sorry," Parm said. "But I bet you can find out online. Just look up 'Tucson popular hot dog' or something. I swear, they're everywhere here."

Gladys scrawled that down—she would have to research the exact name and makeup of this hot dog later, but she was excited to add another variety to her list.

"So, why the interest in hot dogs?" Parm asked. "They don't have you writing about *that* for the *Standard,* do they?"

Gladys explained that they did indeed, and that her review was due the first week of August.

"Well, save me a copy when it comes out," Parm said.

"Won't you be back by then?"

"Nope," Parm said dully. "My parents decided that me and Jagmeet could use more time bonding with our cousins, so they're leaving us here until the middle of next month."

"The middle of August?!"

"Tell me about it," Parm groaned. "Who packs their

kids off to live in the desert during the *hottest time of the year*? Seriously, you can't kick a soccer ball around for five minutes without getting heatstroke. But if I dare complain, all my relatives jump down my throat." Parm's voice went nasal in imitation. "'*You think this is bad? Try growing up in India!*'"

When they hung up a few minutes later, Gladys looked over her list. She'd amassed five solid candidates for world's best hot dog. But the real question was, how many of them would she be able to find in New York City?

She devoted the next hour to finding out—and amazingly enough, every single hot dog on her list was available somewhere in the five boroughs. There was a Scandinavian café with pylsur on the menu, a desert-themed bar that served the Tucson-style hot dog (which, it turned out, was called a Sonoran), a Thai hot dog and iced tea stand, and even a cart called Completos Locos, which dished up the elusive completo Italiano.

Less amazingly, the locations were far apart. Scandinavian Kitchen was fairly close to Nathan's in Brooklyn, but the others were scattered all over Queens, the Bronx, and Staten Island. Gladys was just starting to wonder how she'd manage to visit them all when she heard her parents' car pull into the driveway. She closed the browser and was about to close her Dump-

Mail, too, when a new message in her inbox caught her eye.

From: rabbitboy@dumpmail.com, she read. Sandy!

Gladys clicked to open the long-awaited message. It was only two lines long.

Be at computer tomorrow (Wednesday) at exactly 5 p.m.
I'll video-chat you.

Gladys suppressed a squeal. She had hoped that Sandy would write her a long message when he found Wi-Fi, but this was even better. In less than a day, she'd get to talk to him, and see him!

She shut down the computer and bounced out of the office like a jumping bean.

# Chapter 20

# MORE LEAFY GREENS

AT PRECISELY FIVE P.M. THE NEXT DAY, the video-chat alert rang out of Gladys's computer. She clicked "Accept Chat," and a blurry brown-and-green image filled her screen.

"Gladys!" Sandy's voice cried.

"Sandy?" Gladys stared at the screen. "Oh, no—I think something's wrong with my computer. I can't see you. It's all—"

She stopped short. What were those bright blue things moving in the middle of the screen? They looked almost like eyes. But if those were Sandy's eyes, then the brown-and-green thing had to be . . .

"Sandy!" Gladys shrieked. "What happened to your face?!"

Sandy laughed, and Gladys saw a brief flash of white that must have been his teeth. "Camouflage," he said finally. "Did I do a good job?"

He backed away from the screen a bit, and finally Gladys was able to make out the outline of his face. His forehead, chin, and round cheeks were all coated with mud, and his blond hair was hidden under a messy cap of leaves.

"Um, yeah," she said. "You did an amazing job. But . . . why?"

Gladys caught Sandy's white grin again, but when he spoke next, his voice came out hushed.

"I'm in the bushes right outside the camp office. It's empty now; every day at five, the director makes a grocery run into town. But still, I don't want to be surprised while I'm breaking the rules, so I figured a little camo would help me, you know . . . blend."

"Got it," Gladys said. She shouldn't be surprised that Sandy had come up with a good plan for sneaking around—after all, he was always helping her figure out how to do it.

"Anyway, sorry it took me so long to get online," he said. "They keep us really busy here, but I've been searching for Wi-Fi whenever I've had a chance. I finally hacked into this network yesterday—the password turned out to be 'Camp123,' if you can believe it! I thought that chatting live would be more fun than e-mailing."

"It's *way* more fun," Gladys said. "So how are you? How's camp?"

"Forget about me, Gatsby!" Sandy hissed. "Tell me about you, and this hot dog thing!"

But Gladys shook her head. If her encounters with Hamilton had taught her anything, it was how annoying it was to listen to someone prattle on about their life without them ever asking you about yours in return.

"We'll get to my stuff in a minute," she said. "But seriously, first I want to hear all about camp."

Gladys listened patiently as Sandy told her about waking up at sunrise to do karate drills, challenging his cabinmate Dane to spar for top-bunk privileges (he lost), advancing from blue belt to red belt, and suffering through bland meals at the refectory. "They're all super-healthy," he said with a groan. "Our sensei says that a sugar-free body is a strong body. But I *really* miss my mom's brownies. I mean, there are only so many buckwheat noodles a boy can eat!"

Gladys giggled.

"Okay, so that's it for me," he said. "What about you? What's going on with this hot dog review?"

She told him everything—about the two different e-mails from Fiona, about her day in the city with her dad, and about her freak encounter with Gilbert Gadfly on the train.

"Do you think he could have gotten my assignment switched somehow?" she asked finally.

Dried mud cracked across Sandy's forehead as it creased. "I don't know . . ." he said, "but even if he did, someone still has to write that hot dog review, right? So why not you? If you do a really great job, you'll prove that he's wrong about you . . . and, hey, maybe then Fiona will send you on even more cool quests. Like 'find the best brownie in America'! I could help you with that one."

Gladys smiled in spite of herself. "The thing is, I don't know how to do 'a really great job' on this assignment. Even just trying to find the best dog in Manhattan was impossible—and there are four more boroughs I haven't visited yet!" She could feel the panic rising in her voice.

"Okay, Gatsby, take some deep breaths. That's what our sensei always has us do, and it really does help you calm down. Here, I'll do them with you."

Sandy looked straight into the screen, sucked in an enormous breath, then let it out, causing his streaky cheeks to puff like a chipmunk's. Gladys couldn't help it—she burst out laughing. And maybe that wasn't exactly the way Sandy intended his exercise to work, but it *did* make her feel better.

"Well, I do sort of have a new plan," Gladys said once her giggles were back under control. She told him about all the international recommendations she'd received.

"Gatsby, that's excellent!" Sandy cried. "So, what's

the problem? You can still sneak away during camp, right? You'll probably need at least one day for each borough, so that's five trips. Do you think you'll be able to squeeze those in by the end of the month?"

"I'm just not so sure about the sneaking out any-more," Gladys said. "Things have gotten a little complicated at camp."

"Complicated? What do you mean?"

"Well, I sort of got myself put in charge of making better lunches for the people who work there . . ."

Sandy sighed. "Of course you did." He thought for a moment. "Okay, well, why don't you map all the restaurants and e-mail me the link? I should be able to sneak out to check my e-mail again after lights-out. Maybe I can come up with a route that'll make them easier for you to visit. Then we can video-chat again tomorrow and figure out a new way to get you into the city."

"Okay!" Gladys cried. Then she repeated a phrase that she had already said to her friend many times before. "What would I do without you?"

He snorted, sending a dried leaf fluttering from his forehead to the ground. "Don't start with that again. Though if you really want to thank me . . ."

"What?" she cried.

"Well," he said, "my mom *refuses* to break the camp's no-sugar rule. But . . . if you have time . . . maybe you could send some brownies?" He shot her a hopeful smile. "Just make sure you disguise them as something else, in case Director Samuels opens the package first. Okay?"

"Done," Gladys said.

The clock on her computer read 5:29 now, which Gladys grudgingly pointed out to Sandy. "You'd better go before your director gets back," she said.

"All right, but I'll see you tomorrow—same time, same place."

Gladys nodded, and they each waved at their screens. Then Sandy's camouflaged face disappeared.

# Chapter 21

# ALL BUTTERED UP

THE NEXT DAY AT CAMP STARTED OFF with morning announcements and the singing of the camp song—which, after a week of repetition, Gladys had finally committed to memory.

*Camp Bentley, Camp Bentley,*
*the greatest camp of all!*
*We wish it was always summer,*
*never spring or fall!*

*The values of friendship*
*and fun are e'er our guides . . .*
*Loyal we shall remain*
*with purple-shirted pride!*
*(Yay, camp!)*

"It's brainwashing," a voice muttered behind Gladys as she crossed the field to her swimming lesson. "All these oaths and songs."

She glanced over her shoulder and nearly tripped when she saw how closely she was being followed.

"Oh," she said. "Hi, Hamilton." Ever since Monday, Gladys had been trying to find an opportunity to quietly thank him for standing up for her cooking. She glanced around now; there were no CITs around to overhear her. "So, hey," she continued, "I just wanted to say—"

But Hamilton hadn't finished. "We're always being forced to praise the camp, to glorify the color purple. I mean, our parents have already paid the summer's tuition. We're stuck here, aren't we?" He sighed. "This place is more like Cult Bentley."

Gladys wasn't sure how to respond. She'd had similar thoughts herself but never dared to say them out loud.

"Look . . . I don't disagree," she said finally in a low voice. "But don't let Charissa hear you saying things like that, okay? You don't want to be on her bad side, and . . ." She trailed off, already feeling rotten about what she'd been about to say. *Some way to thank him for standing up for you,* she thought, *by telling him that the most popular kid at camp can't stand him!*

But Hamilton already seemed to know. "Yeah, I can tell she doesn't like me," he said. "I'm not surprised—Charissa Bentley is clearly the jealous type. What baffles me, though, is why *you're* friendly with her, Gladys." Under the rim of his fedora, his brow furrowed. "Unless my powers of observation are way off, you two don't seem alike at all."

Gladys was, once again, taken aback by Hamilton's directness. Did he always just say everything he was thinking? And now he was staring at her, waiting for a response. "Well, our friendship is kind of hard to explain," she admitted. "But Charissa can be really nice once you get to know her."

Hamilton shrugged. "If you say so."

They were fast approaching the pool enclosure, and Hamilton's long legs put him within reach of the gate first. He undid the latch and swung the gate open, but then he stepped aside in a gallant sort of way, letting Gladys walk through first.

"Oh—uh, thanks," she mumbled. She could already feel an unexpected flush creeping up her neck, and it only blazed hotter when, instead of saying *you're welcome* like a normal person, Hamilton swept his fedora off in a bow.

"After you, Madame Muse."

Gladys ducked her own head and hurried to drop her backpack onto the bleachers. Thankfully, Rolanda had been too busy adjusting lane dividers in the pool to notice their awkward exchange at the gate.

A moment later, Coach Mike was barking instructions as usual. "Beginning swimmers!" he shouted. "You'll be retaking your swim tests in a mere three weeks! Your results will determine whether you'll be able to join Free Swim, or will need additional lessons in your last weeks of camp!"

Hamilton's disbelieving voice rose up from the back of the group. "Additional lessons?"

The coach's beady eyes lasered in on him. "Yes, Herbertson," he growled, "additional lessons! If you cannot pass your swim test, you'll need to spend an extra two hours here every morning."

Gladys's stomach dropped. She hadn't realized that so much depended on passing the next test. If she failed, she would have to spend her remaining mornings in the pool. One hour a day would not be enough time for her to make lunches! And Hamilton was probably thinking about how remedial lessons would cut into his writing time.

"Now, line up along the lanes!" the coach said. "Let's see how you would do if your tests were today!"

"What?" But Gladys's voice was swallowed up by the sounds of scuffling as the little kids around her raced toward the pool. Strangely enough, they all wanted to be first in line—Kyra Astin shoved past little Benny "Swim Diaper" Regis to get to the pool's edge. Trudging behind them, she and Hamilton brought up the rear.

They ended up swimming at the same time in neighboring lanes. Gladys tried to put her floating lesson with her mom to good use, and generally succeeded at staying buoyant, but she knew that her form was closer to a doggy paddle than the clean crawl stroke

Rolanda always demonstrated. And Rolanda once again got to show off her rescuing skills when Hamilton disappeared under the surface one-third of the way across the pool.

"Lane three, Herbertson, FAIL!" Coach Mike shouted as Rolanda towed him toward the pool's edge. The coach shook his head like Hamilton was a lost cause—and Gladys had to admit she agreed.

When class ended at nine thirty, Gladys saw Hamilton jam his fedora over his still-sopping hair and storm out of the pool area. He didn't shrug off his failure like he had at the first swim test. Less had been at stake then.

Before she could even think twice, Gladys grabbed her lobster backpack and dashed after him.

"Hamilton!"

He looked back and stopped in his tracks.

"You need to practice floating more," Gladys said breathlessly.

"Sorry?"

"It'll help," she continued, "with your swimming. My mom taught me, and today I knew that even if I started to sink, I could just flip over onto my back and float instead of . . . you know . . ."

"Panicking?" A bitter laugh escaped Hamilton's lips.

"Well, yeah."

Hamilton contemplated her advice; in fact, Gladys wasn't sure she had ever seen him stay silent this long when there was somebody nearby he could be bragging or speechifying to. Finally, he cleared his throat. "Floating," he said. "All right, Gladys, I'll give it a try. After all, as my muse, you haven't steered me wrong yet." And then, with a tip of his hat, he loped off toward the patio, pulling his notebook out of his bag.

*Well*, Gladys thought, *now we're square.* Hamilton had tried to help her win over the campers at lunchtime, and she had tried to help him with his swimming. Now she could go back to ignoring him with a clear conscience—which, she told herself, was exactly what she intended to do.

Because he was still super-annoying.

Right?

In any case, she didn't have time to dwell on the question.

Back in the kitchen, her new ingredients had finally come in, and she threw herself into chopping carrots, roasting eggplant chunks, and mixing up a peanut sauce for gado-gado, an Indonesian-style vegetable salad. The lunch drew raves from the staff and CITs, and while Mrs. Spinelli insisted on eating one of her own meat sandwiches, Gladys did catch her licking peanut sauce off a ladle before she loaded it into the dishwasher.

After another afternoon at the archery range and a ride home with her mom that hit every red light on Landfill View Road, Gladys was finally in front of the computer. She had sent Sandy the map right after their call yesterday, and she really hoped that he'd come up with a brilliant solution for her.

At 5:02, the video-chat alert sounded, and Sandy's face popped up on Gladys's screen, once again streaked with dirt. "Secret Agent Anderson, reporting from the field!" he whispered. "How's it going, Gatsby?"

"Not bad," Gladys said. "How are you?"

"Oh, fair," he said, but his eyes kept shifting back and forth. "Look, I don't know how much time I'll have today," he said. "There's a cold going around, and yesterday Director Samuels caught it. He's been in his bunk all day . . . and his bunk is right next to his office . . . which is right next to this bush."

"Uh-oh," Gladys said.

"Well, he's asleep now, I peeked in his window—so I think we'll be okay. But let's get right down to business. The good news is I've noticed a pattern in the restaurant locations."

"You have?" They had all looked pretty randomly placed to Gladys.

"Yep," Sandy said. "They're all close to beaches."

"Beaches?" Gladys snatched up her printout of the map.

"Yep," Sandy said. "Nathan's is at Coney Island—I mean, everyone knows that—but look at the others. In Queens, your Thai place is just a block from Rockaway Beach. And then up in the Bronx, Completos Locos is at Orchard Beach!" He was sounding more excited by the second. "Arizona Arthur's bar, with the Sonoran hot dogs, is only three blocks from South Beach on Staten Island. And then back in Brooklyn, Scandinavian Kitchen, with the pylsur, is just a mile from Nathan's in Brighton Beach!"

It was an interesting pattern, and Sandy seemed exceptionally pleased with himself, but Gladys wasn't sure how it could help her. Was she supposed to rent a boat and sail from one hot dog joint to the next along the New York waterways? "So, what are you thinking I should do with this information?" she asked.

"Sorry," Sandy said. "I thought it would be obvious. You should ask your mom to—"

Suddenly, the picture on Gladys's screen went crazy. "Gotcha, you little sneak!" an angry voice cried—but Gladys couldn't see who it belonged to. Instead, her view bounced around from grass to bushes to sky; then it swooped again, and the face of a man with unkempt black hair and a very red nose came into view. Gladys fell back in her swivel chair in surprise.

"You!" the man shouted into the screen. "Yes, I mean you, young lady! I see you!"

Gladys groped for her mouse with a shaking hand.

"Who were you talking to?" the man demanded. "Which camper has broken the no-screens rule?!"

*Click.* Gladys closed her web browser, and the camp director's face disappeared.

She sat frozen in the swivel chair for a full minute longer, until her heart finally slowed down to a normal pace.

If the director didn't know who had been using the tablet, Sandy must have gotten away. That was good. However, Gladys's tablet was now in possession of the director. That was bad.

Could the tablet be traced back to Sandy? Probably not—Sandy was smart about using anonymous-sounding user names and encrypted passwords. His DumpChat log-in was "rabbitboy," and at a camp with hundreds of boys, that could be anyone.

Gladys was relieved about that. But their video-chats had clearly come to an end—and just before Sandy had revealed his plan!

What was the last thing he had told her before they'd been interrupted? *You should ask your mom to—* To what? How could her mom help her visit beaches all around New York City?

Then, like a pie to the face, it hit her. Sandy knew that Gladys's mom had been a champion swimmer when she was young—and Gladys had told him about her own swimming lessons at camp. She could ask her mom to take her to all those beaches . . . under the cover of wanting to go swimming with her!

"Sandy, you're a genius!" Gladys cried, jumping out of her chair. Her mom would be home in an hour, and then Gladys would put the new plan into motion. But first, she had some dinner to start.

Convincing her mom to continue their swimming lessons at beaches in New York City turned out to be easy.

"This will be so much fun!" her mom cried when Gladys proposed the plan over dessert that night.

Of course, at that point her mom was stuffed with buttered noodles, asparagus sautéed in garlic butter, and fresh strawberries with buttery shortcake. Gladys had literally buttered her up.

Gladys's dad, though, was frowning. "I don't see why you're so excited to go into the city with Gladys when you never want to go with me," he said.

"Oh, George," Gladys's mom replied, "you know that what I hate about the city is the crowding, and the noise, and the crime. But beaches, that's another thing entirely! Lydia and I used to swim at Coney Island and Brighton Beach all the time when we were children. Won't it be fun to share that experience with Gladys, too?" She smiled at her daughter, and then at her husband. "And you'll come with us, won't you?"

"Yeah, of course you should come, Dad!" Gladys chimed in.

Gladys's dad's grimace softened. "Well . . ." he said. "If I'm invited, too . . ."

Up in her room that night, Gladys tore a fresh page out of her reviewing journal.

*Dear Sandy,* she wrote, then paused. She planned to hide this note, and his brownies (triple-wrapped in plastic to stifle the smell), in a package that looked like it was carrying something else. But she still needed to be careful about what she wrote, just in case it was discovered.

> *Thanks for your advice. Our friends George and Jennifer are taking me to Brooklyn this weekend. Hopefully, they'll have such a great time that they'll be willing to venture even farther next weekend.*
>
> *G.G.*
>
> *P.S. I hope that this extra underwear will be useful to you at camp!*

She folded the note in half, then in half again. Tomorrow after camp, she would pop by next door to visit the Hoppers—and steal some of Sandy's left-behind undershirts and shorts. As much as she didn't want to touch her friend's underwear, she had to hope that the camp director would want to dig through it even less.

Chapter 22

# SALT AND SAND

THANKS TO EXTENSIVE PLANNING BY
Gladys, that Saturday morning went off
without a hitch. Determined to arrive at
the beach in time for lunch, Gladys lured
her parents out of bed early with hot coffee and a breakfast of blueberry crepes.
She had packed their beach bags the
night before, and hustled them into the
car as soon as breakfast ended. An hour
later, they were in the mostly Russian-
speaking Brighton Beach neighborhood
of Brooklyn.

Her dad muttered darkly as he searched
for a parking spot, but Gladys was ready
for everything. She had printed a map of
the neighborhood, and now pulled it out
of her own beach bag. "Hey, Dad, I found
a lot online that charges only ten dollars
to park all day."

She showed him the location on her map, and her dad's mood immediately improved. "That's our Gladdy," he said, swinging the car in a wild U-turn to head for the intersection she had indicated. "Always prepared!"

Gladys didn't know about always, but in this case, she had made sure to find a parking lot close to Scandinavian Kitchen. Sure enough, her family walked right past the restaurant on their way to the beach. In contrast to the other shops in the area, its sign was in English, and it flew Swedish, Danish, and Icelandic flags over the door instead of Russian or Ukrainian ones.

"Ooh, look at this place," Gladys said, pausing in front of the menu posted in the window. "Food from Scandinavia! Hey, Dad, have you ever heard of an Icelandic hot dog before?"

"An Icelandic hot dog? What's that made of, whale?" he asked.

"It's not a good idea to swim on a full stomach," her mom said.

Gladys made a show of reluctantly pulling herself away from the window. She hadn't really expected them to buy her a hot dog this early—but she wanted to plant the idea for later.

Once they found a good spot on Brighton Beach, everyone lathered up with sunscreen. That was when

Gladys's stomach started flip-flopping. She knew the hardest part of the day was coming: swimming with her mom.

While Gladys's dad lay on their beach blanket with his copy of *Zombietown, U.S.A.*, Gladys followed her mom down to the ocean, gulping in nervous lungfuls of salty air. But she needn't have worried. They started off easily, and for twenty minutes, Gladys practiced breathing out as she put her face in the water, then turning her face to the side to breathe in. "The arms and legs can come later," Gladys's mom said. "It's the breathing that you have to learn first."

Gladys had always known her mom had a passion for swimming, but she'd never really had a chance to experience it. In fact, their two lessons so far were the most one-on-one time they'd spent together outside of the car in a long while.

"I thought you two would never come out," her dad said when they finally emerged from the ocean. "I'm starved!"

"Let's head down to Coney Island and visit Nathan's," her mom said. "That's where Lydia and I always used to eat."

Gladys hadn't even had to say a word.

Nathan's Famous sat on the edge of the Coney Island boardwalk, the great green letters of its sign standing out against the cloud-streaked blue sky. Towering over it were the amusement park's Ferris wheel and roller coaster, but the Nathan's line was longer than the lines for both rides combined. Gladys expected her parents to moan and groan about the wait, but to her surprise, they simply joined the queue and started reminiscing about the hot dogs of their childhoods.

Gladys paid attention to their conversation—who knew what material she might be able to use in her article? But, annoyingly, her parents couldn't answer her most important questions.

"Do you remember what brand the hot dogs were?" she asked her dad in the middle of a story about grilling illegally with his brother on their fire escape in Jersey City.

"What brand?" Her dad frowned. "How do you expect me to remember a thing like that?"

"Well, do you remember what they tasted like?"

"Sure, they tasted like char—we built the fire too high!" He laughed. "And then the smoke alarm went off, right inside the apartment . . ."

Gladys's mom's memory was a little better—at least she knew that the hot dogs she and Lydia loved eating came from Nathan's. But getting any more details out of her was like trying to catch granules of couscous in a colander.

"What condiments we got? Oh, Gladys, who remembers these things?" She paused. "Well, maybe Lydia got mustard once, because I remember that she came home with a big yellow stain on her shorts and your Grandma Rosa made a huge stink . . ."

When they finally reached the register, her parents were still so far down memory lane that Gladys had to do the ordering.

"I'll take an original hot dog, a chili dog, and a corn dog," she told the man behind the counter. "And a large order of fries."

When their food came up, Gladys's dad carried their boxes over to a condiment station, where he loaded up on little cups of ketchup, mustard, and relish. Then they headed out to the beach.

Gladys had never eaten a meal on a beach—especially not a meal she was trying to review—and found it more difficult than she'd expected. Without a table, there was nowhere to put the food, and nowhere to hide her reviewing journal. Laying her hot dog's carton down gently in the sand, she tried to open her journal secretly in her lap. But then a gust of wind sent the pages flapping—and, even worse, blew a pile of sand over the dog.

"Gladdy, you're going about this all wrong," her dad said, snatching up the hot dog and shaking sand from it. "It's called fast food for a reason. You've got to eat it quick, while it's hot and not too sandy. Here, like this!" And he took such a huge bite that he immediately choked, shooting a wad of green stuff right out of his nose.

Gladys and her mom nearly fell over laughing. Once her dad stopped coughing, he laughed, too, though not quite as loudly. "That was relish!" he insisted. "Relish, I swear!" But that only made them all laugh harder.

The next ten minutes were filled with food swaps, dives to protect the French fries from seagulls and sand, and more laughter. Gladys couldn't remember her family ever having so much fun together. Unfortunately, when the food was gone, she also couldn't remember which dish had tasted like what. Was it the French fries that had oozed grease onto her fingers— or was that the batter around the corn dog? Had the all-beef hot dog tasted better under a thick layer of chili, or a thin drizzle of mustard and relish? *Fudge,* she thought. She'd been so busy having a good time that she'd nearly forgotten about her assignment.

After a couple more hours playing Skee-Ball in the arcade and riding the Wonder Wheel, the Gatsbys made their way back to Brighton Beach. In her planning, Gladys had come up with all sorts of potential tricks to convince her parents to take her to Scandinavian Kitchen: She could feign exhaustion from a lack of protein, or tell them the theme of this year's camp color war was "Battle of the Baltic Sea" and that she needed to stop in for research. But as they turned onto the block with the restaurant, Gladys decided that, on this great day of swimming, laughter, and to-getherness, she would try the truth.

(Well, the truth minus the whole *New York Standard* thing.)

"Hey, Mom, Dad," she said, "I'd really like to pop into that Scandinavian place. I've never had an Icelandic-style hot dog before, and as long as we're here, I think it might be really interesting to try."

It turned out that was all she needed to say. They entered the café, which had simple white walls and paper menus, sat at a counter on wooden stools, and ordered three pylsurs. The franks were pink, the sauces soaking into the buns brown and red, and the onions both crispy and crunchy.

Gladys's parents dug in, comparing this hot dog with the ones they'd had earlier. Gladys agreed that the flavors were pleasantly surprising. But in truth, they weren't half as surprising as the fact that her parents had come in here with her at all. Just a few months ago, trying something as crazy and unfamiliar as an Icelandic hot dog would have been unthinkable for them.

It was like they were finally growing up.

Chapter 23

# SOMETHING FISHY

HONESTY HAD WORKED SO WELL FOR Gladys in Brooklyn that she decided to try it out again the next day at breakfast. "I've been doing some research online," she told her parents, "and there are actually a lot of really interesting hot dogs at the beaches of New York City. I thought maybe we could make it a kind of family project to try them all out."

"Ooh!" said her mom through a mouthful of coconut waffle. "Visiting more beaches means more swimming! We can really work on your skills, honey."

Her dad agreed to the plan, too. "You know, I'm impressed with you, Gladdy," he said. "First, you ate all those hot dogs with me in Manhattan, and now you want to try hot dogs in other boroughs.

It's like you're finally learning how to eat like a kid!"

So they made a plan to visit beaches in Queens and Staten Island the next Saturday, and to go to Orchard Beach in the Bronx the Saturday after that. For once, Gladys wouldn't be scrambling at the last minute to finish her assignment; she would have more than a week after the Bronx trip to get her review into perfect shape before Fiona returned from her vacation.

During swimming lessons the next week, Gladys managed to tune out Coach Mike's shouts and concentrate on the tips her mother had given her at Brighton Beach. She found that if she spent the first few minutes of class getting her usually panicked breathing under control, she could breathe in the water much better.

Life in the kitchen with Mrs. Spinelli was going more smoothly, too, since they each had their own projects to work on. And, if Gladys wasn't mistaken, the cook was starting to look a little less skeletal. Maybe that was because she was now eating two lunches a day: the one she made herself and the one Gladys made.

Gladys had more free time after camp each day, too, now that her hot dog research trips were squared away, so she decided to make another care package for Sandy. She stopped by his house on Monday afternoon to steal more underwear, baked peanut-butter-chocolate-chip cookies for him on Tuesday, and on Wednesday boxed everything up and cycled to the post office to mail the package.

On the way home, she stopped at Mr. Eng's. Postage for Sandy's packages had cost her more than fifteen dollars, so her funds were pretty low, but she did have just enough change left to buy a copy of that day's *Standard*. Even on weeks when she didn't have a review scheduled, Gladys liked to read the Dining section. Maybe today there would be a delicious new recipe, or a report on an emerging culinary trend.

"Anything good in there today?" she asked Mr. Eng. She knew he always read the Dining section first thing in the morning—he was the one who had originally gotten her hooked on reading it.

"Not if you're a restaurant called Café Accra," he replied. "Honestly, I'm not sure why your editor even sent Gilbert Gadfly there. It's pretty clear from the first sentence of his review that he despises African food."

"Wait—Café Accra?" Gladys had already seen Mr. Gadfly's notes for Ristorante Massimo in his reviewing notebook, but Café Accra was the *other* restaurant Gladys was supposed to review! She flipped the paper open on Mr. Eng's counter and saw the headline "Cuisine of West Africa Disappoints."

Gladys only had to skim the first few lines to confirm that Mr. Eng was right. Mr. Gadfly wasn't critiquing Café Accra's menu so much as the culinary traditions of western Africa as a whole. *Too many beans make the belly grow gassy,* he wrote, and then, later, *The chef might want to replace some of the chopped pea-*

nuts in his signature stew with a tastier protein—like pork.

Gladys's teacher, Ms. Quincy, had grown up in western Africa, and her geography lessons had been particularly memorable. Thanks to her, Gladys knew that peanuts were a major crop grown in several West African countries, but that pigs were not widely raised, in part because the region's large Muslim population didn't eat pork.

Had Mr. Gadfly done *any* background research before slamming the new café?

And had Fiona edited this review before she left for vacation? Somehow, Gladys didn't think so. This was the kind of sloppiness readers might expect to see in the *Dumpsford Township Intelligencer,* but not in the country's top newspaper. Gladys wondered how long the eatery would stay in business with such a poor write-up in the *Standard.*

"I could have done a better job with this review," she grumbled.

Mr. Eng smiled. "You always do."

"Thanks, Mr. Eng."

When she got home, Gladys found that he had slipped a free peach into her bag.

She sliced it up to eat while perusing the rest of the Dining section. There were three recipes, an interview with a vegan chef, and an article about a new super-fruit from Malaysia. All of it seemed to be up to the *Standard*'s usual . . . well, standard. Only the Gadfly review stood out.

Something seemed fishy about this whole situation.

More than ever now, Gladys wished that Sandy was home from camp—she was sure they could get to the bottom of this mystery together. But she didn't expect to hear from him anytime soon. She imagined her tablet sitting in the camp director's office, propped up against the wall like a magic mirror that would reveal her to him the moment she signed in to video-chat. Which, of course, she had no intention of doing. In fact, she'd made sure to change her DumpMail privacy settings to never reveal when she was online. She thought Sandy would be proud of this move, but of course she had no easy way to tell him about it now.

She supposed she could talk to Parm, but her friend probably wouldn't find the Gadfly review as weird as she did. "Beans?" she imagined Parm saying. "Peanuts? Ugh! No wonder he gave it a bad review—that all sounds disgusting!"

Charissa would be more understanding, but Gladys still wasn't ready to trust her with her secret. Charissa seemed like the kind of person who would keep quiet about something until you got in a fight with her . . . and then the rumors would start. No, it was still too dangerous to confide in her.

But who did that leave?

The next day, Gladys caught up with Hamilton as he crossed the lawn after their swimming lesson. "Hey, Hamilton," she said.

"Gladys!" He immediately swept his fedora off his head. "My favorite muse. Do you have more swimming advice for me today?"

"Er . . ." Gladys hadn't expected that question, but she supposed that passing along another tip from her mom couldn't hurt. Quickly, she explained the breathing technique she had practiced at Brighton Beach.

"Now," she went on, "I have a question for you."

"Fire away."

"You have an editor, right?" Gladys asked. "For your books?"

"Of course I do. She's terrific."

"And your editor—does she work with other writers, or just with you?"

"Oh, she has other authors, too."

They had reached the lunch patio now, and Hamilton pulled his notebook out of his bag. "Have you read any of their books?" Gladys asked quickly. "These other authors your editor works with?" She was trying to get some insight into how editors operated, to see if she could figure out whether Fiona had actually edited Gilbert Gadfly's review before it was published.

"I've read a few," Hamilton said, zipping his bag back up. "But if I'm honest, none of the other books are that great. So if you're looking for a good read, I really must recommend *Zombietown, U.S.A.*"

An all-too-familiar feeling of exasperation flooded through Gladys. "That's *not* what I—" she started, but she managed to cut herself off before saying something rude. Hamilton was the only other published writer she knew, the only person who might be able to answer her questions.

"What I meant to ask was, can you tell when your editor has worked on a book?"

Hamilton frowned as he flipped his notebook open. "Well, I'm sure my editor helps her other authors. But if you're asking whether every book she edits is up to my standards, then I'd have to say no." And with that, he uncapped his pen, hunched his long torso over his notebook, and began to scribble—a sure sign that their conversation was over.

Gladys fumed as she marched into the kitchen. It had been ridiculous to think that her questions would get through to Hamilton. Charissa was right—she'd need a supersonic fighter jet to navigate around an ego that size! The goodwill she'd been feeling toward him over the last week was disappearing fast.

Gladys's sour mood even seeped into the lunches that day. "Whew!" Mrs. Spinelli cried when she took a bite of her seared tofu and pomegranate seed salad. "Maybe use a little less vinegar in that dressing next time, huh, girlie?"

When the weekend finally arrived, Gladys couldn't wait to get to Rockaway Beach in Queens. For once, she actually *wanted* to hang out with her parents. She might not be able to talk to them about her confusing Gilbert Gadfly problem, but she was pretty sure that another day of sun, sand, and hot dog tasting would at least help put it out of her mind. She wasn't even that nervous about swimming—two weeks of practicing her mom's techniques in the pool had really improved her confidence.

Gladys and her mom spent the morning in the ocean, working on the crawl stroke. "Slice! Chop! Whip!" her mom called out, reminding Gladys what she should be doing with her arms and legs. Once her mom was satisfied with her progress, they moved onto the breaststroke, which Gladys actually found much easier.

Gladys's dad joined them for a while, and by the time they found the Royal Bangkok stand on the boardwalk, they had all worked up an appetite. Gladys made a conscious effort to focus on her delicately fried hot dog on a stick and supersweet cup of Thai iced tea, but she couldn't help but get distracted. The sun's reflection on the water was bright and beautiful, and the shrieks of little kids racing down the board-walk were loud and excited. And then there were her parents, who kept shooting straw-wrapper missiles at each other until Gladys yelled at them for littering and made them find a trash can.

Maybe they weren't growing up as quickly as she'd thought.

In the afternoon, they drove across the Verrazano Bridge to Staten Island and swam for another couple of hours at South Beach. Here, Gladys's mom taught her how to fill up her lungs and dive under the surface, covering extra distance with a few strong underwater strokes. "Pretend you're one of those turkey baster doodads," her mom said. "Just make sure it's air you're sucking in before you dive, not water."

After swimming, the Gatsbys dropped in at Arizona Arthur's for an early dinner. A large concrete-floored space with sauce-splattered, cafeteria-style tables, it was full of loud beachgoers swigging margaritas and digging in to dripping burritos. Gladys's dad took care of the ordering and came back to their table with three Sonorans—bacon-wrapped hot dogs tucked inside oval buns and smothered with pinto beans, onions, tomatoes, mayonnaise, mustard, and jalapeño sauce. Gladys reached for her journal in her beach bag, excited that she could actually take notes this time since they were at a real table.

"You know, your father took me to a place a lot like this one for our first date," her mom said loudly over the bar noise.

Gladys's dad nearly choked on his first bite of hot dog. "It was *nothing* like this!" he insisted.

"I guess you're right," Gladys's mom said, glancing around at the neon cacti that decorated Arizona Arthur's walls. "This place is much, much nicer."

Pretty soon, Gladys was giggling as her parents argued about their first night out together: Her dad made their destination sound like a four-star restaurant, while her mom described something closer to a filthy dungeon. Whatever the truth, their debate definitely got Gladys's mind off her crazy reviewing assignment.

Too far off. It wasn't until the last bite of her own Sonoran hot dog had disappeared that Gladys realized she'd completely forgotten to take any notes. Again.

*Fudge.*

# Chapter 24

# THE ONION TRICK

"IS SOMETHING THE MATTER?" HAMILTON asked Gladys through the lunch window that Monday at camp.

"What?" Gladys snapped. "No, why?"

"Well," Hamilton said, "I just asked you for a ham sandwich, but you gave me turkey. Usually you're sharper than that. Also, I noticed you struggling in the pool this morning, which is surprising after your week of solid improvement."

Gladys snatched the sandwich back from his tray and passed him the right one. "Here. And why were you watching me so closely, anyway?"

Hamilton shrugged. "If I'm basing a character on someone, I have to observe them closely. It's my job."

"Yeah, well, you're not the only one with a job to worry about," Gladys mumbled.

"What's that?"

"Nothing." She had already said too much.

Gladys was still angry at herself for paying such poor attention to that Sonoran hot dog on Saturday. Why did she keep letting herself get distracted? The *New York Standard* already had one critic who didn't give his work the attention it deserved; it didn't need another.

It rained that afternoon, and Charissa once again dragged her CIT friends to the Arts & Crafts Tent to work on pottery projects. Predictably, the conversation soon turned to Hamilton.

"He's such a creeper," Rolanda said as she brushed glaze over a lopsided vase. "You guys should see the way he stares at Gladys during their swim lessons."

Gladys, who had been rolling pieces of clay into spaghettilike strands, froze.

"Oh, it's not just at swimming," Mira said. She set her paintbrush down and laid a purple-stained hand on Gladys's arm. "I *totally* saw him checking you out in the lunch line last Friday. Owen and Jake just cut right in front of him, and he didn't even notice! He was, like, on another planet."

Leah giggled. "Yeah, Planet Gladys."

"Omigosh," Marti cried. "Do you think he *like*-likes you?"

Noses all around the table wrinkled in disgust, and Mira mimed sticking a purple-coated finger down her throat. Gladys's cheeks burned.

"O-of course he doesn't," she stammered. "If he's staring at me, it's . . ."

She was about to explain that it must be because he was basing a character on her—but suddenly that sounded awfully weird, too.

Luckily, Charissa chose that moment to intercede. "Leave Gladys alone, guys," she said. "If that nutcase has taken a liking to her, it's not her fault. Gladys just happens to be extremely *likable,* that's all. I mean, don't *we* all like her so much?"

The other girls at the table agreed immediately.

"Oh, yeah!"

"Definitely!"

"She's *so* super-likable!"

Gladys didn't buy it, but she shot Charissa a grateful smile anyway. Charissa didn't smile back, though—in fact, her glossy lips were now set in a very thin line.

"But this business with Hamilton Herbertson has gone on long enough," she told the group. "I promised that if he messed with Gladys again, I'd make him pay."

"Oh," Gladys said. "No, Charissa, I really don't think that's—"

"You're my friend," Charissa snapped, "and no one messes with my friends. It's that simple."

But it wasn't so simple to Gladys. Hamilton certainly wasn't her favorite person, but she didn't hate him anymore, either. How could she explain that to

Charissa, though? If she said something nice about Hamilton in front of this group, they'd make fun of her forever.

"I don't know exactly what I'll do about him yet," Charissa went on, "but once I have a plan, I'll expect everyone here to pitch in. Got it?"

"Absolutely!"

"Can't wait!"

Gladys shuddered. It sounded like Hamilton's fate was sealed.

Over the next few days, Gladys tried to keep an extra eye on Hamilton to see whether he might be keeping an extra eye on *her*. To her dismay, Rolanda and the other girls were right. When her head popped out of the water during the crawl stroke, there he was, watching her from the next lane. As she served campers in the lunch line, he lurked by the garbage cans, observing. And when she stepped out onto the archery range in the afternoon, she noticed that he had seated himself under the tree right next to it with his notebook, all but blending into the shadows in his black camouflage.

Was this the way authors normally worked?

That Thursday, Hamilton came up beside her as she crossed the field after swimming lessons. "Hello, Gladys," he said, sweeping his fedora off as usual. "I've been meaning to ask you something."

Gladys glanced around, but there were no CITs in

sight—no one to tell Charissa that she was talking to him. "Okay," she said, "what is it?"

He shoved his hands into the pockets of his black jeans, pulled them out, then shoved them in again. Was he actually *nervous* about something?

He cleared his throat. "Well, next Friday is the big swim test, and I'm hoping that, once it's over, we'll both have something to celebrate. So . . . I was wondering if you might . . ."

Suddenly, Gladys knew that she didn't want to hear the end of this question. "Oh my goodness, a seagull!" she cried.

Hamilton looked bewildered. "A . . . what?"

Gladys pointed at the garbage bin outside the camp kitchen. "There's a seagull! In the Dumpster!"

"There are always seagulls in that Dumpster," Hamilton said. "Haven't you seen them before?"

"*What?*" Gladys cried in mock outrage. "We have an infestation of seagulls? Mrs. Spinelli isn't going to like that. Sorry, Hamilton, but I've got to run and tell her right away!"

Without another word, she tore across the field and burst into the kitchen; in fact, she didn't stop running until she was alone in the pantry with the door shut tightly behind her.

Gladys sank down onto the floor beside a giant box of quinoa. Could Marti have been right? Had Hamilton actually been about to ask her out on a *date*?

"Aghhhhhhh!" She buried her head in her hands. Thanks to Sandy, she'd finally gotten used to the idea of having boys as friends—but going out with a boy was a whole other idea. Really, she'd had no choice but to run away. What would she have answered when he finished asking his question?

If she said yes, Charissa and her cronies would never let her hear the end of it. And anyway, if she went on a date with Hamilton, what would they talk about? More about his book, and his book signings, and his fabulous life as a celebrity kid author?

No thanks.

But somehow, no didn't seem like the right answer, either.

The pantry door squeaked open, and Gladys scrambled back—but it was only Mrs. Spinelli. "I thought I heard moaning and groaning in here. You sick, girlie?"

Gladys shook her head, and Mrs. Spinelli clicked her tongue. "Must be boy trouble, then. Ah, yes, I know all about that." She was nodding to herself now, her loose gray bun bouncing against the back of her neck. "Let me guess—the one who hangs around on the patio and stares at you from the lunch line?"

Gladys's mouth fell open. Had *everybody* figured out that Hamilton had a crush on her before she had?

Mrs. Spinelli held out a hand and pulled Gladys to her feet. "Come on. I know just the thing to help you out today."

"You do?"

Mrs. Spinelli raised an eyebrow. "Don't look so surprised," she said. "Even I was nine years old once."

"I'm twelve," Gladys told her.

"Sure you are, girlie." Mrs. Spinelli led Gladys out of the pantry and pointed to the far counter, which was covered with baseball-size onions. "As a special favor, I'm going to let you slice all those up. That way, when everyone notices that your eyes are red and puffy, you can say truthfully that it was the onions that made you cry, rather than that boy."

"I wasn't crying," Gladys pointed out, but the cook didn't seem to hear her.

"No need to thank me," she said breezily. "I'll just be over in my chair with my magazine; you let me know when you're done."

# Chapter 25

# PURGATORY PANTRY

GLADYS SPENT A LOT OF ENERGY ON Thursday and Friday carefully avoiding Hamilton, but it wasn't until she was sitting on Orchard Beach in the Bronx that Saturday that she felt truly at ease. There was no way he would find her here. Even her own parents had a hard time finding the beach, taking several wrong turns off the parkway before stumbling upon it.

Orchard Beach was more crowded than the others they had visited, but that didn't stop Gladys's mom from chasing her into the water. "We'll work on your backstroke today," she said. "Pretend you're a . . . um . . . well, there must be something you cook face-side up, right?"

It wasn't her mother's best cooking-meets-swimming metaphor.

The Completos Locos stand was more

pleasant than the beach. Its hot dogs looked fresh and appetizing, nestled into toasted buns and topped with bright green avocado chunks, ripe red tomatoes, and artistically swirled mayonnaise. They were served up by a tattooed man who spoke Spanish at about a million miles an hour with most of his customers.

The dogs were even tastier than they looked, though once again, Gladys wished that she'd paid closer attention while sampling the other vendors' products. She would just have to decide which hot dog deserved the top spot when she started writing her review.

Gladys and her parents washed their dogs down with a traditional Chilean drink called mote con huesillo, which was kind of like iced tea, except that each cup also had half a peach and a bunch of barley floating in it. Gladys's parents weren't fans, and even Gladys had to admit that it wasn't her favorite, but she had read about it in her background research on Chilean food and appreciated the chance to try it. She was already thinking about including a section in her review on pairing your hot dog with the perfect drink when thunder sounded in the distance.

"I think we're done here," her dad said, and Gladys didn't object.

Gladys hunkered down with her journal on Sunday and the hours slipped by, but the words didn't flow as easily as usual. She had no shortage of material to work with—she'd eaten hot dogs in all five boroughs, after all—but what exactly should she say about them? When she thought about Nathan's, for instance, the memories she'd heard from Mr. Eng and her mom filled her mind rather than the tastes of the hot dogs and fries she'd had there. And when she tried to picture the Thai dogs, all she saw was her parents shrieking and frolicking in the sand.

It was like the hot dogs themselves wanted to fade into the background of whatever scene they'd been eaten in.

By dinnertime, Gladys had only managed to write a handful of sentences, half of which were crossed out. Thank goodness she had a whole week left to work on the review! She trudged downstairs when her mother called, grabbed a Sticky Burger from the take-out sack on the counter, and settled between her parents on the sofa for the latest episode of *Purgatory Pantry*.

The camera zoomed in on Chef Rory Graham, clad in chef's whites from head to toe except for her long, green-polished fingernails, which drummed on a countertop as the contestants filed into the kitchen. Every week, someone got eliminated, and now there were only four contestants left.

"Chefs!" Rory barked. "A particularly hellish challenge awaits you this week! A brand-new restaurant will be opening its doors in Times Square *this Friday*, but its menu is one item short. Each of you will attempt to fill this hole with your own original creation."

Four chef hats bobbed up and down as the contestants attempted to out-nod one another.

"The restaurant's owner will help me judge your entries," Rory continued. "The highest-scoring creation will be featured on his menu on opening day, and its chef will receive a five thousand dollar bonus. But the chefs who create the lowest-scoring items will find themselves"—the camera zoomed in on Rory's bloodred-lipsticked mouth as she pronounced the show's famous catchphrase—"*in purgatory!*"

Gladys's parents gasped, as if Rory didn't say this every single week.

"Come on, get to the cooking," Gladys muttered. All this preliminary hoopla always drove her crazy. She wanted to see what BeBe Watkins would come up with this time. BeBe had the fastest chopping technique Gladys had ever seen, and no challenge had flapped her yet. On last week's episode, she'd defeated Clay Martolucci—Gladys's least favorite contestant—in an onion dice-off for immunity.

But Rory droned on. "And here comes our guest judge for this week: Chef Christoph von Schnitz!"

Gladys excused herself to refill her water glass. The celebrity chef bios were always so boring.

She was about to turn the kitchen faucet on when the announcer's voice said, "But can the Sausage King of Dusseldorf succeed in his latest venture—an upscale hot dog restaurant in the middle of Times Square?"

Gladys's cup clattered into the sink as she raced back to the den.

Sure enough, there was Times Square on the screen, its theater marquees and Jumbotrons blinking and blazing. The camera showed workers heaving a huge sign into place. VON SCHNITZ'S HEAVENLY HOT DOGS, it said, and then, in slightly smaller letters: THE BEST WÜRST IN NEW YORK!

Gladys gripped the back of the sofa as the camera cut back to the *Purgatory Pantry* kitchen, where Chef Rory welcomed Chef von Schnitz with a kiss on each cheek.

"Christoph!" she cried, batting her purple-tinged eyelashes. "You're opening a restaurant in New York at last!"

"Yes, yes," von Schnitz commented airily. "This has been in the works for a while, but it's all very top secret, you know? My menu already has five fabulous gourmet varieties of hot dog, but I am looking to add just one more." He turned to the show's contestants. "This is where you come in!"

"That's right," Rory said. "Christoph von Schnitz's highly anticipated hot dog emporium opens to the public *this Friday*. Will your creation be on its heavenly menu? Or will you find yourself"—the camera zoomed in again—"*in purgatory?*"

Gladys's parents gasped again—but this time Gladys gasped with them. A huge new hot dog restaurant, run by a German sausage expert, was opening in the heart of Manhattan this Friday? Her review was due the following Monday, and obviously wouldn't be complete without a sampling from Heavenly Hot Dogs.

The show cut to a commercial, and Gladys cleared her throat. "Wow," she said, circling back around the sofa. "That new hot dog place looks pretty great, huh?"

"Sure does, Gladdy," her dad said. "We'll have to try it at some point."

"Well, how about next weekend?" Gladys asked.

Gladys's mom shook her head. "A place like that, on opening weekend? It'll be mobbed! No, honey, let's wait a few weeks, at least."

"And anyway," her dad said, "we're going to Pennsylvania on Saturday for an overnight, to visit Grandma, remember?"

*Fudge!* Gladys had forgotten about that trip. "Right," she said. "Well, maybe we could stop through the city quickly on the way there?"

Gladys's dad chuckled. "Only if they're open at eight a.m. We'll need to get going early, to beat the traffic."

Gladys nodded mechanically, but inside, her brain felt like it had been set ablaze with a crème brûlée torch. How could this be happening? After all her expeditions to try hot dogs in the far corners of the city, she was going to have to skip the one right smack in the middle of Times Square?

The show came back on, and Gladys sank into the sofa's cushions as Rory and Christoph explained the rules of the hot dog challenge. But she couldn't enjoy watching the contestants cook, even when BeBe hacked at pickles and hot peppers like a crazy slicing machine. There was a countdown clock in the screen's corner, and Gladys felt like a timer had been set for her, too. Every second that passed was a second closer to when her review was due—a review that would be incomplete without a visit to Heavenly Hot Dogs. But how was she going to get there?

Chapter 26

# OPERATION TOP DOG, TAKE TWO

"HEY, CHARISSA," GLADYS SAID AS THEY walked through the archway at camp the next morning. "Remember when your parents rented that limo and we all went into the city together?"

Charissa's face scrunched into its you're-talking-like-a-crazy-person look. "Of course I remember. It was my *birthday*."

"Right," Gladys said quickly. "Well, it was so much fun! Do you think they might want to do something like that again soon? Like, maybe on Friday?"

"I *wish*," Charissa said. "But Daddy said that was a one-time thing. He commutes into the city for work on the days he's not here, and he hates going in when he doesn't have to."

*Fudge,* Gladys thought. There went that idea.

The morning announcements began, and after everyone finished singing the camp song with a rousing "Yay, camp!" Mrs. Bentley retook the microphone. "Now remember," she said, "interim swim tests will take place this Friday—and any camper who doesn't pass the Basic Beginners test will be required to take extra lessons for the remainder of the camp session. There will be no makeup tests or do-overs!"

"I hope you don't have to take extra lessons," Charissa said as they stood up. "Though if my plans go right, you won't have to worry about that jerkface either way after Friday." She looked pointedly at Hamilton, who was standing at the edge of the crowd—alone, as usual.

"What plans?" Gladys asked.

Charissa lowered her voice. "Let's just say that Rolanda might find herself having heatstroke on Friday during a *certain somebody's* swim test. She'll definitely need Coach Mike to help her, so there won't be anybody on hand to save Mr. Bigshot Author when he starts to slip under the water." Charissa made a glugging sound and wiggled her hands over her head in a cruel impression of Hamilton sinking.

Gladys felt like someone had just slipped an ice cube into her bloodstream. "Charissa," she said. "You can't let Hamilton *drown!*"

Charissa lowered her hands, laughing. "Of course not! That would cause all kinds of legal hassles for my parents. Ro will just leave him in the pool long enough to give him a good scare. He'll get so traumatized that even his parents won't be able to force him to come back to camp!"

Gladys could hardly believe what she was hearing. "Look," she started, but just then, Charissa checked her watch.

"Ooh, I've got to run to the office," she said. "Catch ya later, Gladys!" And with a whip of her ponytail, she was gone.

All day, Gladys tried to corner Hamilton to warn him about Charissa's plan, but she never got the chance. He swam on the opposite side of the pool, quickly took off across the field after their lesson, and barely mumbled "thank you" when she served him his ham sandwich at lunchtime—with bonus arugula from her own ingredient stores.

Was *he* avoiding *her* now? He must have been as embarrassed by the almost-date-asking conversation as she was. *Well, okay,* Gladys thought to herself. *Maybe if Charissa sees that he's leaving me alone, she'll call off her terrible plan.*

That afternoon, Gladys finally found what she'd been looking for all month in the mailbox: an envelope addressed to her from the *New York Standard* containing the payment for her second published review.

*At least I got to it before my parents did,* she thought, and sank down onto her front stoop. As she shredded the check into papery strips, her brain focused on the new review that was due in a week. Her parents weren't going to take her into the city this weekend, and neither was Charissa. Who could help her now?

Gladys tried to imagine what Sandy would say to her in this situation. He'd probably start with "Come on, Gatsby." Or "Get it together, Gatsby." Or—

"Jeez, Gatsby, you look awful."

Gladys looked up. Right in front of her stood a glowing apparition of Sandy, grinning from ear to ear.

Great—now she was seeing things. The stress had gotten to her, and she'd finally cracked.

Except that her angelic vision of Sandy then took a step to the side and lost his halo. Gladys blinked as the sun flashed into her eyes, and she turned to find plain old Sandy kicking at her front stoop with his sneaker. "What, I don't even get a 'welcome home'?"

Gladys leapt to her feet and—without pausing for even a moment to consider whether she should or shouldn't—flung her arms around him.

"Whoa, Gatsby, careful!" Sandy laughed. "You don't want to break this—I went through a lot of trouble to get it back for you."

When Gladys finally released him, she saw he was holding her tablet.

"How did you get that back?" she said. "And what are you doing home?"

"Well, those are actually both parts of the same story," Sandy said. He ran a hand through his messy blond hair. "It may also involve me getting caught breaking into Director Samuels's office, and, uh . . . possibly being thrown out of karate camp."

"No!" Gladys cried.

"Yeah." Sandy glanced back toward his own house and lowered his voice. "My mom is not thrilled with me right now. But I don't care. I'm happy to be back!"

Gladys laughed—she couldn't help it. Sandy was home! Her heart felt as light as a meringue.

"Okay, now you're pretty much caught up on my news," Sandy said. "So what's going on with you? Have you made it to all those hot dog places yet?"

"Yes . . . and no." Gladys told him about her last-minute discovery of Heavenly Hot Dogs. "I don't know how I can possibly get there on Friday," she said. "Unless . . ." An idea was coming to her, and she paused to let it ripen. "Unless you can convince your mom to take us! Do you think she would?" It seemed like the perfect plan—Mrs. Anderson liked foreign foods, and they'd already chatted about interesting hot dogs.

But Sandy didn't share her enthusiasm. "There's no way," he said glumly. "She's really mad at me.

Technically, I'm grounded—no phone, no Internet. I'm probably not even supposed to be talking to you, but Mom's at yoga, so I figured I could risk it. I'm sure she'd never agree to anything as fun as a trip to the city." He shook his head. "Sorry, Gatsby."

"Don't be sorry," Gladys insisted. "It's my fault you got in trouble! You wouldn't have broken those rules if I hadn't snuck you my tablet in the first place."

"Eh, I don't know," Sandy said. "Life without screens was *really* hard. I probably would've broken into the office eventually, just to get online for a few minutes."

Gladys was skeptical, but she didn't push the issue.

"And anyway," Sandy continued, "at least we got away with some stuff. Director Samuels never sniffed out my brownies or cookies. Thanks for those, by the way. Wrapping them up in my underwear was a really good trick."

Gladys felt herself blush at the mention of underwear, and she shifted her gaze away from Sandy. "So, um, have you got any ideas for getting me into the city this week?"

"Just the same old plan we came up with at the beginning of the summer," Sandy said. "Sneak out of camp! I mean, wasn't that the whole reason you agreed to go in the first place? So you could *sneak out* when you needed to?"

"I . . ." Gladys started. "I just . . . don't think that sneaking out will be as easy as we thought."

"Sure it is," Sandy said. He reached down, plucked a twig off the lawn, and started rolling it back and forth in his hands. "You can just call into camp fake-sick. Then, when your mom drops you off, instead of going inside, you sneak off to the train station. That way, camp will think you're home, and your mom will think you're at camp."

"Yeah, but I have responsibilities there now," Gladys said. She reminded him that she made lunches every day, and added that Friday was her big swim test. "If I miss it, I'll have to take extra lessons, which means I won't have time to cook lunches anymore. Plus, there's Hamilton—"

"Who's Hamilton?" Sandy asked.

"Just . . . a kid," Gladys said. "But he's, um, not the best swimmer, and I kind of wanted to keep an eye on him on Friday. You know, to make sure he does okay on his test." For some reason, Gladys didn't feel like launching into the whole story of Hamilton's crush on her and Charissa's swearing her revenge. She'd already burdened Sandy with enough of her problems.

Sandy flung his twig out onto the lawn. "I don't get it, Gatsby," he said. "I thought that writing for the *Standard* was your dream. Are you really saying that taking a swim test at Charissa's stupid camp is more important than nailing this review?"

"I . . . no, of course not." When Sandy put it like that, the choice seemed obvious. "Of course you're right," she said, trying to make her voice sound as firm as possible. "I don't know what I was thinking."

"That's okay," Sandy said. "I guess things kind of fall apart when I'm not around to remind you of your posterities."

"My . . . *posterities*?" Gladys asked, momentarily baffled. "Oh—I think you mean my priorities."

"Right, those," Sandy said, and Gladys laughed. She hadn't realized how much she'd missed hearing Sandy's regular abuse of the English language.

"So, we're agreed?" he asked. "You'll sneak out of camp Friday and go to Heavenly Hot Dogs?"

"Yeah," Gladys replied. "I mean, that's definitely the right thing to do."

She just wished she believed it herself.

Over the next two days at camp, Hamilton continued to avoid Gladys, and Gladys did her best to point this out to Charissa. "Wow," she said at the lunch table on Wednesday. "I've hardly seen Hamilton around at all this week. Which means he definitely hasn't been bothering me."

"Good," Charissa replied. "But we want to make sure the message *really* sinks in on Friday. Don't we, Ro?"

Across the table, Rolanda bared her teeth in a sharklike grin.

It was hopeless. Gladys didn't see how she could possibly avert disaster on Friday . . . unless she told

Charissa the truth. But would Charissa be willing to stay friends with a person who liked someone she hated?

Gladys steeled herself. Rolanda might be a good junior lifeguard, but Gladys didn't trust her to know the difference between letting someone "get scared" and letting them drown for real. And now that Gladys wasn't planning to be at camp on Friday, she knew that staying silent was just too dangerous. She had to confront the plan's mastermind head-on.

"Charissa," she said as they dropped their trays off at the kitchen window. "I need to talk to you in private. It's urgent."

"Sure," Charissa said. "You girls go on to the pool without me."

The scowling group of CITs slunk away, and Charissa guided Gladys down the wooded path where Gladys had entered camp on her first day. They stopped under the biggest oak tree. So far, so good— they were out of earshot of any other campers.

"Charissa," Gladys said, "Hamilton doesn't deserve to be scared out of camp. He hasn't been following me around or bothering me. He's actually a pretty nice person, once you get to know him."

The irony didn't escape Gladys that she had used almost the exact same words to describe Charissa to Hamilton a few weeks back. Hamilton had seemed to take her word for it—but how would Charissa react?

Gladys looked into her friend's gray eyes, anticipating a flash of fury. But instead, she saw the very last thing she would have expected: tears.

"Do you like him better than me?" Charissa asked, her voice barely louder than a whisper.

"What?" Gladys was truly taken aback by this reaction. "No, of course not! I mean, I barely know him, really. I just don't think he deserves to be punished."

Charissa blinked rapidly. "You swear?" she said. "Because it just wouldn't be fair if you liked him better. I mean, I know he's a celebrity, but I'm the one who picked you to come to my birthday party, and who got you into camp."

"Charissa," Gladys said, "I don't like people because they're famous, or because their parents own camps. I just like them if . . . you know, they're nice to me, and we have fun together."

"I don't think any of my other friends like me for those reasons," Charissa said, her voice growing smaller with every word. "I think they only like me because . . . well, they're afraid not to."

Gladys didn't know what to say—so she simply gave her friend a hug.

It took a moment for Charissa to hug her back, but when she did, she held on to Gladys for a long time. When they finally separated, Charissa pulled a tissue out of her shorts pocket and used it to dab at her eyes.

"So," Gladys said cautiously, "will you call off the

plan for Friday? And . . . maybe consider giving Hamilton another chance?"

Charissa, looking more like her normal self now, considered these questions. Finally, she said, "Look, Gladys—I just don't know. I mean, first impressions are very important to me. Once I make my mind up about somebody, it's made up forever."

"But that's not true!" The words were out of Gladys's mouth before she'd had time to think. "You changed your mind about me. A few months ago, I was just like Hamilton to you. But then we got to know each other . . . and now we're friends."

Finally, a hint of a smile crossed Charissa's face. "Yeah," she said, "now we're friends. Best friends."

*Well,* Gladys thought, *Sandy is kind of my best friend already*—but this didn't seem like the right time to bring up that technicality. So she just smiled back.

"Okay," Charissa said. "In the name of our best friendship, I'll tell Rolanda that she needs to save Hamilton on Friday if he starts to sink. *But,*" she added, before Gladys could even thank her, "let's not have any more secrets between us. If you've got a problem in the future, just . . . *tell* me about it. Isn't that what friends do?"

Gladys looked into Charissa's eyes again, and felt like something had changed between them. She was no longer afraid of Charissa dropping her, or of what kind of revenge she might exact if she thought Gladys had crossed her. They were beyond that now. Charissa had been honest about her fears and feelings . . . and, for the first time, Gladys realized that she wanted to be completely honest back.

"There's one more thing I should tell you," she said quietly. "See, I sort of have this top secret job working for the *New York Standard* . . ."

Miraculously, Charissa stayed quiet as Gladys explained the entire situation; then she let out an excited sort of squeal.

"Gladys!" she cried. "That is so, so awesome! Oh my goodness—and I helped you research your first two reviews, even if I didn't know it!"

"Yeah," Gladys said, "I couldn't have done either one without you."

"So, hey, is that why you asked if my parents would take us into the city this weekend? Because you have to do another review?"

"Sort of," Gladys admitted. "Though it would have been totally fun to hang out with you, too."

Charissa waved this pronouncement away with one hand. "You were totally using me," she said, "but, whatever—it's not like I haven't done that plenty of times."

*Hmm,* Gladys thought. Maybe she and Charissa were even more alike than she'd realized.

"Anyway," Charissa said, "we need to make a plan to get you into the city on Friday."

"Oh," Gladys said. "Actually, I've already got one. I just . . . well, I was going to call in sick to camp." An hour ago, she would have been terrified to say that. But now, Gladys wasn't worried. Charissa would understand . . . wouldn't she?

"Yeah, sounds like that's the only way," she said. "Luckily, you've got a friend in the front office." She winked. "I'll just make sure that you get marked as present when I file the attendance sheets."

"Wow," Gladys said. "Thanks, Charissa!"

Charissa nodded, brisk and businesslike now. "I'm not going to be able to do anything about your swim test results, though," she said. "Those come straight from Coach Mike, and he'll know if you aren't there."

Gladys sighed. There was no getting around it—she was going to be stuck in remedial lessons for the rest of the summer. She'd have to give up her CIT duties. But if that meant finishing her hot dog review, it was a trade she had to be willing to make.

"How can I ever pay you back?" she asked Charissa.

Her friend smiled. "Let me tag along on your next reviewing assignment?" she said.

"Absolutely," said Gladys, though she added *if I ever get another one* in her head. Suddenly, nailing her hot dog story, proving Gilbert Gadfly wrong, and getting assigned another review seemed more important than ever.

# Chapter 27

## A STUDY OF TECHNIQUE

ON FRIDAY MORNING, GLADYS CAREFULLY stuffed her lobster backpack with all her regular camp gear, just in case her mom peeked inside.

"Hey, Mom," she said when she reached the kitchen. "Do you think you might be able to drop me off at camp early this morning? Today's my big swim test, and I thought I might squeeze in some extra practice."

"Swim test?" her mom said. "Oh, honey, why didn't you tell me? I could have planned to come with you, but now I have an early appointment."

"That's okay," Gladys said quickly. "It's really not a big deal."

Gladys's mom wrapped her muffin in a napkin. "Well, with the improvements you've made lately, you're sure to pass,"

she said. "But if you want to squeeze in one last practice, I understand. Let's go!"

When they pulled up in front of the Camp Bentley
arch ten minutes later, the place looked deserted. "Oh,
goodness—are you sure it's all right for me to leave
you here?" Gladys's mom asked. "I don't see anyone
else around."

"Don't worry, Mom," Gladys said. "Charissa said
she'd meet me at the pool, and she's a junior lifeguard.
I won't go in unless she's there."

"Okay," her mom breathed. "Well, have a good day.
And good luck on that test, even though I know you
won't need it! I'm so proud of you." She reached across
the seat and squeezed Gladys into a one-armed hug.

"Thanks, Mom," Gladys murmured. She was feeling
guiltier by the minute. She really would have had a
good shot at passing—if she were actually planning to
take the test.

As her mom's car zoomed away, Gladys glanced
around again. There was no one under the arch or
in the parking lot—no one to see her sneaking away.
Hitching her lobster backpack higher up on her back,
she started toward the train station.

"Gladys!"

*Fudge.*

Hamilton stepped out from under a tree. "I thought
that was you," he said.

"Why are you *always* doing that?!" Gladys cried.

"Doing what?"

Gladys tried to control her breathing. "Hiding. In. The. Shadows!" she gasped. "And sneaking up on me!"

Behind his black-rimmed glasses, Hamilton blinked. "Am I? I don't mean to be. I suppose it's just my authorial nature, always prompting me to stand back and observe."

Gladys groaned. She couldn't very well stroll out of the parking lot now that he'd seen her. "Well, your authorial observational skills have probably cost me my job," she snapped, "so thanks a lot."

"Your job?" Hamilton asked. "You mean your drudgery in the camp kitchen? How? That lunch lady you work for usually doesn't arrive until 8:47, and"—Hamilton glanced at his watch—"it's only 8:22."

"Do you always lurk under a tree and time everyone's arrivals?" Gladys asked bitterly.

Hamilton looked down at the pavement. "I have to pass the time somehow," he said. "I write a little, too, but it usually gets too noisy once the campers start arriving."

The old tug-of-war started up inside Gladys again: be annoyed with Hamilton, or feel bad for him? In spite of herself, she could feel sympathy winning out. "Do your parents drop you off this early every morning?" she asked.

"Oh, earlier than this," he said. "I'm always here by 8. My parents are both authors, too, and they need to start their writing by 8:30. I've learned my discipline from them!" He smiled. "Anyway, what brings you to camp at 8:22?"

Gladys was about to lie and say that her mom had to get to work early, but then she paused. She knew Hamilton had no great love for the rules of Camp Bentley. Could she trust him to cover for her?

"Look, Hamilton," Gladys started, "if I told you that I was considering sneaking out of camp today . . . what would you think?"

"Ah," Hamilton said, "I know what this is all about."

"You do?" Gladys panicked as she tried to remember if her reviewing journal might have ever accidentally fallen into Hamilton's hands. Telling Charissa her secret had been one thing, but she had no plans to let anybody else find out.

Hamilton nodded. "Of course I do. You're worried about the swim test, like me."

"What? No, I'm not," Gladys huffed, but Hamilton kept talking right over her.

"You shouldn't be nervous," he said. "I've been observing you carefully in the pool, though I have to admit that it's been for selfish reasons. Those swimming tips you gave me really helped, so I thought you might have more to teach me and have been studying your techniques. I even thought for a while that observing your posture out of the pool might teach me something about poise and balance, but I eventually gave up on that theory."

"You've been watching me . . . to learn my swimming techniques?" Gladys couldn't believe it. "Why didn't you just ask me for more help?"

"Well," Hamilton said, his cheeks reddening slightly, "I did try to ask once, but then you spotted a seagull and took off. You seemed stressed out with everything else on your plate, so I decided not to bother you about it again."

Gladys was dumbfounded. So he hadn't been trying to ask her out on a date at all!

"Anyway," Hamilton continued, "I hope you won't ditch camp today, of all days. I was planning to observe you in the pool one more time before taking my test."

"Look," Gladys said, "I don't really want to skip the test, either, but . . ." On instinct, she decided to trust him. "There's somewhere I really need to go in New York City, and today's the only day that I can get there."

"Oh!" said Hamilton. "How interesting. I'll actually be in New York City tonight, for the Kids Rock Awards."

Gladys stared at him. "The what?"

"For the Kids Rock Awards," he repeated. "It's an awards ceremony for kids who have made great accomplishments in areas of the arts usually reserved for adults. I'm nominated for Best Kid Author. Haven't you noticed the sticker on my book's cover?" Hamilton reached into his backpack and pulled out a copy of *Zombietown, U.S.A.* to show her. "So, the awards ceremony is tonight in the city, and I'm heading there right after camp. My agent says I'm basically guaranteed to win!"

Gladys wasn't sure what to say about any of this. "Um, congratulations?"

"Thank you," he said. "The support of my muse means a lot to me."

Gladys glanced at her watch: 8:27. The next train into Manhattan left at 8:45, and the station was three blocks away. She had to get moving if she wanted to make it.

"Say, Gladys," said Hamilton, "this is last minute, but . . . would you want to come with me to the ceremony tonight?"

"What?"

Hamilton sighed. "I'm afraid that all that drudgery has affected your hearing somehow." He took a step closer, so that there was barely an inch of space between them, and ducked down to bring his face right to her level. "I SAID," he bellowed in her ear, "WOULD YOU LIKE TO COME WITH ME TONIGHT TO WATCH ME GET MY AWARD?"

"Jeez!" Gladys cried, taking a step back. "I heard you the first time! I was just . . . surprised, that's all." She glanced around. There still weren't any cars nearby; despite his booming voice, no one else could have heard him shout-ask her to come to the ceremony.

"Yes, well, that's understandable," Hamilton said. "It's not every day that you get asked to a fancy event at one of Manhattan's most famous theaters."

Gladys took a second to absorb this new piece of information. Manhattan's Theater District was right near Times Square—and therefore right near Heavenly Hot Dogs! This seemed almost too good to be true.

"My parents are sending a car to pick me up at 4:30," Hamilton continued.

"Are they coming, too?" Gladys asked.

Hamilton shook his head. "My dad was going to—but then he told me yesterday that he, um, was too busy with his deadline. My mom, too. That's why I have an extra ticket. So . . ." He looked at her hopefully. "Would you like it?"

Gladys considered her options. On one hand, spending an entire evening with Hamilton while he got another ego-stroking award sounded unpleasant. But on the other hand, this way she could take her swim test and still get into the city. Maybe she could even get Hamilton to come with her to Heavenly Hot Dogs and order a couple of things off the menu so she wouldn't look suspicious getting six hot dogs just for herself.

"Sure," she said finally. "I would love to come."

Chapter 28

# LIKE A KNIFE THROUGH BUTTER

JUST BEFORE THE MORNING ANNOUNCE-
ments started, Gladys caught sight of
Charissa in the crowd and waved her
over.

"What are you doing here?" Charissa
hissed.

"Change of plans," Gladys said quietly.
"Believe it or not, Hamilton is going to get
me into the city tonight. He's nominated
for something called a Kids Rock Award."

Charissa gripped Gladys's arm, her
purple-polished nails digging in hard.
"The Kids Rock Awards??" she squealed.
"Omigosh, are you *going*? I'll have to look
for you on TV!"

*Wait. What?*

"TV?" Gladys asked.

"Of course!" Charissa said. "On Channel

12—they've been advertising all week! Haven't you noticed?"

For the first time ever, Gladys kicked herself for spending her free time reading cookbooks instead of watching TV. "I guess not," she said. "So is this awards thing a big deal?"

"Um, *yes*," Charissa said. "There are going to be *so many* celebrities there—Jeffy Marx, Sasha McRay. I'm so jealous. What are you going to wear?"

"Uh . . ." Gladys looked down at her purple camp T-shirt and shorts. Somehow, she didn't think they were going to cut it. "I'm not sure."

"Don't worry," Charissa said. "You can borrow a dress from me. Daddy's at camp today—I'll just send him home at lunchtime to pick it up. You'll look amazing. This is so cool!"

But Gladys was feeling anything but cool; in fact, nervous sweat was now streaming down her back. The number one rule of restaurant reviewing was to stay anonymous and avoid making a spectacle of yourself—but she had just signed up to attend a televised awards ceremony. What had she gotten herself into?

She hardly had time to think about it, though—because, before anything else, she had to take her swim test.

"No beating around the bush!" Coach Mike bellowed when the Basic Beginners reached the pool. "Your tests will begin right away! First up: Astin, Chu, Corning, and Gatsby—we'll be using lanes one through four! Remember, you need to swim a full length of the pool cleanly to pass!"

Gladys shuffled toward the edge of the pool, blood pounding in her ears. *You've got this,* she told herself. *You're ready.* She was actually looking forward to the whistle, if only because no one would be able to see her knees shaking underwater.

Finally, a sharp blast sounded, and she crouched and sprang. As her body soared, she caught a glimpse out of the corner of her eye of a tall boy in a black swimsuit, giving her a thumbs-up. "Go, Gla—" he called, but the rest of his words were swallowed up by a rush of water in her ears.

For an agonizing second, the pool water felt like honey, or molasses, or some other thick liquid meant for baking, not swimming in. Gladys's arms and legs, feeling simultaneously heavy and weak, beat against it, like the whisks of an electric mixer stuck in too-goopy batter. But then her mother's words came to her: "Swim like your limbs are knives, cutting through soft butter."

Her arms and legs sliced through the water, and she broke the surface.

Just a few short knife-strokes later, Gladys's hand touched the far wall of the pool. She'd done it! She'd used the crawl stroke and swum an entire lap!

But she wasn't ready to stop. Shoving off from that

wall, she dove under the water again, undulating her body like a flexible spatula. When she broke the surface again, she started a breaststroke, pretending that she was pulling apart bread dough and kneading it back together with each circle of her arms. Then, when she hit the wall where she'd started, she flipped over onto her back for a lap of backstroke, churning through the water with her arms like it was cream she was turning into butter.

When she hit the far wall again, she flipped over and pulled herself up out of the pool. Kyra Astin, Mason Chu, and Deric Corning were all gawking at her, and Rolanda had her hands on her hips like she couldn't believe what she'd just seen.

But Coach Mike was beaming. "Gatsby, pass!" he cried. "I've never seen so much improvement in such a short time."

Gladys grinned back. She'd passed! No thanks to Coach Mike, of course—but she kept that thought to herself.

"All right!" he shouted. "Group two will be Herbertson, Jacoby, Jenkins, and Malone! Go on my whistle!"

Gladys looked back across the pool as Hamilton stepped up to the edge, his focus on the water. On her side of the pool, the little kids from the first group cheered for their friends.

"Come on, Hamilton!" Gladys heard herself yell. "Just pretend that zombies are chasing you!"

Hamilton glanced up and shot Gladys a big smile. Then the whistle sounded, and the second group jumped into the water.

Given that his body was practically twice as long as the other kids' in the pool, it was a little embarrassing that Hamilton finished dead last in his heat. But he did finish—and his form was impeccable. Gone were the thrashing, flailing strokes Gladys had seen on the first day of camp, now replaced by long, smooth movements and even breaths. Had Hamilton really learned how to do all that just from watching her?

"Herbertson, pass!" Coach Mike cried as Hamilton pulled himself out of the water, and Hamilton's face froze in shock.

"Really?" he squeaked. "I really passed?"

"You really did," the coach said, and Hamilton pumped a fist into the air. Then he turned toward the kids assembled on that side of the pool, took a huge breath in, puffed his chest out . . .

"Aw, cripes," Mason Chu muttered. "He's gonna make a speech."

But just as Hamilton cleared his throat, Coach Mike's voice boomed: "Third group, on your marks!" His whistle blasted.

Gladys sidled up to Hamilton. "Just save your speech for tonight," she whispered.

"Ah, good idea," Hamilton said, turning toward her. "Thank goodness I have my muse looking out for me."

Gladys was suddenly aware of how close they were standing; his ribs poked out through his pale skin like the pleats of a very tall accordion. She took a step back. "Well, um, great job out there."

"I was inspired by the best," he said.

The rest of the day passed in a blur. For lunch, Gladys chopped and roasted peppers to make a paste she spread on focaccia and served with white-bean soup; then, after lunch, she called her mom from the kitchen's phone to tell her about the swim test and that evening's plans.

"Congratulations! I knew you'd pass," her mom said.

"Thanks, Mom," Gladys replied. "I couldn't have done it without your help."

"And the famous author Hamilton Herbertson asked you on a date, too?"

"It's *not* a date, Mom," Gladys insisted. "It's just sort of a . . . thank-you outing, I think, since I helped him with his swimming."

"Well, have a great time," her mom said. "We'll look for you on camera!"

Gladys hung up, then quickly dialed Sandy's number. So far that week, Mrs. Anderson had been true to her word, and hadn't let Sandy near the phone or the Internet. She hadn't nailed his bedroom window shut, though, so he and Gladys were still able to talk face-to-face if they were careful. Just last night, they had firmed up her plans for sneaking into the city on the train, but she wanted to let him know that those plans had changed.

Unfortunately, it was Sandy's mom who picked up the phone. "Hi, Mrs. Anderson," Gladys said. "Any chance I could talk to Sandy? Please?"

Mrs. Anderson sighed at the other end of the line. "Not yet, Gladys. Sandy still has some thinking to do about the choices he made at camp."

"Okay, well, could you give him a message for me? It's important."

There was a pause as Mrs. Anderson contemplated this. "All right," she said finally. "Go ahead."

Gladys opened her mouth—but then realized that she actually had no idea what to say. How could she pass the information along to Sandy without his mom getting wind of what they'd been planning?

Only the truth was going to work.

"Could you tell him that I'm going to be on TV tonight?" she said. "I got invited to the Kids Rock Awards by a friend from camp. So I'll be heading into the city for the ceremony—and for dinner."

"Well, isn't that exciting!" Mrs. Anderson said. "I'll make sure to look for you, though I'm afraid Sandy isn't allowed to watch TV right now, either."

"Oh, right," Gladys said. "But . . . could you still tell him for me?" She wanted to make sure Sandy understood that, even though her plans had changed, she was definitely still going to eat at Heavenly Hot Dogs that night.

Mrs. Anderson agreed to tell him, and they said good-bye.

At the end of the camp day, Charissa met Gladys in the changing room by the kitchen. She was carrying a dress bag in one hand and a large purple plastic case in the other. "C'mon," she said. "Let's get you TV-ready! Put this on."

Gladys slipped into a stall, shimmied out of her camp uniform, and unzipped the dress bag. There, staring back at her, was the blazingly red flamenco dress Charissa had worn to Gladys's birthday party.

"Isn't it great?" Charissa called from the other side of the stall door. "I told Daddy to bring that one especially. *Everyone* was staring at me when I wore it to your party, remember?"

"Um, yeah," Gladys answered. *Because it was the brightest thing in the room!*

"Okay, hurry up and put it on—I want to see it on you!"

Gladys didn't have much of a choice. She released the froufy dress from its bag and pulled it over her head. It was kind of long—Charissa had a couple of inches on Gladys—and when she emerged from the stall and caught sight of herself in the mirror, she winced. The dress practically glowed.

"You look amazing!" Charissa screeched. "Now we just have to do your hair and makeup."

"What?"

But Charissa was already opening her purple case on the counter. Inside were more shades of sparkly lip gloss and eye shadow than Gladys had ever seen.

She considered bolting, but she wasn't much of a sprinter—Charissa would surely catch her. It was better to just submit now; Gladys could always undo the damage in the car.

Or so she thought. Fifteen minutes later, her lips were stained red with all-day lipstick ("Won't fade for eighteen hours!" Charissa exclaimed), and her hair was sculpted into a sort of cinnamon roll–esque swirl with extra-strong, super-hold hairspray. When Gladys pressed a finger to it, it felt crispier than a fried noodle from Palace of Wong.

"Don't touch!" Charissa commanded. "You'll ruin it. I wish you had enough hair for a high ponytail, but this'll have to do." She took a deep breath of the now-hairspray-scented air. "Okay, Gladys—you're ready. Go meet some celebrities and eat some awesome hot dogs! Wave to me on TV!"

Gladys nodded, noticing that her sprayed hair didn't move at all as her head did. "Thanks, Charissa," she managed to say. Even if this new look wasn't really her style, she did appreciate her friend's effort.

Luckily, Charissa's dad had brought her flats instead of high heels, so at least Gladys could walk without tripping. Grateful that the camp had already cleared out for the day, Gladys slowly made her way to the parking lot.

Hamilton was waiting for her beside a sleek black car—but for once, he wasn't clad in all black himself. Instead, he wore a white collared shirt, a brown bow tie, a gray sweater-vest, and a hideous tweed jacket with leather elbow patches.

"Wow," Hamilton said as she approached. "You look . . . different. I mean, nice! Very nice."

"Uh, thanks," Gladys said. "You too."

Hamilton stood up straighter. "I'm so glad you think so," he said. "This is my 'author formal' outfit. I can't just wear my everyday writing clothes to special events like this."

"Sure," Gladys said.

"Well, shall we?" Hamilton gestured toward the car door being held open by a uniformed driver. They climbed into the dark, air-conditioned interior, and a minute later were heading toward the expressway.

Even sitting down, Charissa's dress poufed out well past Gladys's knees, and she felt like she was being swallowed by crinoline. "So," she said, desperate to talk about something that had nothing to do with her appearance, "who else is nominated for Best Kid Author?"

"There are two other nominees," Hamilton said. "A twelve-year-old named Caroline Giotta wrote a memoir about her life growing up in a Mafia family—but her prose really isn't up to the same standard as mine. And the other author, Max Finkelstein, is just four years old, so clearly he's out of the running."

"He's four?" Gladys asked. Her own publications were feeling less significant by the second. "What did he write?"

Hamilton snorted. "He wrote and illustrated a picture book called *I Like Rainbows*. Even the title is horrible, don't you think? But somehow he got himself nominated—or his parents did. Rumor has it that they're the driving force behind his whole career."

Gladys wasn't sure what to say about that.

"In any case," Hamilton continued, "the actual awards ceremony doesn't start until seven, but there are some preliminary events I need to attend. A photo shoot and some schmoozing with the organizers. Do you think you'll be able to keep yourself busy?"

"Oh, absolutely," Gladys said. Actually, this was the best news she'd heard all day. She could walk over to Heavenly Hot Dogs and sample a couple of dogs before the show even started! Then, she and Hamilton could go back together after and order more.

The rest of the ride passed mostly in silence, though

Gladys noticed that the closer they got to the Midtown Tunnel into Manhattan, the faster Hamilton's right foot tapped against the back of the driver's seat. Was he getting nervous? She was about to try to comfort him when she realized that their car had just shot past the exit for 42nd Street.

"Hey," she said. "Didn't we need to get off there?"

"Where?" Hamilton asked.

"Forty-Second Street. You said that the awards ceremony was at a theater, right? Aren't all the big Broadway theaters around Times Square?"

"Oh, the Kids Rock Awards aren't held at a Broadway theater. They're at the Apollo," Hamilton said.

"The Apollo?!" Gladys cried. "Where's that?"

"In Harlem, I think." Hamilton leaned forward. "Hey, Marcus, where's the Apollo?"

"West 125th Street," the driver answered.

Hamilton sat back. "West 125th Street," he repeated helpfully.

But she'd heard the first time. They were going to be eighty-three blocks away from Heavenly Hot Dogs!

The car whipped past the 61st Street exit, then the 96th Street exit. Even with an hour and a half to spare before the show, there was no way Gladys could get down to Times Square and back. Now she just had to hope that Hamilton would really be in the mood to eat a celebratory hot dog (or four) after his big win.

Gladys slumped back in her seat, her huge skirt

billowing up around her. The car finally pulled off FDR Drive onto 125th Street, then jerked to a stop a few minutes later in front of an ornate white building. Under a huge red APOLLO sign, letters on a lightbulb-laden marquee spelled out "Tonight: The 3rd Annual Kids Rock Awards!" And under the marquee, spread out on the sidewalk, was . . .

"Come on," Hamilton said, reaching for Gladys's hand as he opened the car door. "Time for us to walk the red carpet."

# Chapter 29

# MORE ROTTEN THAN ROTTEN EGGS

GLADYS BARELY HAD TIME TO BLINK before the first camera flashes exploded in her face.

"You didn't tell me there would be a red carpet!" she hissed as Hamilton tugged her out of the car. She ducked her head down, wishing more than ever that Charissa had not shellacked her hair back from her face. She knew it was a long shot, but if a photographer somehow learned her name and paired it with her photograph, her future as a restaurant critic could be in jeopardy.

Gladys could still see flashes out of the corners of her eyes as they moved down the carpet, but she didn't dare lift her head. "Don't worry," Hamilton said in her ear. "The paparazzi are mostly here for the actors and pop stars. Though if we play our cards right, maybe we'll end up on some literary blogs tomorrow morning!"

Someone shouted, and a moment later, feet pounded all around them. Gladys took a peek and saw that the photographers on either side of the carpet were abandoning their posts and rushing to crowd around a limousine pulling up to the curb. "Sasha!" they cried. "Sasha, Sasha, over here!"

Hamilton nudged Gladys. "See what I mean?"

The limo door opened, and when a silver platform-heeled shoe emerged, the photographers went wild snapping pictures of it. A second shoe touched pavement, and finally Sasha McRay, twelve-year-old pop singer, emerged. A shiny silver minidress showed off her perfect caramel skin, which was accented by silver bangles up her arms and silver eye shadow that reached all the way to her eyebrows. As she stepped onto the red carpet, she shook her signature Afro—teased tonight into a mane worthy of a lion—and struck a few poses before teetering forward on her platforms toward the door.

Seeing how the photographers were following Sasha's every step, Gladys yanked Hamilton toward the theater entrance, too. If they could beat Sasha inside, she might avoid being in any more photos.

She was just pulling him through the open doors when a voice cried, "Ham! Ham, is that you?!"

It took Gladys a moment to realize that the person shouting those words was Sasha McRay.

"You know her?" Gladys asked Hamilton incredulously.

"Of course," Hamilton said. "We met at the Preteen Choice Awards."

Sasha was running toward them now—or trying to run, if only her shoes would let her.

"She's really smart," Hamilton said. "She writes all her own songs, you know."

Somehow, Gladys didn't think you had to be *that* smart to rhyme *maybe* with *baby*, but before she had a chance to say anything, Sasha hobbled across the threshold and threw herself into Hamilton's arms.

"It's so good to see you!" she cried.

Gladys glanced nervously out the door, but it seemed that the photographers were not allowed to follow them inside. Sasha grabbed Hamilton's hand and started to pull him across the lobby to a table covered with fancy shopping bags. "C'mon, let's get our swag," she said, "and then we can sit down. These shoes are already killing me!"

"Sasha," Hamilton said, "this is Gladys."

Sasha dropped Hamilton's hand and whirled around. "Oh!" she cried. "Gladys! It's so great to finally meet you!"

Then, before Gladys knew it, one of Sasha's bangle-encased arms was wrapped around her shoulders. "Ham has told me so much about you!"

"He has?"

"We e-mail sometimes," Hamilton explained.

Sasha punched Hamilton lightly on one tweedy arm. "That's an understatement," she said. "We're, like, online besties! Ham's been telling me all about camp. I wish I could go to camp, but I get followed *everywhere* now, so normal kid stuff like that is out." She said this not in a braggy way, but just sort of matter-of-factly. And based on what had just happened outside, Gladys could see she was telling the truth.

As they joined the line of people waiting for "swag"— whatever that was—Sasha continued to talk. "It's kind of ironic, though, because if *anyone* here should be a household name, it's Ham. I mean, have you read his book?"

"Um," Gladys said—but Sasha didn't wait for her answer.

"Well, *of course* you have—so you know it's brilliant. I mean, I spend a ton of time on my tour bus, so I'm always reading. And Ham's book is, like, my favorite book *ever.*"

Hamilton's cheeks turned slightly pink at this. "Sasha, you're embarrassing me," he said.

"Ham, I told you my summer reading list, and your book is better than all of them. Seriously!" she cried.

She turned back to Gladys. "So, which part is your favorite?"

"Oh," Gladys said. "Um, I don't know. I mean, all the parts are so . . . good."

Hamilton beamed at her. "You really think that? You've never told me before."

"Yeah, well . . ." Gladys blundered on, "I didn't want you to think I liked you just because of your book."

What was she saying?

They had reached the front of the line, and a man holding a scanner gun ran it over the bar code on Gladys's ticket. Then he handed her one of the fancy shopping bags and said, "Enjoy."

"Okay, let's see what they're giving us this year," Sasha said. She plunked herself down onto a nearby velvet couch and kicked off her platforms, then started pulling items out of her bag. "Look, there's something representing every nominee."

Gladys dug into her own bag. There was a DVD set of the first season of *Cory Missouri* starring Jeffy Marx, a CD of Sasha's own nominated album, a giant cellophane-wrapped oatmeal raisin cookie . . .

"A cookie?" Gladys couldn't help asking. "Who does that represent?"

"Oh, probably one of the nominees for Best Kid Chef," Hamilton said, taking a seat on the couch. "Have you heard of Notorious Gloria's Cookie Kitchen? Gloria is only nine."

"I guess not," Gladys said. She had never really thought about there being other kid chefs out there. *What do you have to do to get your cooking nominated for one of these awards?* she wondered.

A tall woman with a clipboard strode over to the couch. "Sasha! Hamilton!" she said. "Come with me, please—time to take photos."

Sasha groaned. "All right." She shoved her feet back into her shoes—but before she stood up, she turned toward Gladys again and laid a glittery-nailed hand on her arm. "It's been great meeting you, Gladys," she said seriously, then lowered her voice so it was barely above a whisper. "So many people just want to get close to people like me and Ham because we're celebrities, but he's super-lucky to have someone who likes him just for *him*." She pushed herself up to her feet then and gave Gladys a finger wave before following the woman around a corner.

"I'll meet you out here before the show, okay?" Hamilton asked. Gladys nodded, and then he was gone, too.

Alone at last, Gladys stared down at her poufy red skirt. She felt more rotten than an entire carton of rotten eggs after what Sasha had just said. And Hamilton had looked so excited when Gladys said that she'd read and liked his book. Of all the lies she'd told to get herself here today, that one felt the most awful.

She reached absently into her swag bag, thinking

that that cookie might make her feel better. But when she pulled her hand out, it was holding a copy of *Zombietown, U.S.A.*

Suddenly, Gladys knew exactly what she was going to do until the awards show started.

# Chapter 30

# ICING ON THE CAKE

OVER THE NEXT HOUR, GLADYS TORE through the pages of *Zombietown, U.S.A.* It turned out to be the story of Grady Masterson, a twelve-year-old boy who lived in the seemingly normal town of Appleton in upstate New York. But then one day both his parents became zombies and forgot their son existed.

Slowly, they turned all their friends into zombies. Then they turned all of *Grady's* friends into zombies. But even when Grady was standing right in front of them, they wouldn't give him the zombie bite.

Grady tried to fit in with the zombies. He changed his walk to a shuffle and, in one disgusting chapter, tried to develop a taste for brains. But nothing he did could get his zombie parents' attention.

Gladys didn't have time to read the whole thing, so when she noticed that kids were starting to return to the lobby from the photo shoot, she flipped quickly to the end. In the final pages, Grady realized he would never again fit in in his "zombietown" and set off for New York City in search of nonzombified people who would understand him.

Gladys closed the book slowly. She had never been so depressed by a story's ending, and was glad that Hamilton was working so hard on the sequel. Maybe, in the second book, Grady and his parents would finally figure out how to communicate with each other.

She was just dropping the book back into her swag bag when shouts sounded from outside the building.

"Randy!"

"Delilah, over here!"

"Darren, which award are you presenting?!"

The adult celebrities were arriving.

Gladys recognized a few of the people who were now sweeping into the theater lobby. There was Randy Ritter, the sequined fringes of his signature cowboy shirt glinting beneath a dinner jacket; Oscar winner Delilah Banks, dazzling in a gold evening dress; and a tuxedoed Darren Carmichael, whose face Gladys recognized from a highway billboard advertising his latest sappy romance novel. But there was one adult who wasn't very dressed up: a tall lady in pink sweatpants. She was wheeling a hot-pink suitcase around, and amid all the glittering celebrities, she looked lost. She also looked kind of familiar.

More than familiar. Gladys had seen her before—in the lobby of the *New York Standard* building earlier that year.

She was looking at her editor, Fiona Inglethorpe!

A million thoughts flashed through Gladys's mind. She should run away—as fast as possible! No, that might draw unwanted attention. She should sit completely still and try to look nonchalant. But then what if Hamilton or Sasha came back and called her name loud enough for Fiona to hear?

Before she could decide what to do, a shrill voice called a different name from across the room. "Fifi! Yoo-hoo, Fifi!"

Fiona looked up, and Gladys followed her editor's gaze until she was staring at yet another face she recognized: *Purgatory Pantry*'s very own Rory Graham, dressed in a sea-green gown that hugged her hips and legs.

Rory glided across the lobby and kissed Fiona on each cheek, leaving deep-crimson lipstick marks.

"Well, would you look at who the cat dragged in?" she exclaimed. "Now, Fifi, I know that you like to be comfortable at your desk—but really, when co-presenting an award on TV, one usually tries to spruce up a little, no?"

It looked to Gladys like Fiona might be on the verge of sprucing up her punching arm and testing it on

Rory's face. "I'm not dressed this way *on purpose*," she hissed. "I didn't even know I was coming here until twenty minutes ago! I'd just barely made it through customs at the airport when who should I find waiting for me but—"

"Speak of the devil!" Rory cried, and waved over Fiona's shoulder. Fiona spun around, and Gladys felt her jaw drop even lower. Gilbert Gadfly, his gold button shining at his midriff, was striding across the room and parting the cluster of dressed-up adults like it was a celebrity Red Sea.

"Ah, Inglethorpe," he said when he reached them, "I'm sorry to have abandoned you like that on the red carpet. Had to use the side entrance—can't let a picture of this face get out in public, you know!" He turned then to Rory. "Rory, you're looking smashing this evening—like the Little Mermaid's evil cousin."

Rory cackled with delight. "Gil, you have such a way with words!"

Now Fiona looked like she wanted to punch *both* of them in the face.

"Fifi was just telling me how you were sweet enough to surprise her at the airport," Rory continued.

"I did not—" Fiona started, but Gilbert cut her off.

"It wouldn't have been a surprise if she had bothered to check her e-mail," he said. "I sent her a message three days ago saying that I volunteered her to copresent with you!"

"Gilbert, you knew full well that I was unplugging during my vacation," Fiona said. "Honestly, of all the irresponsible things you could have done—"

"Irresponsible?" Gilbert gasped. "Was it irresponsible of me to try to help poor Rory, high and dry and in need of a copresenter? After all, it's not like *I* can be seen on camera, or I surely would have volunteered myself!"

Gladys stifled a groan. The more she saw and heard Gilbert Gadfly, the more she loathed him; she couldn't blame her editor for barely managing to hang on to her cool.

"Well, I guess I'll head backstage and see what I can rustle up to wear," Fiona grumbled. "At least I had my laundry done before I flew home."

She had barely wheeled her suitcase around the corner when her two former companions burst out laughing. Then, to Gladys's horror, Gilbert took Rory by the elbow and escorted her right over to the *very couch on which Gladys was sitting*! Gladys immediately grabbed *Zombietown, U.S.A.* from her swag bag and opened it in front of her face. What if Gilbert recognized her from the subway?

But the critic didn't even spare her a glance. Apparently, unless she was throwing up on his shoes, she was invisible to him.

"Gil, you devil," Rory purred, taking a seat on Gilbert's far side. "Are you really going to send that poor woman onstage in her pajamas? Do you really think your publishers will fire her over just one embarrassing television performance?"

Gladys froze. Gadfly was trying to get Fiona *fired*?

"Of course not," Gilbert said. "But her ridiculous appearance will be icing on the cake. Don't forget that I've had other plans in motion the whole time she's been away."

"With that other restaurant critic?"

Now Gladys hardly dared to breathe.

"How did you end up taking care of her?" Rory asked.

"It was a stroke of genius, really," Gilbert said. "Sneaking onto Fiona's computer right before she logged off for her vacation. At first I was just going to e-mail Gatsby and cancel her assignments, but then I thought it would be even better to send her on an impossible quest—keep her busy, you know? So she's been running all over town for a month, looking for the perfect hot dog."

"The perfect hot dog?" Rory snorted. "Ha! As if the *Standard* would ever print that review!"

It was a good thing Gladys was sitting down, because now she felt dizzy. She had suspected that Gilbert Gadfly disliked her—and that he even, somehow, might have stolen her original assignments. But she'd never imagined that her entire project had been made up!

"After all," Rory continued, "it's not like any dish centered on such an inferior, overprocessed meat product could ever be considered perfect."

"Well," Gilbert said, "your friend von Schnitz gave me a bit of a scare with his new Heavenly Hot Dogs venture—but you've assured me that his offerings are awful."

"Oh, yes," Rory said, and Gladys felt her heart sinking down into her fancy flats. "He brought some samples into the studio this week, and they were absolutely inedible. Even with BeBe Watkins's new recipe on the menu, that place won't last a month, I assure you."

"Good," Gilbert said. "Then I have nothing to worry about. Gatsby will fail at her assignment, and there will be no review to publish next Wednesday. They'll both be fired—"

"And you'll be made the new head of the Dining section!" Rory crowed. "Oh, bravo!"

But Gilbert's bulbous nose wrinkled. "Oh, heavens no, Rory. I don't ever want to become an editor! I just want to keep my position as head critic and have more control over my assignments. And that'll be much easier with Jackson Stone in the chief editor's chair. He's a pushover—he'll let me write whatever I like."

Rory shook her head in wonderment. "And if you don't try to take her job, Fifi will never even suspect that it was you pulling the strings!"

"Exactly." Gilbert flashed her a toothy grin. "Now,

don't forget the role you have to play in all this," he added.

"Yes, yes," said Rory, tossing her blond curls over a bare shoulder. "I'm to look gorgeous and confident onstage, and show Fiona up at every opportunity."

"Which should be the easiest thing in the world for you," Gilbert said throatily, and Rory blushed.

If Gladys had had anything in her stomach at that point, she was pretty sure she easily could have retched it up for a repeat barf bombing. Blech!

But, more seriously, she needed to find Fiona. She needed to warn her that they were being sabotaged, that their jobs were at stake, that—

"Gladys!" Hamilton was waving at her from across the room, Sasha by his side. They were lining up at the theater entrance for the awards ceremony.

*Fudge!*

As fast as she could, Gladys whipped her reviewing journal and a pencil out of the fancy purse Charissa had lent her. She scrawled a note, tore it out of the journal, grabbed the rest of her stuff, and started across the room. Now she just had to get her message to Fiona.

Joining the crush of people at the theater door, Gladys sidled up close to Sasha. "Hey, Sasha," she said quietly. "Could you do me a huge favor?"

Sasha's silver-tipped eyelashes blinked. "Sure."

Gladys glanced over her shoulder to make sure that

Gilbert and Rory were still on the other side of the room, well out of earshot. "When you go backstage for your performance, do you think you could give this note to Fiona Inglethorpe?" she asked. "She's one of the presenters for Best Kid Chef—the one who's not Rory Graham."

"Sure," Sasha said again. "What is it—like, a fan letter?"

*Sasha, you* are *brilliant!* Gladys thought, and she felt bad for ever having thought otherwise. "Exactly, a fan letter," she said. "I didn't want to bother her in person when she was out here, but I just want to let her know how great I think she is. Um, preferably before she goes out onstage."

"No problem," Sasha said. "Oh, but I don't know what she looks like. How will I find her?"

"She's tall and wears glasses," Gladys said. "I'm not sure what she'll be wearing—but there's a good chance it'll be pink. That's her favorite color."

Sasha smiled. "You really are a big fan!" she said. "Okay—tall lady, glasses, pink outfit. Got it." Sasha took the folded-up note from Gladys and tucked it into her tiny silver purse. "I'm heading back there right now."

"Thanks so much," Gladys said, and then she stepped over to Hamilton's side.

"It's nice to see you two becoming friends," Hamilton said as he waved good-bye to Sasha.

"Oh, yeah, Sasha's great!" Gladys said. "I'm really glad I met her." *And not just because she has backstage access,* she added in her head. Hamilton's famous friend really did seem like a nice person.

Together, she and Hamilton stepped through the doors into the Apollo's main theater. It was a massive space, filled with more than 1,500 red-upholstered seats and dominated by a wide black stage. Giant television cameras on wheels zoomed up and down the aisles, and excited chatter reverberated around the room, broken up here and there by the notes of an orchestra warming up.

With the amount of glitz and glitter all around them, Gladys now felt like her dress hardly stood out. Maybe Charissa's makeover hadn't been so over the top after all. Gladys directed a little wave at the nearest TV camera for her friend and her parents.

As they waited to be ushered to their seats, Hamilton kept turning to Gladys every few seconds and grinning. It was weird.

"How did the photo shoot go?" Gladys asked.

"Oh, fine," Hamilton said. "I'm getting pretty used to these things. Max Finkelstein threw a fit when they made his parents leave the room, though. He really is unhealthily attached."

Finally, an usher in a gleaming blue dress beckoned them forward. Their seats were only five rows back from the stage, and right on the aisle. Because of their angle, Gladys could see behind the curtain on one side of the stage, where people wearing headsets and carrying clipboards were rushing around. Was Sasha somewhere back there? Had she found Fiona?

Gladys and Hamilton had barely settled into their seats when the house lights dimmed. "Ladies and gentlemen!" an announcer's voice boomed. "Live, from the Apollo Theater in New York City, it's the Third Annual Kids Rock Awards!" The orchestra struck up a lively song, and the audience burst into cheers. The show was officially starting.

# Chapter 31

# THE BITTERNESS OF DEFEAT

GLADYS SAT THROUGH THE FIRST HALF hour of the ceremony as patiently as she could. The emcee, a famous comedienne, talked about the history of the Kids Rock Awards ("three years of kids voting online for their favorite artists and entertainers!") and poked fun at some of the famous people in the audience.

When it was time for the first award—Best Kid Supporting Actress in a Movie—Delilah Banks and action star Gabrielle Crawford swept onstage and read out a list of nominees. Gladys did her best to clap politely as she craned her neck to see if she could catch a glimpse of Fiona, Rory, or Sasha in the wings, but the only people she saw were a fresh pair of presenters she didn't know.

More awards followed the first one,

and when the winner in the Best Kid Modern Dancer category finally left the stage with his trophy, the emcee retook the mike. "When we come back," she announced, "the awards for Best Kid Chef and Best Kid Author!" The orchestra played a few quick notes, and then they were on a commercial break.

Her heart thumping now, Gladys peered again into the wings, but still she saw no one she recognized. She did, however, catch a glimpse of Hamilton next to her as she twisted half out of her seat. He looked deathly pale and was staring down at the note card in his hand. Gladys read the first line: *I would like to thank my parents, without whom I never would have become the author I am today.*

Remembering Sasha's words—and Grady's painful relationship with his parents in Hamilton's novel—Gladys settled back into her seat and patted Hamilton on the shoulder. "Hey," she said. "You have nothing to worry about. I've heard you make loads of speeches!"

Hamilton let out a breath. "Thanks, Gladys," he said. "I'm really glad you're here."

A minute later, the lights dimmed, and the orchestra struck up again. "Ladies and gentlemen," the emcee cried, "please welcome your presenters for the Best Kid Chef Award: *Purgatory Pantry* host Chef Rory Graham, and *New York Standard* Chief Dining Editor Fiona Inglethorpe!"

The audience applauded as Rory swept onstage

from one wing and Fiona entered from the other. Gladys was relieved to see that her editor looked perfectly respectable in an only slightly rumpled pale pink pants suit. Her previously ponytailed hair was swept up now into a simple bun, and her sneakers had been replaced by pink stilettos, which gave her an inch or two on Rory when they met at the microphone in the center of the stage. A flash of annoyance crossed Rory's face as she took in Fiona's appearance; clearly, she and Gilbert had not expected the editor to pull herself together so easily.

But when Rory turned to face the crowd, she was all smiles. "The nominees," she read from a teleprompter, "for Best Kid Chef are . . ."

Rory and Fiona traded off reading out the names, and cameras zoomed around the audience to get close-up shots of each nominee in his or her seat. Some of the kid chefs' products sounded really good, and in spite of everything that was running through her mind, Gladys couldn't help but make a mental note to look up Masie Alfonzo's Fresh Pie Company and Avery Paul's Jammin' Beef Jerkies when she got home.

Fiona leaned in to the microphone. "And the winner is . . ." She reached into her suit pocket. But instead of pulling out a white envelope, like all the other presenters had, she pulled out a small lined sheet of paper and passed it to Rory.

A wave of horror crashed over Gladys. That wasn't the winner's name—it was her very own note!

*Noooo!* she wanted to scream. She couldn't believe that, after pulling off an almost-perfect performance, Fiona had messed things up so spectacularly. Now Rory was reading Gladys's words to herself.

*Fiona,*

*Gilbert Gadfly is plotting against you. He broke into your e-mail account to steal Gladys Gatsby's assignments, and tonight he's conspiring with Rory Graham to embarrass you onstage, so be on your guard against any funny business.*

*Please don't worry about Ms. Gatsby, though—she'll have a replacement review for you this week that'll blow Gadfly right out of the water!*

*—A Friend*

In despair, Gladys slid down low in her seat—but up onstage, Fiona wasn't acting like she had made a mistake at all. In fact, one of her hands had moved to her hip, and she was now regarding Rory smugly. Meanwhile, Rory's green-taloned fingers—the ones holding the note—had started to shake.

And then, all at once, Gladys realized what was going on. Fiona had passed Rory the note *on purpose*, to let Rory know that she was on to her! Now, instead of Rory embarrassing Fiona onstage, it was the other way around.

While Rory's crimson lower lip trembled, Fiona reached into a different pocket and pulled out the winning envelope. She ripped it open herself, leaned into the microphone once more, and announced that Masie Alfonso was the category's winner. The orchestra swelled as pint-size Masie made her way up onstage. Rory, meanwhile—still clutching Gladys's note—stumbled into the wings.

During Masie's speech, Gladys took a moment to reassess the *New York Standard* situation. Her editor had escaped public humiliation, and would hopefully be able to look into the e-mail break-in and assignment-stealing situation quickly. The only piece left in the puzzle now was the replacement review Gladys had promised in her note. Maybe no one at the *Standard* had ever thought hot dogs were worthy of a review before . . . but she would have to change their minds.

Of course, there was the small issue of Gladys still not having a top dog to feature in her article. Could Heavenly Hot Dogs really be as bad as Rory said? Gladys hoped the chef had just been letting her nasty side show when she'd insulted the new hot dog joint.

Before she knew it, Masie was off the stage, and writers Darren Carmichael and Serenity James were at the microphone. Hamilton found Gladys's arm and squeezed it as they introduced the Best Kid Author category.

"The nominees," Serenity announced, "are . . . Caroline Giotta, for her memoir *My Father the Hitman!*"

Across the aisle from Gladys and Hamilton, a camera focused on a girl with thick dark hair, and a second later, her smiling face flashed up on the huge screen at the corner of the stage. Next to her, a gray-haired man was grinning, too—or, at least, Gladys thought he was grinning. He had so many scars on his face that it was kind of hard to tell.

". . . Max Finkelstein, for his picture book *I Like Rainbows!*"

The camera swept off to the right to show a tiny boy who was practically bouncing up and down in his seat. On either side of him sat adults who must have been his parents—they kept squeezing the kid's chubby little arms and pointing up at the jumbo screen excitedly.

". . . and finally, Hamilton Herbertson, for *Zombietown, U.S.A.!*"

A camera zoomed in on Hamilton and Gladys. But in spite of her instinct to duck under the seat—or at least pull her arm out of Hamilton's sweaty grip—Gladys stayed put. Her fellow CITs from camp were surely watching, and would probably jump to the wrong conclusion. She'd be in for a lot of teasing on Monday. But after everything else she'd dealt with so far tonight, she was pretty sure she'd find a way to deal with that, too. There had to be worse things in the world than people thinking you were on a date with Hamilton Herbertson.

Up on stage, Darren Carmichael pulled an envelope out of his jacket. "And the winner is . . . Max Finkel-stein, for *I Like Rainbows*!"

The orchestra burst into song, the audience cheered, and little Max catapulted out of his seat. He started to climb the stairs to the stage, tripped halfway, then looked back at his parents for help. Hamilton's grip on Gladys's arm finally slackened as Max's father picked the boy up and carried him to the podium.

"I won!" Max screeched into the microphone. Max's mom laid a hand on his shoulder, but there was no calming the kid down. "Mommy, Daddy, I *won*!"

A titter rose up from the audience at this, but Hamilton didn't laugh. "I feel sick," he murmured.

That was exactly what poor, friendless Grady had said in *Zombietown, U.S.A.* the first time he'd forced himself to eat brains.

"Come on," Gladys whispered, scooping up her purse. "Let's get out of here."

She reached for his hand, and when he took it, she pulled him up and out into the aisle. Luckily, the audience seemed so engrossed with little Max onstage that no one paid any attention to them. A camera was blocking the exit at the back of the theater, but there was an emergency exit just a few feet away. Praying that it wouldn't set off an alarm, Gladys led Hamilton out into the alleyway.

The door slammed shut behind them—no alarm had gone off, thankfully—and Gladys collapsed against the side of the building in relief. The sky had grown dusky, and next to her Hamilton took deep gulps of the cool night air.

"I just can't believe it," he said finally. "How could the judges give that twerp the award over me? He didn't even *need* it. Clearly his parents would be proud of him whether he won or not."

Gladys took her own deep breath. "Look," she said. "I know what it's like to have parents who don't appreciate you. Mine were like that for years about my cooking. But if you just spend some more time together, and try to learn to trust each other . . ." She thought about her beach outings this summer and couldn't help but smile. "Things can get better. I promise."

A tear streaked Hamilton's cheek. "Maybe with your parents," he said, his voice a quiet rasp now. "But not with mine."

Gladys didn't know how to respond to that. She'd never met Hamilton's parents, so she couldn't tell him he was wrong. After all, they hadn't even found the time to come support him tonight. Gladys, meanwhile—despite everything she'd just told Hamilton—

hadn't trusted her own parents enough to share her biggest accomplishment with them. Had that been the right decision?

Hamilton dried his face on the sleeve of his jacket. "Can we get going?" he asked.

"Definitely," Gladys said.

# Chapter 32

# A TASTE OF THE RSA

AS THEY EMERGED FROM THE ALLEY onto 125th Street, Gladys noticed a handful of photographers and journalists perched on stools and lawn chairs around the red carpet. They were watching the theater's entrance intently; she and Hamilton would be able to sneak right past them, unnoticed.

But then Hamilton waved a hand high in the air and yelled, "Marcus, over here!"

Their car swerved toward them—and the journalists' heads snapped toward Hamilton like sharks catching the scent of blood. Maybe they wouldn't have swooped in so quickly if there had been other celebrities around, but it was still the middle of the show, so everyone else was inside.

"Mr. Herbertson!" a squat journalist

cried, pulling a notepad out of her pocket, "Marjorie Daly from the *New York Sun*. How did it feel to be beaten by a four-year-old?"

Another journalist—a lanky blond man—all but shoved Marjorie aside to stick a microphone in Hamilton's face. "Hamilton, I'm Eli Winterspoon with Manhattan Municipal Radio. Our listeners would love a comment on the literary merit of your competitors!"

A third journalist elbowed her way forward. "Jillian Worthy with the *Empire State Reporter*!" she cried. "Hamilton, is this your girlfriend?"

There was a photographer standing next to Jillian Worthy, and Gladys saw him lift his camera.

*Fudge.*

She spun around just as the flash went off, only to find herself facing another photographer on the other side.

The sound of squealing brakes had never been as sweet as when it came from their black sedan jerking to a stop at the curb. "Let's go!" Gladys cried. She yanked the door open, and they tumbled into the car. Marcus pulled them back out into traffic as more cameras flashed, and Gladys thanked the gods of car service for tinted windows.

"Where to, kids?" Marcus asked.

Gladys was about to tell him the address for Heavenly Hot Dogs when Hamilton passed a slip of paper up to the front seat.

"This address, please, Marcus. I don't think it's far."

Marcus hit the brakes at a stoplight and took the paper from Hamilton. "Not far at all," he said. "I'll have you there in just a few minutes." He flicked his signal on and turned left, crossing West 124th Street, then West 123rd.

"Where are we going?" Gladys asked.

Hamilton's expression betrayed nothing. "It's a surprise."

Marcus pulled the car to the curb at the corner of West 114th Street and Frederick Douglass Boulevard, and Gladys followed Hamilton out of the car.

At first, she barely noticed the place; it was squished between a bank and a dollar store, with an entrance barely wider than the lobby holding the bank's ATMs. It didn't have an awning or a lighted sign, either— just some faded letters in the window that read CAPE FLATS: A TASTE OF THE RSA. When she looked through the window, Gladys spotted a lone metal table and two chairs, and behind that, a counter with a few stools.

"Is this . . . a restaurant?" she asked Hamilton.

"Yep," he answered.

"Okay, but I kind of had a different place in mind for dinner," she said quickly. "This new place in Times Square. The owner is a famous German chef, and—"

"You'll like this place better," said Hamilton, reaching for the door. "Trust me."

*What nerve this boy has,* Gladys thought. *Picking*

*out a restaurant and insisting I'll like it!* She had half a mind to storm back over to the car and insist that Marcus drive her to Times Square, Hamilton or no Hamilton. But when she looked up at him holding the door—and saw a hint of a smile on his face for the first time since he'd lost the Kids Rock Award—her resistance dissolved.

"All right," she said, and followed him inside.

A grizzled old man with deep-brown skin and white hair stood behind the counter, but otherwise, the place was empty. Hamilton waved Gladys over to the metal table, collected a pair of laminated menus from the old man, and brought them over.

"So what's the RSA, anyway?" she asked. Her menu was covered with sticky spots, and its edges were frayed.

"The Republic of South Africa," Hamilton said.

*Okay*, Gladys thought. *Kind of random, but interesting.* "Why did you want to come to a South African restaurant?"

Hamilton made an impatient kind of noise. "Would you just read your menu, please?"

"Fine." She started at the top, scanning down a list of unfamiliar dishes. Number one was Bobotie, described as "A Cape Malay specialty: meat loaf with raisins and egg, served on rice with tropical garnishes." Number two was Bunny Chow: Durban-style vegetarian curry served in a hollowed-out bread loaf. (No actual rabbit, Gladys noted with relief, so Sandy would be okay with it.) Number three was Peri-Peri Chicken: marinated in the traditional spicy pepper sauce and grilled.

Now Gladys's mouth was watering, and not just because she hadn't eaten anything since noon. These were dishes she didn't know—but they all sounded delicious! Heavenly Hot Dogs suddenly far from her mind, she wondered how many items she could order without looking greedy.

And she also wondered how Hamilton had found this place. Could the boy whose favorite lunch was a ham sandwich actually be a secret gourmet food lover?

She glanced up over the top of her menu and saw that he was staring at her. Immediately, she looked back down, but felt herself starting to blush.

"Have you chosen yet?" he asked.

"No, I . . . well, everything sounds so good."

"Well, if you can't decide," he said, "I'd recommend you try number five."

"Oh, thanks. I haven't gotten that far." Gladys looked down the list again—but when she reached number five, her breath caught.

It was called the Gatsby.

Chapter 33

# GLADYS GATSBY'S SIGNATURE SANDWICH

GLADYS BLINKED, BUT WHEN SHE OPENED her eyes, her name was still there, staring up at her from the dilapidated menu.

"I don't get it," she said. "Did you . . . call the restaurant and tell them to put my name here?"

"Nope," Hamilton said. "It's a real thing. Did you read the description?"

*The Gatsby*, it said. *A foot-long sandwich filled with hot chips, Vienna sausage, and Indian curried pickle. A specialty of Cape Town.*

"It's your signature sandwich," he said.

Gladys was truly speechless now.

"You kids ready?" the old man behind the counter called out to them.

When Hamilton called back, "We'll

split a number five, please," Gladys wasn't even annoyed that he had ordered for her.

"One Gatsby, comin' right up!"

Gladys finally pulled her eyes away from the menu and forced herself to look at Hamilton. "How," she asked hoarsely, "did you know that they sold this sandwich here?"

"Well, that's a funny story," he answered. "See, I was observing you at work in the kitchen one day, and I had a kind of epiphany." He paused. "Do you know—?"

"*Yes*, I know what an epiphany is."

"Right." He cleared his throat. "Well, it struck me that for every hour I'd spent working on my new book, you'd spent the same amount of time making lunches. And it just seemed kind of unfair that I—an author—should have a sandwich named after me, but that you—an actual sandwich-maker—should not.

"So, originally, I was going to contact the Tipsy Typist and ask them to invent a signature sandwich for you. But then I thought I should check online and make sure that a Gatsby sandwich didn't already exist somewhere."

"And when you did the search, you found this place?"

Hamilton shook his head. "First I found a lot of articles about South African food. In Cape Town, there's a stand selling Gatsby sandwiches on almost every corner! So then I wondered whether there might be any South African restaurants here in the city. And *that's* when I found this place."

"Which just happens to be in Harlem," Gladys said.

"Exactly," said Hamilton. "Once I mapped it and saw how close it was to the Apollo, I knew I had to bring you here."

"But, Hamilton," Gladys said, "you only just invited me this morning. You couldn't have done all that research today."

Hamilton lowered his eyes to the smudgy tabletop. "You're right," he said. "I've actually known for weeks that my parents weren't coming. I wanted to invite you all along. I just . . . never found the right opportunity."

He looked back up, and Gladys felt her earlier blush return. So he probably *had* been trying to invite her out last Friday—on an outing to New York City, to try the "signature sandwich" he had found just for her. And how had she repaid him? By avoiding him, so Charissa's stupid friends wouldn't make fun of her.

Their order arrived just then, saving Gladys from having to talk. The Gatsby was a huge, messy thing: a foot-long roll with all sorts of stuff sticking out. There were crispy French fries—Gladys supposed those were the "hot chips"—and a lot of reddish-orange bits, which Gladys assumed were the curried pickle. And then, peeking out from between the chips, Gladys saw something that made her heart leap.

"Are those hot dogs?" she cried.

The old man, who had been limping back to his counter, turned around. Gladys pulled a chunk of cylindrical, red-brown meat out of the sandwich and held it up to help him see.

"Those're the Viennas," he said, "but you Americans, yeah, you'd call 'em hot dogs. Same thing."

Gladys could hardly believe it, but when she took a bite of her half of the sandwich, she knew for sure.

Forget Times Square—Hamilton had found her the best hot dog in New York City.

Forty minutes later, her stomach full to bursting, Gladys leaned up against the sink in the restaurant's tiny restroom and pulled out her journal.

*The Gatsby sandwich at Harlem's Cape Flats restaurant features snappy sausages, just-fried-enough "chips," and a sour-sweet pickle topping. This combination of textures and flavors creates an almost-perfect hot dog–eating experience.*
   ★★★★ *(truly delicious)*

At long last, her hot dog review was coming together. She jotted down a final thought and was flipping her book shut when a review she had written earlier that summer caught her eye.

*Hamilton Herbertson is the worst!!!*
   *No stars! (completely irredeemable)*

Gladys paused, then gently drew a line through her words.

Hamilton was waiting for her by the restaurant door. "I took care of the bill," he said, and when she began to protest, he held up a hand. "I just put it on my parents' credit card. If they couldn't make the effort to come, then I think paying for dinner is the least they can do."

"Hamilton," Gladys said, "if you wanted your parents to come, maybe you should have just *told* them that it was really important to you."

He shook his head. "No, I wanted you to come. Honest." He paused. "Well, maybe it would have been nice if you *all* came."

Gladys smiled. "Well, next time, I think you should tell them how you really feel, instead of pretending it doesn't matter to you, or . . ." She took a deep breath. "Or writing about it as a metaphor in a novel."

Hamilton gaped at her. "How did you know?"

Gladys wanted to say *Because I'm a writer, too,* but

stopped herself. First, before she told any more friends her secret, she needed to come clean to her parents. She would send in her review to the *New York Standard* this weekend; then, after it was published, she'd have a long talk with her mom and dad.

As she resolved to do this, Hamilton spoke. "So you're saying I'll feel better if I tell the truth to the people I care about? That I shouldn't hold my feelings about them inside anymore?"

"*Exactly*," Gladys said. Then she reached forward and squeezed her friend's hand. Finally, he was listening to her instead of talking over her, and she was proud of him for it.

"Okay," Hamilton said. He nodded, like he had just talked himself into doing something. "Okay." Then, still holding Gladys's hand, he leaned forward and kissed her square on the mouth.

Tiny explosions went off in Gladys's brain. The first thought she had was that the paparazzi must have found them somehow and were now taking pictures . . . of *this*. Horrified, she stumbled back, pulling her lips away from Hamilton's slightly-curry-flavored ones. But once they were apart, she realized that there was no one else in the room with them; even the old man was out of sight, washing dishes loudly in the back kitchen.

Hamilton smiled then, showing off a smidgen of

pickle between his two front teeth. "You're right," he said. "It feels good to share your feelings."

Gladys felt like someone had flash frozen her in place, but Hamilton didn't seem bothered by her reaction. "Come on," he said, opening the restaurant door. "Our car is waiting."

# Chapter 34

# NOT SO STALE

DURING THE LONG RIDE BACK TO EAST Dumpsford, Gladys stayed as silent as possible—and Hamilton, thankfully, stayed on his own side of the spacious backseat. He was definitely in a good mood, though, sighing a lot and shooting Gladys moony-looking smiles. "How are you feeling?" he asked her about a dozen times, and each time she managed to squeak out a "Fine."

Hamilton's loss at the Kids Rock Awards appeared to be completely forgotten, but Gladys still felt stunned about what had happened at the restaurant. It was one thing to worry about her fellow CITs thinking she and Hamilton had been on a date . . . but it was quite another to think that *Hamilton* had been under the same impression. He'd probably even thought Gladys wanted him to kiss her.

*Had she?*

Gladys pushed the preposterous thought out of her mind.

When the car pulled up in front of her house, Gladys said good night and jumped out before Hamilton could even think about leaning her way again. She hurried up the path toward her front door, her hand fumbling around in Charissa's purse for the keys. It wasn't until the door shut behind her and she heard Hamilton's car roar off down the street that she was able to take a proper breath.

The house was dark, and Gladys crumpled against the heavy door. She had only meant to lean on it for support, but the slippery fabric of her dress sent her sliding down to the floor. She couldn't help but giggle when her butt hit the carpet—but a moment later, her laugh turned into a sob.

Was she happy? Was she sad? She didn't even know. She had outsmarted Gilbert Gadfly, saved her boss's job, and found the best hot dog in the city.

She just might have accidentally gained a boyfriend in the process.

"Gatsby!"

The whisper was so faint that Gladys thought she

might have imagined it—but then she heard it again, coming from the bushes outside the open window in the living room.

She pushed herself up off the floor and wiped at her eyes, her hands coming away streaked with makeup. *Fudge.* She snatched a tissue from the box on the end table as she tiptoed over to the window.

Sandy was peeking up out of a bush, barely visible in the moonlight—though, thankfully, he had skipped the camo face paint this time.

"Come inside," Gladys insisted, but Sandy shook his head.

"Too risky!" he hissed. "What if your parents catch me? I'm finally getting back on Mom's good side—I don't want to ruin it."

Gladys had to smile. "What are you doing out here, then?"

"I snuck out after she went to sleep—I couldn't miss my chance to talk to you before you left for the weekend." Sandy shoved a leaf away from his face. "*So,* how was it?"

"The Kids Rock Awards?" Gladys asked.

"No, Gatsby, the hot dog place in Times Square!"

"Oh," Gladys said with a laugh. "We actually ended up going somewhere else—a place that Hamilton found." She stopped there, not sure she could describe the Gatsby sandwich without her brain getting stuck on what had happened to her mouth just a few minutes after she'd finished eating.

"Wait," Sandy said, "after all that work we did to plan your trip to Heavenly Hot Dogs, you didn't even go?"

"I . . . no," Gladys admitted. "The night didn't exactly go the way I thought it would. But this other hot dog place was really good," she added quickly. "The best in the city, I think. So it all worked out."

Sandy shook his head, causing the leaves around him to rustle. "That is so *you*—throwing out all your plans at the last minute only to come up with something even better."

"I didn't mean—" Gladys started, but Sandy cut her off.

"I'm not saying that's a bad thing. I mean, it's probably the only way you *can* operate, given the circumstances."

"What circumstances?"

"You know," Sandy said, dropping his voice even lower. "Keeping all your reviewing a secret from . . ." He nodded up in the direction of Gladys's parents' bedroom window.

Gladys took a deep breath. "Actually," she said, "I think I'm going to tell them."

Sandy nearly fell over in the bush. "WHAT??"

"Shhh!"

"Sorry," Sandy whispered, righting himself. "But . . .

Gatsby, that sounds like the worst idea in the world. Remember how badly they freaked when you had your little crème brûlée accident?"

"That was ages ago," she said. "We've spent a lot of time together this summer, and now . . . well, things feel different."

"So you think your parents will suddenly be okay with the fact that you've been sneaking around for months, keeping secrets and breaking rules? Because in *my* experience, parents don't like that."

It was true that Sandy's mom had not reacted well to his behavior at camp—and generally, Gladys considered Mrs. Anderson to be a lot cooler than her own parents.

"Well—" she started, but Sandy wasn't finished yet.

"Not to mention all that money you stole from their account on your birthday," he continued. "How do you think they're going to react when they find out that was you?"

"Okay, you have a point," she said. "But if I *keep* lying, it's only going to get worse. And what if they find out all this stuff some other way, from someone else?"

It was hard to read Sandy's expression in the dark, but he didn't look terribly convinced. "I dunno, Gatsby," he said. "You've got a good thing going now. I wouldn't mess with it if I were you—not unless you get some kind of huge sign that they'd suddenly be okay with it all, or something."

Gladys sighed. "Well, thanks for the advice," she said. "I'll take it into consideration."

Sandy gave her a lopsided grin. "Anytime. And hey, congrats on finding New York's best hot dog. I can't wait to read your review." He yawned then. "Okay, I'd better go back to bed."

Gladys watched him crawl out from the bush and run across the yard, and then she slipped upstairs to her room, where she could finally change out of the awful red dress and into her favorite writerly uniform: her pajamas.

Gladys stayed up until the wee hours drafting her hot dog review in her journal. As a result, she was so tired the next day that she slept through the car ride to Pennsylvania, then nodded off again in the afternoon during a particularly boring game of Scrabble with Grandma Rosa.

"Look sharp, Gladys!" her grandma cried, jolting her awake. "You could have played that *Z* for three times the points in the corner! Your parents told me you were very good with words . . ."

Grandma Rosa gleefully scored seventy-six points using that corner spot, but Gladys didn't care. If her parents had been bragging about her writing just based on her essay from school, wouldn't they be proud to learn that she'd already been published for a national audience? Maybe this was exactly the sign Sandy had told her to look for!

When they finally returned home on Sunday night, Gladys made a beeline for the computer, telling her parents that she had made plans to chat online with Parm. *My last lie,* she told herself. She was feeling even more confident now in her decision to come clean on Wednesday.

Back at camp on Monday, Gladys noticed Hamilton writing in his usual spot on the patio during morning announcements. For once, she was glad he didn't have any friends at camp other than her—at least that meant he had no one to tell about what had happened between them on Friday night.

Charissa and her friends, meanwhile, kept Gladys surrounded in a near-constant mob.

"What's Sasha McRay like?"

"Did you get Delilah Banks's autograph?"

"Is it true that Jeffy Marx is even cuter in person?"

The girls seemed to have forgotten that Hamilton had even been there, and their questions only stopped when Gladys disappeared into the kitchen for CIT duty. Grateful for the break, she threw herself into transforming last week's stale baguettes into a moist panzanella salad.

Floating in a quiet corner of the pool that afternoon

during her first Free Swim, Gladys was finally able to reflect on things. She had e-mailed her review to Fiona before camp that morning, lunch had earned her raves from the staff and CITs, and she still had two days before the time would come to reveal her secret to her parents. There was really only one unresolved issue gnawing at her, and when she looked toward the bleachers at the edge of the pool, she spotted him, dressed all in black.

He was hunched over his notebook as usual, but he wasn't scribbling at his regular speed. Maybe Hamilton hadn't planned to write this afternoon; maybe he'd thought Gladys would want to spend her free time with him. Or that she'd at least have said more to him today than "Here's your ham sandwich" at lunchtime. All at once, she felt terrible for avoiding him. He had been brave enough to admit how he felt about her—couldn't she at least do the same for him?

With a few efficient crawl strokes, Gladys reached the pool's ladder. She climbed out, wrapped a towel around herself, and jogged up the bleachers to where Hamilton sat.

"Hey," she said, sliding in next to him.

Hamilton finally looked up from his notebook. "Oh," he said. "Hello, Gladys." But he didn't stand, or sweep his hat off, or even hold her gaze. In fact, he scooted a tiny bit farther away from her on the bench.

"Look, Hamilton," she said. "I've been thinking

about Friday, and—well, I think it would be better if you and I just stayed friends."

"Oh!" Hamilton sat up a bit straighter. "I was actually going to suggest the same thing."

"You were?"

Hamilton cleared his throat. "Gladys, an artist and a muse don't usually . . . um . . ." He shook his head, as if that might convince his brain to send the right words to his mouth. Gladys knew the feeling.

He tried again. "I mean, I'm at a point in my career where I really need to just . . . well, focus on my career. You understand, don't you?"

"Absolutely," Gladys said. After all, she had a career to focus on herself.

About twenty furrows seemed to disappear from Hamilton's brow all at once. "Oh, good," he said. "So everything can go back to the way it was before . . . um, before we—"

"Yes!" Gladys said, cutting him off as quickly as she could. "Just like before."

He nodded, then glanced down at the pool. "So, how's the water today?"

"It's not bad, actually," Gladys said. "Swimming is a lot more fun without Coach Mike shouting from the sidelines." She paused. "Do you want to come in?"

"Oh," Hamilton said. "I . . . I shouldn't. I'm right in the middle of this crucial scene, and—"

"Come *on*," Gladys said. "You have years of writing

ahead of you, but who knows how many more sum-mers at 'the funnest camp ever'?"

They both laughed, and Hamilton looked toward the pool again.

"You're right," he said. "I'll go change into my swim-suit. Meet you in the water?"

Gladys nodded and led the way down the bleacher steps.

*Chapter 35*

# THE STARS OF SUMMER

THAT WEDNESDAY, GLADYS'S HOT DOG roundup was published in the *New York Standard*'s Dining section.

## BEYOND THE CORNER CART:
### A Quest for New York City's Best Hot Dog
by G. GATSBY

Did that headline surprise you?

Many regular Standard readers may be baffled to see a feature about hot dogs in these pages. After all, they aren't exactly haute cuisine. And I'll admit that, when I first received this assignment, I was disappointed, too. Hot dogs, I thought, were kid food—salty meat on white bread, and undemanding of a sophisticated palate like my own. I thought that I already knew all there was to know about them.

But I was wrong.

The article went on to detail Gladys's experiences around the city, tasting hot dogs from all corners of the world. She had ended up giving her experience at Nathan's a solid two and a half stars, the Icelandic pylsur, the Thai dog, and the Sonoran hot dog three stars each, and the Chilean completo Italiano three and a half. She then awarded the Gatsby a full four stars before closing her review with this reflection.

The weeks I spent on this quest taught me that sometimes you have to give things a second chance. Sometimes you need to take the time to dig in deeper, to learn about a food's variations and try it under different circumstances. If you do, you may discover that what made an unsavory impression on you the first time around actually has a lot more potential than you think—including the potential to bring people with different tastes to the same table. If my own outings with family and friends are any indication, lovers of fancy food and simple food, gourmet food and fast food can come together to enjoy the specialty dogs reviewed here.

This year, hot dogs turned out to be the stars of our summer menu. What will they do for yours?

The review was by far the longest and most detailed one Gladys had ever written, and it took up almost the entire front page of the Dining section in the printed version. In fact, the only other item on the page appeared in a small square in the bottom right corner.

## LONGTIME RESTAURANT CRITIC GILBERT GADFLY RESIGNS
### by JACKSON STONE, Deputy Editor

Gilbert Gadfly, head restaurant critic for the *New York Standard* for the past fourteen years, has resigned his position with the department, effective immediately. Mr. Gadfly cited "overwork and exhaustion" as his reasons for leaving the paper. When asked about rumors that he has been offered a job cohosting the reality cooking show *Purgatory Pantry* with celebrity chef Rory Graham, Mr. Gadfly declined to comment.

As for the future of the *Standard*'s world-class reviews, Chief Editor Fiona Inglethorpe insists that readers have nothing to worry about. "Thankfully, we have a stable of devoted freelancers who will have no trouble picking up the slack until a replacement full-time critic can be found," she said. "In fact, I wouldn't be surprised if one of our freelancers ended up taking over the permanent position."

"So," Mr. Eng said as he bagged Gladys's newspapers for her that afternoon, "are you going to throw your hat into the ring?"

"For what?" Gladys asked.

Mr. Eng raised his eyebrows. "For the full-time critic's position, of course!"

Gladys snorted. "Right."

"They couldn't find a better candidate."

"Yeah, well," Gladys said, "I think you're forgetting about a little thing I have coming up in September called *middle school.*"

But this revelation didn't stop Mr. Eng in his tracks the way she thought it would.

"There are ways around that," he said. "Homeschooling, for instance. Did you read that interview in the *Intelligencer* with Hamilton Herbertson, the twelve-year-old author? He said he never would have been able to write his novel if he'd had to attend regular school."

Gladys hadn't actually read the interview. *Hamilton was homeschooled?* She had never thought to ask him about school. Then again, if he'd never been around kids his own age before camp, that explained a lot.

"Well, I wouldn't hold your breath," Gladys told Mr. Eng, "but I'll keep you posted."

Ten minutes later, Gladys parked her bike in the garage and heaved her canvas bag full of newspapers out of the basket and onto her shoulder. Normally she'd head straight for Sandy's and stash them there, where her parents had no chance of finding them. But today, her plans were different.

She unlocked the front door and headed straight for the dining room, where she carefully laid out a copy of the newspaper, open to the Dining section, at each of her parents' places. They weren't home from work yet, but when they did get there, they wouldn't be able to miss her review.

Things were about to change, and Gladys knew there might be a hefty price to pay for telling the truth. She wondered if, as part of her punishment for lying to them, she might get banned from watching *Purgatory Pantry*. That would be no great loss, especially if Gilbert Gadfly really did become the cohost. She would happily give it up. In fact, there was a lot she'd be willing to give up, just as long as her parents let her keep the one pastime she really cared about: reviewing restaurants for the *New York Standard*.

# ACKNOWLEDGMENTS

*THE STARS OF SUMMER* WOULDN'T EXIST without the help of the following people, all of whom deserve homemade strawberry-lime cupcakes:

My husband, Andy, to whom this book is dedicated—you are the best. Extra special thanks for taking over chef de cuisine duties on the nights when deadlines were looming.

My editor, Shauna Rossano, my agent, Ammi-Joan Paquette, and all the good folks at Penguin Young Readers Group— thank you all for giving an emphatic "Yes!" to a second Gladys adventure.

My critique partners Ann Bedichek, Jenny Goebel, Jessica Lawson, and Lauren Sabel—thank you for your hugely insightful and timely feedback. Without you, this book would make much less sense.

My friend Katie Wade—many thanks for helping me navigate the world of Spanish tapas (who knew there were so many types of pork?!).

My compatriots in the #write-o-rama, OneFour Kidlit, and Emu's Debuts groups—thanks for keeping me writing, and keeping me sane, over the past few years.

The Paul sisters: Evelyn, Lucia, and Emily—thank you for continually challenging me to write books up to your extremely well-read standards.

Kelly Murphy, cover artist extraordinaire—thank you for your boundless attention to detail.

And thank you to everyone who has read *All Four Stars* and asked for Gladys's adventures to continue.

Hmm . . . that's a whole lot of cupcakes!

# COMPLETO ITALIANO
## *(Chilean Hot Dog)*
### Serves 4

Though it may sound Italian, this is actually a hot dog you'd find in Chile—it's called "Italiano" because its green, white, and red toppings are the colors of the Italian flag.

### Ingredients:
4 hot dogs of your choice (the longer the better—in Chile, completos can be huge!)
4 hot dog buns
2 avocados, mashed
2 fresh tomatoes, diced
mayonnaise to taste

### Instructions:
*If you are a young chef,*
*ask an adult to work with you on this recipe.*

Cook the hot dogs via your favorite method (boiling, grilling, etc.).
If you like, toast the buns lightly.
When everything is ready, set the hot dogs in the buns. Slather the hot dogs with a layer of mashed avocado, a generous layer of mayonnaise, and a layer of diced tomato.

*Serve immediately and enjoy!*

# THE "GATSBY"
## *(South African Hot Dog Sandwich)*
### Serves 2–4
(one Gatsby is meant to be shared by multiple people)

This is not only Gladys Gatsby's choice for best hot dog in New York but also the signature sandwich of Cape Town, South Africa. There are many, many varieties, but this one featuring hot dogs is Gladys's favorite.

### Ingredients:
2 cups of French fries (fresh or frozen)
4 hot dogs of your choice
1 foot-long crusty roll
1 cup shredded lettuce
*achar* to taste (Indian curried pickle—see note)

**NOTE:** There are many types of *achar*, made by pickling foods ranging from mangoes to carrots to chilies! You can find them in jars at Indian grocery stores or find recipes online for making your own.

### Instructions:
*If you are a young chef,
ask an adult to work with you on this recipe.*

Cook the French fries via your favorite method (baking, deep-frying, etc.).
Cook the hot dogs via your favorite method (boiling, grilling, etc.). Cut each cooked hot dog into 3 or 4 chunks.
Split the crusty roll open, but don't cut it all the way through. Toast lightly if desired.
Open the roll on a plate and layer in the hot dog chunks, French fries, *achar* (and/or other condiments of your choice), and shredded lettuce.

*Cut into multiple portions and enjoy!*

TURN THE PAGE FOR
A TEASER OF GLADYS'S
NEXT FOOD ADVENTURE!

# Chapter 1

## LOBSTER LOCKDOWN

GLADYS GATSBY FELT LIKE A LIVE FISH was flopping around in her stomach.

All around her in the schoolyard stood strangers, talking and laughing—incoming seventh-graders from the four other elementary schools that fed into Dumpsford Township Middle School. They couldn't possibly all know one another already, but somehow it felt like they did, or like everyone there knew at least *one* other person. Gladys didn't have a lot of friends, but she wished now that she had made plans to meet up with one of them this morning before middle-school orientation started.

"Nice stuffed animal," said a snarky voice.

Gladys looked up just in time to see a girl with a super-short haircut and a green messenger bag melt into the crowd. Who had she been making fun of? Gladys didn't see any kids nearby holding a stuffed animal. Seriously, you'd have to be pretty clueless to bring one here—might as well announce to the world that you were a giant baby.

Still, the drive-by comment had rattled her. Was that the kind of thing she had to look forward to in middle school? Taking a deep breath to compose herself, Gladys stroked the fuzzy strap of her lobster backpack—and froze.

She yanked the backpack off to examine it. Its belly was sunken today, since there wasn't anything inside it other than a lock for her new locker and her restaurant-reviewing notebook and pencil, which she kept with her at all times. But the lobster was made of bright red plush fake fur.

That girl had thought her backpack was a stuffed animal.

In sixth grade, Gladys's lobster backpack had been . . . not cool, exactly, but her classmates had accepted it, probably because they all knew she was a foodie. Sometimes they even came to ask her for cooking advice at recess. But the new kids here wouldn't know that; they wouldn't know she was a professional restaurant critic, either, with several reviews published in the country's biggest newspaper, the *New York Standard*. To them, she was just a juicy piece of fruit, ripe to be picked on. And if her skin wasn't thick enough, her soft insides could come bursting out at any moment.

"Gladys!"

Gladys spun around and saw Parm Singh racing up to her. *Oh, thank goodness.*

"Parm!" she cried, and when her friend finally reached her, they embraced. "I didn't know if you'd be back from Arizona in time to come today!"

"We just got back last night," Parm said breathlessly. "Though I considered skipping it altogether. Jagmeet went through this same orientation three years ago and said it was pretty useless."

Jagmeet was Parm's brother, and they had spent the entire summer in Arizona together, visiting cousins. Gladys hadn't seen Parm since her own birthday in June, but it seemed that a summer in the desert sunshine still hadn't managed to turn her cynical friend into a bright-eyed optimist.

"So," Parm said, lowering her voice, "what's going on? How was the rest of your time at camp? And your hot dog assignment—did you get your review done for the *Standard*? Did you end up telling your parents about your secret job?"

There was so much to catch Parm up on—but just as Gladys opened her mouth to respond, a bell rang and the doors to the middle school burst open. "I'll tell you everything later," Gladys promised as they got swept up among the kids pushing into the building.

The first stop for orientation was the school auditorium, which was just opposite the school's front door. Gladys barely had time to look around the crowded lobby before being herded inside by a man she assumed was a teacher. All of the adults were wearing matching blue T-shirts that had a picture of what looked like a comet on them and the words *Dumpsford Township Middle School: Where everyone's a star!*

"I sure hope the science teachers at least know the difference between a comet and a star," Parm muttered, "or else we're in for a pretty mediocre educational experience."

They took two seats, and soon a woman dressed in the shooting-comet T-shirt walked onto the stage. "Welcome to DTMS, seventh-graders!" she cried. "My name is Dr. Sloane, and I'm going to be the principal for your next two years here." Dr. Sloane went on to explain how the students' schedules would work: seven forty-eight-minute class periods in a day, plus lunch and homeroom.

Gladys glanced around the vast auditorium. She spotted another friend, Charissa Bentley, sitting up near the stage with Rolanda Royce and Marti Astin. She also saw a few kids she knew from last year and from camp scattered around. But there were many more new faces, and Gladys wasn't sure how she felt about that. After all, it had taken six years of elementary school just to get used to the old ones.

Once Dr. Sloane finished explaining the absolute necessity of getting a hall pass before going to the bathroom, she cleared her throat. "And finally," she said, "I have an announcement to make about after-school activities. Because of budget cuts, DTMS doesn't have as much funding this year for extracurriculars as we've had in years past. There will still be a variety of clubs and teams offered, but if groups want to take field trips, or purchase new equipment, they'll have to raise the funds to do so on their own."

"Oh, no!" Parm murmured.

Gladys turned to her friend. "What?" The budget cuts didn't sound like such a big deal to her, but she wasn't planning to join any clubs anyway—she figured that her job at the *Standard* was after-school activity enough. Parm, though, looked distraught.

"Every spring, the girls' soccer team goes to the big regional tournament in Pennsylvania," she whispered. "I've been looking forward to it ever since I started Pee Wee Soccer." She frowned. "Then again, I might not even make the team."

"Of course you will!" Gladys didn't know the first thing about soccer, but she did know that Parm practiced harder than anyone else. "And Dr. Sloane didn't say you can't go—she just said you'd have to raise some extra money."

"*All* the money," Parm corrected her. "Do you know how much money it takes to send a team of eighteen girls away for two nights?"

Gladys guessed that it was probably a lot.

Parm and Gladys weren't the only ones discussing this latest announcement; the entire auditorium was buzzing.

Dr. Sloane had to tap the microphone to regain everyone's attention. "There are tryout and sign-up sheets posted on the bulletin board outside the cafeteria for those of you who want to get a jump on your extracurriculars. More importantly, though, you'll be able to pick up your class schedules outside these doors here, as well as your locker assignments. Please use the remaining hour to tour the school and look for your classrooms. You can also test out your lockers and place your new locks on them; teachers will be stationed in every hallway to help you out. Enjoy yourselves, and we'll meet again on the first day of school!"

Out in the lobby, teachers were manning tables with boxes of schedules organized by last name. Gladys went to the *G* station, and Parm to the *S*. When they met up again to compare, Charissa bounded over, her high brown ponytail bobbing behind her.

"Hey, Gladys!" she said brightly. "Oh, hey, Parm."

Parm raised one of her thick black eyebrows in

Gladys's direction. While Parm had been away in Arizona, Gladys had spent the summer at Camp Bentley, the day camp owned by Charissa's parents. In that time, she and Charissa had become pretty good friends. But sarcastic Parm and popular Charissa had never really gotten along.

"Hello, Charissa," Parm said coolly. "I trust you had a good summer?"

"Oh, the *best*," Charissa gushed. "I got to swim every day, my team won the color war, and Gladys taught me how to cook West African food *and* let me give her a makeover one night!"

Parm shuddered, though Gladys couldn't tell whether it was over the horrors of makeovers or the horrors of international cooking. Parm was the pickiest eater Gladys knew.

Charissa probably should have then asked Parm how *her* summer had gone, but she didn't. Parm was already too busy comparing her schedule with Gladys's to notice, though.

"I can't believe this!" she grumbled. She held both schedules up to the window, as if illuminating them might change their contents. "How can we not have a single class together? We even both signed up for French!"

This was true, but Gladys had been put into an eighth-period French class, and Parm had French during third period. They didn't even have the same lunchtime—Parm was in sixth-period lunch, and Gladys had her lunch during fourth.

Wait—*fourth* period? Gladys grabbed her schedule back and looked at the times again. Fourth period started at 10:20 a.m. As far as she was concerned, that was barely brunch time. How was a meal at 10:20 supposed to last her through the next four hours of classes?

Gladys groaned. "This is less than ideal."

"You can say that again," Parm said.

Charissa was peeking over Parm's shoulder now. "Hey, Parm," she said, "our schedules are almost identical."

Parm's voice faltered. "Are they?"

"Yeah," Charissa said, holding out her paper. "We've got math, science, English, gym, and lunch together. I'm in third-period social studies and eighth-period French with Gladys, but otherwise, our timetables are exactly the same."

Charissa didn't sound especially thrilled about this, and Parm shot Gladys a look that clearly said *Kill me now.*

"Well," Gladys said quickly, "it's nice that you guys will have at least one familiar face in most of your classes, right?"

She was trying to help her friends see the bright side—but at the same time, the pit of worry that had entered her stomach in the schoolyard now felt like it was sprouting into a full-grown tree of anxiety. Two classes with Charissa and none with Parm left a whole lot of classes with zero friends. Her parents would surely advise her to make new ones . . . but Gladys would rather tackle a hundred difficult new recipes than force herself to talk to one new person.

"Come on, let's go find our lockers," Charissa said. "Marti and Rolanda's are both in the south wing, but mine's in the north. What about you guys?"

Gladys's and Parm's locker assignments were in the north wing, too, so they all set off together in that direction. They reached Gladys's locker first, and she dug into her lobster backpack. In elementary school, they hadn't had lockers, but for middle school, a lock was on the list of required school supplies.

The U-shaped shackle clacked back and forth as Gladys pulled her combination lock out, and its metal felt cold to her touch. She had spent a good half hour the night before practicing her combination to make sure it was branded firmly into her memory; she could think of nothing worse than drawing attention to herself by needing to ask a custodian to break into her locker on the first day of school.

Most kids in the hallway were just slapping their locks onto their empty lockers, not leaving anything inside since they didn't have books or supplies yet. But as Gladys's lock jiggled in her hand, the words *stuffed animal* echoed in her head. Making a snap decision, she shrugged off her lobster backpack and tossed it in. There it slumped at the bottom of her locker, claws drooping. She slammed the door, slid the shackle through the latch, and snapped her lock shut tight.